V.I.P

A NOVEL BY

AZAREL

Life Changing Books in conjunction with Power Play Media
Published by Life Changing Books
P.O. Box 423 Brandywine, MD 20613

Library of Congress Cataloging-in-Publication Data;

www.lifechangingbooks.net
13 Digit: 978-1934230251
10 Digit: 1934230251

Dedication

This book is dedicated to my two gifts from God, my love-able daughters. It's been an incredible year for us all, but we know that He changes things for the better. Stay the course…keep your faith always. We now have another favorite scripture.
Psalm 46:10- Be still and know that I am God.
Love you both more than you could imagine.

Acknowledgements

By now, you all know the drill. First, I'm giving all the glory to my Lord and Savior, Jesus Christ. For without Him, I am nothing and would not have been able to write the words on these pages. Secondly, I have to give loads of thanks to my hubby, Tony who held on tightly through my mood swings, outbursts, and countless nights spent working on V.I.P. This by far has been the most difficult book I've ever written.

Loads of love go out to my immediate family who've been by my side since L.C.B began. To my mother and father, thanks for making me the person I am today. Life's been rough, but you've prepared me. My sis, Tam...love you to pieces... thanks for always having my back. To my brother in law, Don, thanks for being on my Board of Directors...crazy how we've watched all these businesses grow. You know our next project is insane. Keep your wallet tight. To my two wonderful grandmothers, I can't thank you enough for being such an inspiration in my life. You are both forever loved! To my cousin, Jersey, what can I say? Thanks for always willing to help. You are a blessing. To D. Vick, thanks for holding things down in ATL...I truly appreciate it.

Words cannot express how I feel about the following people who help keep my personal life in tact. Keisha George, you do so much to assist me, all I can do is say thank you!! Tasha, you seem to be that woman who wears many hats, not just with LCB, but personally, too. I'm so blessed to have you. Kinae, my niece, the mini-me in training. I'm so proud of how you take instructions and make it happen. Tobe, thank you dearly for keeping me physically able to tackle daily life. I appreciate it.

A special thanks goes out to all the professionals and test readers who worked on this project. To my Director of Operations; Leslie Allen. You've rolled with me from the start, through all the storms, and now the sun is finally shining! Thanks for your help with this book along with everything else. Kellie, you nailed the cover...so hot...so creative. You've been such a blessing to me. Cheryl Moody, Shannon Barnes, Emily Gloster, Tonya Ridley, Aschandria Fisher, Virginia, Jasmine Bell and Ella Curry, I thank each of you for your contributions to this project. The comments were unbelievably hilarious. Honesty was off the charts this time.

A special recognition goes out to all the LCB authors and all the bookstores across the world who carry my books. Hakim, Tyson, Porgo, Akion, Max, Sidi, Henry, Chris B., and whoever else I missed, I am forever grateful. Until next time...

Azarel
Follow me on Twitter: @ceoazarel
www.facebook.com/msazarel

Chapter 1

Royce

"Who wants to go home with me tonight?"

Damn, he's conceited, I thought watching Tango grip the mic, talking to the ladies as if he were God.

The crowd exploded and the females went wild as Tango commenced to singing the last verse of his hit song, *One More Time.* None of it impressed me, but since my girl Tyesha and I had second row seats we had a close up view of this curvaceous, over-sized hoochie who brushed past us to stand in the aisle and throw her panties on stage. *Nasty.* She swung her jiggly arms like a cowgirl releasing her lasso over and over again saying how much she loved him.

"Oh my God! I'll go home with you. Hell, I'll leave my kids and have yo' babies next week wit' yo' sexy ass! Let's do this, Tango!" she screamed like an idiot.

"Why don't people like that have someone to tell them 'don't do it'. And that they look funky and stupid all at the same time?" I asked Tyesha jokingly.

Tyesha yelled back attempting to let her raspy voice resonate over Tango's long, whiny, Keith Sweat sounding note. "Girl, these chicks are desperate." She shook her head. "Thirsty tramps. Have some damn integrity, fat girl."

Tyesha laughed at her own joke.

I frowned.

I couldn't even say anything else as I watched Tango rip off his white, ribbed tank, exposing his tantalizing six pack, then unzip his zipper slightly, teasing the crowd along the way. It was borderline porno the way he slithered like a snake dipping his hands in and out of his pants. Out of the blue my cell rang. It was the call I'd been waiting for. I wanted my baby to say he'd made a mistake and that I should meet him at the airport, pronto. I wanted him to beg for forgiveness and tell me I was now going with him to Miami. Instead, it was his assistant attempting to talk over the loud music.

"Hello, Royce. It's Alexis. Trae asked me to call you. He's running late and has lots to do before his plane leaves for Miami in a couple of hours."

I huffed. "He couldn't call himself?" I belted over the loud acoustics, "I mean this is crazy."

"Ahhh. No. So, here's the run down." She spoke so damn fast it made me angry. "Take the papers that he gave you to the courthouse. Pick his clothes up from the cleaners. Drop Meechie off at the dog pound, and pick up the packages from Fed Ex."

"Are you serious? What about money? Did he leave any?"

"Not that I know of. I don't do accounting. You'll have to ask Trae that?"

"Well, where in the hell is he? I've been calling him all day and the bastard keeps sending me to voicemail."

"Not sure, I've gotta go, hon. My flight leaves tonight, too."

"My heart sank. Everyone was going to see my man play in the Superbowl but me. Before I could ask another question all I got was a dial tone and a disapproving snarl from Tyesha. Suddenly, the singing stopped on stage and Tango ended with a bang, rubbing his genitals even more sexily and dropping the mic for a strong ending to his performance. Oddly, before he jetted off stage he made eye-contact with me.

"Royce, girlllllll, he wants you," Tyesha taunted.

I was stunned wondering why he focused on me out of all the chicks hovering near the stage trying to get his attention and taking one photo after another. I then wondered if someone had told him why I'd actually come to the concert or if he just thought I was some type of slut. I wanted to mouth my favorite line, "I gotta man. One who I wanted to marry," but before I knew it he was gone and the lighting in the arena had changed.

Tyesha yanked me from my seat as more lights flicked on brightly and the MC came on thanking everyone for coming out.

"Let's go. We gotta hurry," she urged. "Romello and JR won't be backstage for long. You know how niccas who gettin' money do. They in and out."

"What?" I had no idea what Tyesha meant and I hated that she and my girl India always substituted the word nigga with nicca. It didn't make it any better in my book.

"Wake up, Royce. Wake up! This is your shot, girl. Why you movin' so slow?"

"Chill out girl, damn."

My adrenaline pumped as I followed, attempting to keep up, while bumping into several people along the way. I knew the plan was for us to go backstage so I could politic with Tango's mangers and a few producers that Tyesha knew. But my nerves had gotten the best of me. Besides, the call from Trae's assistant had me heartbroken, and Tyesha's constant ranting about the do's and don'ts when we got in front of the producers were driving me crazy as we strutted swiftly. My opportunity had finally come. It was really about to go down, I told myself with a smile. I just didn't want to come across as a groupie like the one's we'd stopped behind waiting to get backstage.

"Excuse us!" Tyesha shouted, rubbing against people as we barged our way through the crowd. Her hard walk, broad shoulders and stocky build allowed her to bulldoze her way thru without problems. "We have these," she announced to the big, burly bouncer, guarding the entrance to the back of the arena.

My eyes zoomed in on the laminated passes that read All Access and suddenly made me feel privileged being as though I tried my hand at being a background singer before, so I knew how hard it was to obtain those. I figured Romello, the hottest producer and music exec around had made that happen for her. I couldn't wait to meet him. His name was like gold in the industry and was just who I needed to link up with. Then again, Tyesha was so shady the passes could've come from anywhere.

"Where did you get those?" I mouthed to her.

She quickly shook her head, which was a sign for me to shut up, and to *just go with it, a* term she frequently used.

Soon, the bouncer let us back with ease leaving the wannabes talking crazy from behind us.

"Who them tricks think they is?" a ghetto ass woman called out.

"That bitch stole my pass!" another shouted.

I huffed ignoring their every word. I was so above them. My focus stayed on my opportunity. What if they wanted me to sing? I wondered. What would I choose? I needed something that was fire...that would leave a lasting impression. And what if they asked me to dance on the spot? Hell, I had on five inch, thigh high Valentino boots. As I played around with my thoughts Tyesha felt the need to bust off some disrespectful comments about my man as we rounded the corner headed down a long, narrow hallway.

"So, did you tell that muthufucka Trae you were comin' here tonight? I know that was probably that bastard who called a little while ago."

"No, I didn't. He's headed to Miami tonight. You know the Super Bowl is this weekend. He's probably got his mind on winning a ring."

"I know," she shot back quickly. "I just don't know how you missed out on *another* trip. Girl, you stay on punishment with his ass. You know me and India hate Trae, right?" she informed as we walked directly into a crowd of guys standing in a circle.

I swallowed hard, feeling like some shit. Thankfully, Tyesha's focus got diverted because surely she had more words to share about my relationship with Trae.

"Well, well...well...money making, JR Jones. What's up superstar?"

"Tyesha, what's up, baby?"

I watched them embrace one another feeling pretty good about their relationship. It seemed as though I had a chance of getting hooked up, especially when Tyesha began her introduction.

"JR, this is Royce, my girl I've been tellin' you about."

The entire group of guys got quiet as I became the center of attention. It was like I was the prime piece of steak on display at the meat market. I knew my tight, black Alice & Olivia skirt showed off my thick, firm thighs, and video vixen ass, but my upper body seemed to be of interest, too. The fixated stares made me uncomfortable.

"Oh, this her?" JR asked, slipping his hands into his jean pockets.

"Yessssss, Sir. This is Royce, the one and only. The one you need to sign. She sexy as hell, right?" Tyesha said, batting her eyes. "And yes, I want a cut when you hear the pipes on this babe. At least five percent, but more if we go platinum."

I couldn't believe she was acting like my manager. Yes, it was her idea to come to the show, but we hadn't discussed percentages.

"Oh yeah," JR responded.

"That's right. This is the girl who'll make you famous. I told you about her. Don't you remember? She sang back-up for a short time with Kelly Crisfield."

"Word."

I simply grinned, but I wanted to nudge Tyesha in the back telling her to shut her trap. Everything seemed to be happening so fast I began to sweat under the pit of my arms a bit. This was it…this was it, I kept telling myself. I thought about fixing my hair while Tyesha continued with her sales pitch, but then JR spoke to me directly making me almost piss on myself.

"What's your name again?"

"Ummmmm...Royce," I stuttered. "Nice to meet you." I extended my hand with a little more confidence until he kissed it.

"Naw, the pleasure's all mine."

I smiled. "Thanks."

"Let's talk," JR said, moving slightly away from the other two guys who were now just standing around waiting for Tango to emerge from his dressing room. "So, Tyesha tells me you're a triple threat. You sing, dance, and play guitar."

"Yep," I stated proudly, feeling like this was really going to work.

I imagined myself on the front cover of my breakout CD with my long hair blowing in the wind and my body dripping in diamonds. I wanted to look like a Goddess. I also imagined myself giving Trae an ultimatum. "Now, that I can take care of our son Trae, you will either marry me or just leave. I can take care of myself!"

Even in my imaginative thoughts, I could see Trae saying, he'd have to call me back.

"JR, you want the demo now or you want me to mail it to your office? I really need Romello to hear it, too."

As Tyesha asked him about the demo tape, I pulled it from my purse.

"Hold onto it. I think I need to get to know Royce a little better first," he said, touching my shoulder lovingly. "Besides, I never heard of a black woman, sexy as this little lady who can play guitar. That's some Taylor Swift shit. What else can you do?"

He hit me with a look that I didn't care for. For the first time, Tyesha remained silent. I didn't have any words either. As I felt JR's hand explore my body, I zoned out hoping to ignore the fact that he didn't have his hand in between my thighs. I stood frozen thinking about Trae. Why couldn't he be more supportive? Then I wouldn't have to go through this kinda shit just to get my career off the ground. With the money and connections he had, I was certain he could've made one call and got me a meeting with Sony.

"So, where's Romello?" Tyesha questioned. She probably figured we'd have better luck with getting down to business.

JR shrugged his shoulders with attitude as three, loud females rounded the corner, with a representative from the radio station. It was clear they'd been led back to meet Tango. While I listened to the radio host discuss how things would go down, Tango's dressing room door flew open and the two fans ran up to him with pens in hand. With arrogance, he signed autographs and took two quick pictures before his bodyguard sent everyone away with the exception of me, Tyesha and JR.

6

The hallway cleared faster than a cheetah after its prey leaving the three of us feeling privileged. Tango stood there, staring me in the face; the same way he did as he left the stage earlier.

"What's up?" he asked JR with a nod.

"Nothing, dawg. We were just waiting on you. I was just getting to know this pretty lady here. She's a singer. A pretty good one, so I hear."

Tango smiled. "Oh yeah."

Is that all these guys say? I wondered.

"You tryna go get something to eat before we hit up this after party?" JR asked Tango.

"Yeah. I'm hungry, dawg. Is this pretty lady going?"

Oh hell, Tango was talking about me. "Uh...uh...no," I stepped up to say. I wouldn't dare get caught with some R&B guys and have the news travel to Trae on a weekend where he needed to be focused. "I'm Royce. I just came to drop off my demo," I finally got the courage to say. I held the CD tightly in my sweaty palms.

"So, c'mon beautiful, let's get it dropped off," he told me stepping aside and implying that he wanted me to enter his dressing room.

I paused looking toward Tyesha for approval.

"It's about time somebody wants to conduct business," she announced excitedly, then rolled her eyes at JR. "Let's hurry. Time is money."

I walked inside the room with a glow hearing Tyesha's footsteps behind me. Everything seemed to be looking positive until I heard the door slam, turning to see no one but me and Tango in the room. I felt weird. Everything seemed to move in slow motion as if I were in some low-budget movie. A bad one...frightening me to the core. Tango's eyes were malicious, I knew getting him to think about my music would be difficult.

"Here's the track," I said, handing it to him slowly.

Tango let out a boisterous laugh, which sent chills up my spine. A laugh that was far from funny. Instantly, he snatched the demo from my hand, throwing it, landing on top of an army-green duffle bag. "Sing, butterfly. Let me hear what you got."

Butterfly, I thought as goosebumps popped up on my firm arms. He began to encircle me, taking each step around me creepily, never picking up the pace. "If you're a singer you should be able to sing on demand. You know that, right?"

Scared shitless, I opened my mouth and let the note flow from my lungs. I belted a Jennifer Hudson favorite so he'd see my potential, fast, thirty seconds flat. When I stopped, Tango quit his pacing and gripped my chin.

"Damn, you really got talent."

I sighed, calming my nerves to finish the deal. I needed to know where we would go from here since he liked what he heard. "Where…"

"Quiet! So, what else can you do, butterfly?" His voice bellowed like a beast then lowered all too easily.

My eyes popped from my head. I'd thought too positive too soon. "Uhhhhh…I dance, play guitar. And I even write," I rattled off, with my voice trembling and knowing that wasn't what he meant. I turned to face the door hoping Tyesha would knock. Even JR. Anybody.

"C'mon now, butterfly. I know you're not that green." Tango laughed again. "How's your tongue?"

Immediately, my hands went up as a sign of surrender. I wanted out. The opportunity to connect with Tango and his crew was worth millions but as I watched him unbuckle his pants, my dream of becoming a star dwindled.

"Ahhhh look-a-here, I think you got me all wrong. I just want a chance at singing." I began to back up.

"Did you think you were coming in here to talk? C'mon butterfly, damn. Where you been living…under a rock? You know the game. I heard them say you sang back-up," he preached, dropping his pants to the floor. "You know what this biz is like."

A tear dropped. And I attempted to block out what was happening. Tango's nine inch rod pointed at me as he began taunting me, asking me to do what I came to do. I never moved. I couldn't. I began playing back Trae's words about how the music business was bad for me and how I needed to leave it alone, focusing only on my son, being a mother and a good fiancé. Maybe I should've

8

listened to my man. Then Tango's next set of words resonated through my thoughts. "Pay your dues, bitch."

My dues? All I wanted was a chance to sing.

I closed my eyes and backed against the wall knowing that I would be raped. There was nothing in the room but a long mirror on the wall, two chairs and a couch. So no possible weapons were near. I began singing to myself never allowing even one word to escape from my lips. The lyrics resided only in my head. Just as I'd been able to do my entire toddler years, I erased what was really happening. Tango had managed to attack my lips leaving the lingering taste of Hennesy and pinning my body against the wall.

"Get down on your knees," he belted.

I couldn't move if I wanted to from the way he had me cornered. But I resisted anyway. "Noooo, please….don't do this!" I thought about Tyesha, but before another thought even entered my mind, I was slapped to the floor.

"What's wrong, butterfly?" Tango asked in a condescending, sweet voice. "You don't like me or something?"

Sniffles escaped from my body as I crawled swiftly to the door. Seconds later, I felt my left leg being yanked and my entire body being dragged like a rag doll. I kicked. I shouted, hoping someone would hear me just before getting punched in the eye. I let out a high pitched scream that fell on deaf ears. Then another blow traveled my way with speed, followed by another…and another…

Finally, I gave up just as I'd done many times in life. I closed my eyes singing a song that I'd just written the lyrics to. How ironic- the title, *Take Me Away*.

Chapter 2

India

"Rachel, quit driving so slow, our plane leaves at 6:15 sharp, and we haven't even gotten to the expressway yet." I checked my new Rolex for the correct time, plus hoping my girl would ask me where I got it, and who bought it.

"India, please….stop nagging. We'll get there on time," Rachel told me with attitude. She suddenly whipped her black Porsche Cayenne in and out of traffic as if my words made a difference. Then shot me a nasty look.

"Look, this is the last flight to Miami for tonight, and you did tell me that you have to arrive at least an hour before the doors open at the NFL's Super Bowl Bash tonight, didn't you?"

"I did."

"Well, step on it, bitch. The men are waiting on me," I joked.

Rachel didn't laugh. She killed me, always acting so prissy. I guess that's why I was super pissed that Royce's man banned her from this trip. She was always the punctual one, the one who would've had all three of us at the airport four hours early, and the one who would've chipped in to have a limo drop us off. But that's the shit that happens when you decide to have a baby; your life gets ruined.

I sat up with a wide grin on my face as we turned into JFK

International Airport minutes later. My insides burned at the thought of getting closer to all those men in Miami with multi-million dollar contracts. I could smell the money from the passenger seat of Rachel's ride. Before I knew it, Rachel slammed on brakes in front of the U.S Airways curbside kiosk.

"Get out, I'll go park," she told me.

"No girl. You gotta show your ID. Hop out and let's get the boarding passes first, then you go park."

"Yes sir, master," Rachel told me, mimicking some old down south accent.

I quickly motioned to the skycap, snapping my fingers like I owned the airport. The January wind smooched me in the face immediately, but I wasn't about to let a little cold weather stop me.

"Quick, we need help," I called out to the guy, pointing to our luggage in the back of Rachel's trunk.

It was crazy how Rachel had one, oversized bag but of course I had three of my Louis Vuittion bags compliments of Canal Street in New York City looking like I'd just come off the set of *Coming to America*. No one knew my bags were fake though, not even Rachel, so I held my head high. I'd worked hard to get my shit, following some Korean man with baggy pants and flip flops three, long blocks, up five corridors of stairs, and into a tiny closet to buy my fake designer luggage. So flaunting my shit wasn't an option. I deserved it. See for me, life was about presentation. And as long as my image was flawless, nothing else mattered.

Rachel turned her head in embarrassment as I began to tell the skycap that we were the wives of Shawn Grant and Jason Carr, and that we had to hurry. I'd become a pro at stealing the identity of Shawn's wife to gain entrance into celebrity parties, overbooked restaurants, and first class upgrades on a regular. My stories worked since my name was Grant, too and also thanks to Rachel's inside track with the NFL.

As Rachel placed her French manicured fingertips on my shoulder she whispered into my ear, distracting me like some nagging six year old. "Of all the guys on the team, you pick Jason Carr. He has a slew of women and they're gonna know he's not married."

"Watch your car," I blasted loudly just before shooting the skycap a fake grin. He was busy punching tons of info into the computer, giving me a chance to chastise Rachel one last time. "You want this first class seat, don't you?"

"Not really, India."

"Bitch, I bet you'll sit in it."

"I sure will, but you've got to stop this bullshit sooner or later, and stop living this superficial life," Rachel told me as she watched an airport cop mouth some words to her about her car.

I budded in just as I always did. "Oh, sir, we're moving now." I shot him a smile and a sexy flick of the wrist. "We certainly don't want to cause a nice looking man like you any problems, officer."

Of course he grinned. Then I frowned as the skycap told me he didn't have any first class seats for us.

"It must be a mistake. Can you check the computer one more time?" I asked using my uppity voice. I got a good look at his name tag and decided to make it personal. "Larry, I'm sure my husband's assistant booked us first class tickets. Shawn and Jason just left on a flight last night and we're meeting them in Miami. We always fly first class! Is there a manager on duty?" I questioned, changing my demeanor and checking my watch again.

"Ma'am, I understand your frustration, but you have coach tickets reserved.

"Do I look like I fly coach?" I snapped hard causing a few bystanders to stare.

"Uh, no, you don't, Mrs. Grant," he replied.

My voice became more stern. "Do you watch football, Larry?"

"I sure do, ma'am. I like it a lot."

"So, do you think my husband will be happy with you if you stick me in coach with the general population?"

There was an awkward silence for at least thirty seconds. Larry had begun to look more and more nervous by the minute. He kept surveying the area hoping I wouldn't make a scene. His expression told me the last thing he wanted to do was irritate the wives of popular football players. Time seemed to be running out so I grabbed my sleek new cell phone from my oversized Gucci hobo bag. Larry started sweating like a pig on a hot, sunny day.

"Shawn, you aren't going to believe the skycap here at U.S. Airways can't find our first class tickets in the system," I announced loudly. "Baby, I refuse to sit in coach. You know I don't do that. Maybe you can call his boss," I whined like I was really talking to someone.

"No, wait," Larry said softly using his pointer finger to shush me.

"Oh, hold on a second, honey." I placed my hand over the phone and whispered to Larry. "Would you like to come to a game next season?"

I only got a panicky nod as sweat dripped from his head making me feel victorious inside.

"We're good, honey," I said into the phone and hunched Rachel in her side. "I'll call you if I need you. Smooches." I kissed into the phone and hung up.

Larry began punching keys really fast and glancing from side to side at his surroundings. He knew that his job would be on the line if he upgraded the tickets at no charge. But he also realized that he didn't want to bear the title of the loser skycap that couldn't make shit happen. Quickly weighing his options, he nervously began to grab the new boarding passes from the machine.

"I think I got something you'll be happy with, Mrs. Grant."

Feeling like he was the man of the hour, the skycap leaned forward and said "Mrs. Grant, please tell your husband that I've followed his career since he was at Penn State and it will be my pleasure to place you and Mrs. Carr in first class."

"Thank you so much. I'll make sure that I tell my husband how generous you were to us, and we'll get you those tickets. Here's my email address, just shoot me your info," I announced handing him a card that Tyesha made for me and a twenty dollar tip.

I could see how embarrassed Rachel was and knew the mother hen lecture was coming. Before she could even get a word out, I instructed her to go park. "I'll meet you at the gate, Rachel. TTYL," I said, waving her off.

"Don't talk to me in that Paris Hilton voice, India. I hate when you speak that text message talk."

She grabbed my wrist, pushing me closer to the entrance of the double doors so Larry couldn't hear us. The fact that she was only 5'1 and tryna tell me, a five foot eight bombshell what to do was crazy.

"I'm convinced you have really lost your mind. You've never gone that far as to have a phony conversation with some fake ass husband. I could've paid for us to sit in first class, if it was that important. You're not going to ruin my image or my career because you have dreams of being a celebrity wife. Trust me, they have more problems than they can handle. In my three years of working with all the teams, I guarantee you there are more miserable wives than there are happy ones."

I pulled my naturally long hair to the left side of my neck and said, "Happy or miserable? Who can't be happy with a Black American Express card, unlimited vacations, and a personal shopper? Is that enough to convince your ass that I can be real happy, or shall I continue?"

Rachel looked at me with disgust and stormed off to her car. "And park in the V.I.P section if they have one!" I shouted. "L.U.M," I added just to piss her off.

Of course Rachel flicked me off with her hand. "Love you much…my ass," she shouted back.

I simply switched inside the terminal feeling like the Queen of Sheba even though my ass was flat as a pancake; the one thing I hated about myself. While walking, I kept trying to understand how Rachel and I had become such close friends. Our beliefs were the total opposite. Even though we'd met through my girl Royce over five years ago, it still never made sense how we'd maintained a close friendship. We were so different. Rachel was what you called an asset that most men adored, and appreciated everything she had to offer. She had a master's degree in Communications and was one of the youngest, black female public relations managers for the NFL, while I didn't even have a job. Nor did I want one.

We were both men magnets, but I'd always considered Rachel to be more average looking since she kept her hair short, cut close to the face, with the spiky look on top. That look was played, but she still got looks from hotties and had more connections than anyone I knew. My thoughts were that Rachel's connections had more to do with her degrees and talk game. The girl was a genius. I had to give it to her…always planning for her next career move. I on the other hand was blessed with just D cups and long legs. With honey blonde highlighted hair that flowed like a body wave, my biggest asset was my talk game, which my mother always said would get me nowhere but in the soup line.

As I pranced through the terminal I couldn't help but to have flashbacks of all the horrible things my mother said to me as a child. "You'll never amount to shit, India," she once told me. "Or, you know why I named you India? It was because I've prayed daily that you and your no good ass father would move all the way to India the moment you were born."

Those comments brought tears to my eyes as I pranced through the security line slow enough to grab any free stares. I lived for attention, and was thirsty for a light ego boost from anyone who could feed my soul, even if it had to be the toothless guy moving all the trays off the conveyor belt.

As I proceeded all the way to the gate, I pretended like I was in some beauty pageant, smiling and giving slight waves to anyone who would look my way. My beauty walk was interrupted by the ringing of my cell. I looked down only to see that it was Royce. I hit ignore since I knew she wanted to know if I'd arrived in Miami yet, and if I'd seen Trae. It didn't take long for Rachel to show up and the gate agent to come onto the loud speaker.

"Good evening passengers, thank you for choosing United Airlines, we will now start boarding flight 99 with nonstop service to Miami. We would like to welcome our first class passengers and any other passengers needing assistance to board at this time," the gate assistant said.

I stood proudly with a rare glow in my eyes as the female working the gate called for first class passengers. Grabbing my small carry-on bag, I began to push my way thru the small crowd, not even caring that I'd elbowed an elderly lady to get to the front of the line.

"Rachel, what are you waiting for?" I shouted as I gave my boarding pass to the agent.

Rachel just slid down in the black leather seat behind the kiosk in humiliation, refusing to board the plane with me. She killed me being so conservative. Maybe it was because she grew up in Long Island and had a father who was a lawyer and a mother who was a doctor. I remembered education being a priority in the Owens household, so Rachel had no choice but to become a professional. But acting like I was committing a crime didn't make any sense to me at all.

"Rachel, let's go, you heard the lady," I repeated, "she said first class passengers. That would be us."

She waved me off again so I held my head high and left her prissy ass to board with the common folk. By the time I got on the plane and plopped my new, J Brand jeans in seat 2A, I began to daydream while waiting for Rachel to board the plane. I thought about how good life would be if I lived a first class life. I began to watch myself smile thru the tiny oval window as I thought of owning every designer bag on the market, eating at gourmet restaurants for every meal, vacationing at five star resorts, and living in an estate, not an apartment.

Some older white guy with a receding hair line in the seat across from me broke my trance. Although he needed a hair transplant, he had it going on for an old man. He wore a black expensive looking suit and rocked a Presidential Rolex on his wrist, of course not a fake-me-out like mine. While he sipped on a glass of red wine, he stared at me as if I were some black goddess that was sent directly from above. I played things to a tee, and picked up my cell pretending to call my secretary.

"Michelle, did you handle everything that I asked you to do today?" I turned to see if he was watching. And just like I thought, he was indeed. "Great. Take tomorrow off and make sure everything is clean before you leave today."

I threw my phone into my purse and sat back with pride. Within seconds, Rachel finally boarded the plane and placed her laptop bag in the overhead compartment just as he finally decided to open his mouth.

"So, what's a beautiful young lady like yourself going to Miami for?" the old white guy asked.

"Well, my husband is playing in the Super Bowl this weekend, so my girlfriend and I are flying down for the game."

That shit just rolled off my tongue. But I felt so important while saying it.

"I should have guessed. You look like you are well taken care of. What a lucky young man," the older guy smirked as he reached for his cell phone that was vibrating. "Excuse me, I have to take this call, but it was definitely a pleasure meeting you. By the way I didn't get your name."

"India, India Grant. Shawn Grant's wife."

"Is that so? Very beautiful name for a very beautiful woman."

"Bitch, you watch way too many reality shows," Rachel commented before I could even relish in what the man said to me. "You would think you'd learned from Royce what could happen when dating an athlete."

"Blah blah blah," I told her. "Chello, Chello," I called for the stewardess in my high society voice. "Bring me your best champagne," I told her with a smirk. I reared back in my seat as our plane descended taking me to meet my future husband.

Chapter 3

Royce

My entire body trembled violently from head to toe as I paced barefoot back and forth across my bedroom floor. My arms were wrapped around my upper frame tightly but failing to give me that calm and comforting feeling I was so desperately in need of. Mascara trailed from my eyes and down my cheeks in a shade of black, darker than charcoal. Blotches of it were smeared over my face from the dozens of times I'd wiped never ending tears from my eyes.

My usually neatly kept room was a total mess. CDs and DVDs cluttered the floor. Bottles of nail polish and perfume had been thrown everywhere in the midst of my temper tantrum, leaving portions of the carpet stained. My vanity mirror was shattered and my plasma screen television had a gaping hole through the center of it. The room's damage had all been caused by me, Royce, the woman who couldn't protect herself.

"Fucking bastard!" I shouted at the cause of my pain, although knowing Tango couldn't hear me at all. Even if he did, he wouldn't care. He was probably sitting somewhere at the very moment with his friends laughing and joking about what he'd done to me. "How could I have been so damn naïve?" I kept asking myself repeatedly.

"You son of a bitch!" I screamed, causing each vein in my

neck to pulsate, ready to explode. Out of rage, I slung a glass vase across the room against the wall so hard it shattered to the floor. My body felt dirty and violated as the vision of him forcing anal sex on me filled my memory. Tango taking my pussy was torture enough. But violating me anally was even worse.

Suddenly, I had a flashback of the sound of his hand loudly connecting with the side of my face. It echoed like a firecracker. The strength of it had dazed me, jerked my head viciously to the right, and almost knocked me unconscious. Within a matter of seconds, I remembered being snatched up by my hair from the floor and was soon brutally having every bit of my vagina, pride, and dignity taken. Tango immediately forced my body over the back of the couch and raised my skirt even further up than it already had been.

"Tango, please don't do this," I remembered begging, knowing what was coming. My vision was still blurry and my knees were still feeling like rubber.

"Shut up, bitch!" Tango demanded as he snatched the crotch of my panties to the side and prepared to enter me again. But this time from a different hole.

Before I knew it he inflicted the worst physical pain on me I had ever felt in my entire life as he forced himself completely into my rectum with no mercy and began to pound while pulling me by my long, black hair. The pain was so bad I felt like my bowels were going to release all over him.

"It hurts!" I screamed, while trying to wrestle away from him. "Please stop!"

"Shut the fuck up and take it!"

Then the knock came from the door.

"Tango," I remembered someone calling from behind it.

"Help!" I screamed to the top of my lungs. "He's raping me! Please help me!"

Within seconds, the door opened.

The concert promoter asked Tango what was going on with a quizzical look on his face. Immediately, I shoved Tango off of me and dashed out the door into the crowded hallway of groupies and Tango's entourage. I pushed and shoved them out of my way as I headed directly for the exit sign, nearly five yards away, fixing my clothes all at the same time. My vision was blurred by the tears falling from my eyes as I ran like a runaway slave until I reached the exit sign. Quickly, I took the stairs down four flights, uncertain about where I'd end up. When I finally reached the bottom and burst through the door, I found myself on the street amongst lingering partygoers. All eyes were on me as I darted past them jumping into the first cab I saw.

Suddenly, my eyes glanced at the alarm clock lying on the floor which for some reason snapped me from my ride down memory lane. It was nearly midnight and I was still in my room reminiscing. I grabbed my cell phone from the bed and called Trae. I had called him five times from the cab only to get several rings and his damn voicemail each and every time. What the hell was he doing that was so important he couldn't answer my call? I needed him. My soul needed to hear his voice. He never called back.

With the phone now in my hand again, I dialed his number with trembling fingers. I pressed the phone to my ear to only once again hear several rings and his voice mail.

"Damn it, Trae!" I yelled. "Something bad happened to me tonight. I need you. Call me!"

After tossing the phone on the bed I thought about grabbing it again and calling the police. Short of murder, I wanted to see Tango in jail, tortured, even pumped in the ass by some big, salad-tossing dude. The only thing that stopped me from calling them was my career. If I told them Tango raped me, my face would be all over the television for the wrong reasons. My career would be over before it even had a chance to begin. The whole world would think I was lying. They would think I was just a gold digger out for some kind of a payday. No record label on the entire planet would even think about signing me.

I grabbed my head in disgust and shame, slamming myself down on the side of my bed. Why did this have to happen to me? I couldn't stop wondering. Why me? Anger began to flood my mind as Tyesha's trifling ass consumed my thoughts. She was the true reason for my circumstances. She had to have known I'd fled Tango's dressing room by now. Someone had to have told her. The grimy bitch hadn't even called to check on me and it was now midnight. There was no doubt in my mind she'd tossed me to the wolves. Until she told me other wise, I didn't have anything to say to her. Suddenly, I thought back to how Tyesha had taken money from some random guy who wanted to get hooked up with her brother's girlfriend when we were back in high school. I figured if she'd done that to her own flesh and blood, there was no telling what she'd do to me.

The only feeling that overrode my anger was loneliness at the moment. I had no one but myself. I needed someone to run to, someone to console me. But there was no one. Everyone I loved with the exception of my son was in Miami by now having fun. There were no friends, family, nothing or no one for me to vent to. Having no one in my life that was blood had always hurt. That's why finding my birth mother had been so important to me. I thought about calling my foster mom but shame made me think against it. After what she had found out about my past, she wouldn't want to talk to me. I was utterly alone.

As tears began to fall once again I heard my roommate and old co-worker, Niecy's keys as she came in through the living room door. I could only bury my face in my hands. She was the last person I wanted to see right now, but she had been babysitting my son, and they were just coming in along with her six week old baby. If I told her what happened, she'd probably use it for gossip. After tossing her keys on the dining room table, Niecy headed to my room and stood in the doorway with her son still wrapped in her arms. I knew she was surveying the damage of my room but my heart was too broken to care.

"Uh-uh," Niecy grunted, annoyed by the mess. "What the hell is going on?"

Her voice irked the shit out of me as usual. "You wanna explain this shit?" she asked me, putting one hand on her right, wide hip. "Hellooooo?"

"Now isn't a good time, Niecy," I said with my face still buried in my hands. "Please just leave me alone. I'm not in the mood."

"Look, Royce, I already kept your child tonight so you

could go get your singing bullshit on a roll, but I can't keep being patient about you fucking up the house every time you get mad. You've wrecked this room again and you're three weeks late with the rent. Something's got to give."

Her voice was beginning to piss me off. But I kept calm because I could hear Lil Trae in the living room turning on the television.

"I need the rent money now, Royce."

"I told you, I'm going to pay you, Niecy," I grumbled, wanting her to just go the fuck away. She was so money hungry and I never understood why. "I'm just waiting on my check from Trae."

"You've been saying that for a fucking while now. You know I'm still trying to figure out if he was the one who got caught cheating, why were you the one who got put out. That shit makes no sense."

"It wasn't like I could've put him out of his own house. We're not married yet."

"Well, you shoulda made his cheap ass put you and your son up in some fly apartment in Manhattan. But noooo, you wanna sit here in the dirtiest part of Brooklyn waiting on his late checks every month." She shook her head. "Wow…that's exciting."

"Niecy please. I'm not in the mood."

"Then, to top it off, a damn social worker was over here looking for you today. You know I don't like them white folks in my business, especially white women. Them bitches sneaky."

My head rose immediately at the mentioning of a social worker. It was the only thing that could take my mind off of the rape. "What did she want?"

"I don't know?"

"She didn't tell you?"

"I told you, I don't know. You know I don't discuss no personal business with them damn white folks. They might be the cops. All I know is she was asking a bunch of nosey ass questions about you like she the muthafucking FBI or something."

Niecy could tell I'd gotten nervous.

"Anyway, I thought you were just searching for your birth

mother."

"I am."

"Then why was she asking so many questions? And why are you so nervous? You getting food stamps and ain't telling me?"

There she goes wanting more money. "Don't worry about it, Niecy!" I shouted, not in the mood to be given the third degree. "Just stay out of my business!"

Her face twisted. "You asked me the questions, bitch!"

Suddenly, the doorbell rung.

"Uh-oh," she said. "See, that's the shit I'm talking about right there. It's after twelve o'clock and you still got company ringing the damn doorbell. And come get yo' damn five year old off my T.V. with all that Xbox bullshit. Don't he have a bed time, damn it?"

I fell back on the bed as Niecy rushed off to answer the door. "I hate you sometimes!" I muttered, fed up with her complaining ass mouth.

"Royce!" Niecy yelled moments later from the living room. "You got company out here!"

"Shit," I hissed, not wanting to see anyone. I didn't want to get up but forced myself to. My feet scraped against the hardwood floor as I headed to the living room with my head down. When I finally raised it, I couldn't believe my eyes. My heart jumped to my throat and the pit of my stomach dropped like an elevator. My knees went totally weak, nearly buckling beneath me.

"Well if it isn't Royce, the thief?" he greeted me.

My body was completely paralyzed and my mouth remained speechless as I looked into his eyes wondering what the hell he was doing here and how he had found me. Not a single, solitary syllable fell from my lips.

As my eyes moved between him and Niecy, I wondered if he had told her who he was and how we were really connected. My heart fluttered again as I studied him, hard. Five years had gone by, yet he still looked the same. That same widow's peak, extended forehead, and piercing eyes. Oh, God, this was going to turn out terribly, I just knew it.

He took two intimidating steps toward me.

"Well, don't I deserve a hug?" he asked with heart wrenching sarcasm. His deep, baritone voice had always put fear in my heart, in addition to knowing what he was capable of. I'd seen him murder people with his own two hands.

"We need to talk," he ordered. His eyes rotated toward the door.

There was no way in hell I was leaving with him. "I can't, Latrell," I blurted.

He grabbed me by my arm and glared into my eyes, allowing me to become reacquainted with the numerous tiny black moles covering his dark skin.

"You're coming with me," he told me with his clutch getting tighter.

Of course Niecy's eyes had enlarged like the ones I'd seen on the cartoons. Her baby began to cry and my son stood up and walked toward me. Even though I was terrified of Latrell's frown, I knew I had to protect my child.

"Let me go, Latrell, or I'm calling the police!"

"Mommy, who's this man?" Lil Trae asked.

Oh shit! Nothing could be worse. "A friend," I told my son wearily.

"He seems to be more than a friend," Niecy shot back, becoming concerned. I watched as she extended her hand. "I'm Niecy, Royce's roommate. "What's this all about? You're making her son upset. And mine, too."

"Take him away so he doesn't have to see his mother die," he responded quickly.

Latrell didn't move. His feet remained frozen and his looming eyes locked in on me while Niecy tried to swallow what she'd just heard.

"Take Trae in the other room!" I shouted to Niecy, before speaking to Latrell immediately afterward. "Why are you here, Latrell!"

"You know why the fuck I'm here!"

He let go of my arm after slinging me around so I could face him. I knew what I'd done, but I played dumb. I made sure Niecy was nowhere in sight before I started talking again. I didn't know what he would say and really didn't want her in my past. "Listen, you gotta go. Now!"

"Royce, you either coming with me, or you won't live to see another day."

The next thing I knew I was hit with a haymaker and landed on the floor right next to Lil Trae's feet who'd ran back into the living room attempting to protect me.

Chapter 4

India

The ride took no time. And now I was pumped. After Rachel and I grabbed our luggage from the conveyor belt, we headed to the back of the rental car, shuttle bus line. The whole idea was beneath me, but I didn't want to piss Rachel off so early in the game. Sweat poured down my back as the Miami heat began to dampen my Juicy tank top. I pulled the scrunchie off my wrist to tie my hair into a tight ponytail. At least that would bring some relief to the back of my neck. Rachel wasn't bothered much by the heat or the long line since she was reading her emails and checking messages on her Blackberry that she had missed while in flight. Besides, her dark skin tone told me she was used to heat and sun.

My eyes began to glisten as a black, four door Maybach pulled to the curb beside us. "Rachel, you didn't tell me we were getting picked up in a Maybach, girl. Ooooohhhhh…lala. See this is what I'm talking 'bout, baby. I knew you had some connects up your sleeve. Let's go because my hair can't take the heat."

Rachel began to chuckle, "Girl, I didn't tell you because that's not hardly our car. The only way you will ride in a Maybach is to catch a ride with your old ass friend over there that you met on the plane."

My head swiveled like the chick from the Exorcist. I kept turning, trying to figure out who Rachel was talking about. Before she could say anything, the driver opened the back passenger door, and the old white guy that I'd been talking to on the plane ushered himself toward the three-hundred something thousand dollar car.

"Mr. Haskin, it's a pleasure to have you home, Sir," I heard the clean cut driver tell him.

"Yes, I'm happy to be home. Didn't like the commercial flight though…but who's complaining. I guess I had to take one for the team this time. Hold on one second, Steve," he said to his driver as he looked my way.

My heart raced as he pulled out a business card and walked over to me.

"We meet again so soon, beautiful. I would offer you ladies a ride, but I wouldn't want to offend your husband. Here's my card, give me a call if you're ever in the Miami area again."

"Thanks," I said dryly.

Mr. Haskin walked away leaving his million-dollar scent on the sidewalk. Suddenly, his pace slowed and glanced back my way. "By the way, you're way too classy for rental cars. Tell your husband he should know better."

I felt like two cents watching the driver close the door in my face. I glanced over at Rachel who was bent over laughing her ass off. "Fuck you, Rachel," I said rolling my eyes and glancing at the card Mr. Haskin had given me.

Just like that, Rachel snatched the card, "Mr. Anthony Haskin, Vice President of the Miami Heat. He's NBA baby! No wonder you're over here looking like you wanna throw up. You're pathetic. You really would consider calling this seventy year old man who's old enough to be your granddaddy. Please tell me what you would do with that old piece of dick?"

"Suck it. Massage it. Make love to it. Whatever it takes, you jealous whore." I snatched the card back and looked at Rachel sarcastically. "I'm not as picky as you are. I don't believe in perfect men. They don't exist and that might explain why you haven't had one in years." I sucked my lips and decided to ignore Rachel for a while.

Luckily, time passed quickly. By the time Rachel pulled into the jammed packed valet lane of the Loews Hotel on Collins

Avenue an hour later, I'd transformed into a sophisticated hoochie. From the back seat, I'd slipped on a grey, one shoulder dress stopping mid thigh, and was just putting on a pair of peep toe stilettos when Rachel opened the door and shook her head.

"You really are shameful. And the fact that you changed in the car without a shower is nasty."

"What's a girl to do," I replied in my adopted valley girl voice that was sure to pull an educated and wealthy nicca soon.

"You're a lost cause," Rachel told me just as the valet guy walked up on her.

I applied a little blush to accent my cheekbones, then got ghost on my girl within seconds. While she handled the business of doing the car thingy and checking us in, I waltzed inside with my Prada shades pulled down tight on my nose and began the business of seeing who'd made it to town so far. With hundreds of people scurrying through the lobby you almost needed a Ph.D in Player Identification to figure out who was an athlete and who was not. Of course I was certified so I began my self- created classification process. I'd put men into three categories; those who were here to watch the event, those who had money but were not players; and the elite group; the ballas, those who had contracts.

The crazy part about the situation was, all the people scrambling around were mostly fans and groupies; and definitely an uneven ratio if someone were to ask me; at least eight women to every man.

Damn, this seemed to be getting harder by the second, I told myself through clinched teeth.

As I surveyed the area, I began toying around with what I would say after meeting a potential husband. What lie would I tell first? How would I react? Would I pretend not to know who the guy was if he was a player, or would I confess making him feel like a super-star? So many questions flooded my mind until I spotted Ayden Smoot, fullback for the Carolina Panthers near the bar with a drink in his hand and two off-brand chicks deep in his face. The chick with the leopard print shirt who gave off major cleavage had a set of eyes that batted dollar signs at every word he spoke. He just couldn't see it. I leaned against the column watching from afar when Rachel grabbed me by the elbow.

"You know who that is, right?"

"Yep. That's why you interrupting my scouting process better be important!" I breathed heavily and shot her my pissed off look. "And just so you know Rachel, I've searched this entire lobby and have only seen one player so far. This guy!" I pointed to Ayden. "So, what do you need?"

"Cash would've been nice. I just checked us in and realized your portion of the hotel fee was still missing."

"Girl, I told you, I got 'chu. Just give me a day or two. By Saturday I'll have the money."

"India, this is..."

"Shut up Rachel, damn! Look, you just gave another bitch an opportunity to land what I'd planned on snagging," I pointed. "He's got his hand gliding up her skirt. And now she's all in his ear. They're getting up to leave, togetherrrrrr," I stressed. "See."

"Good. She saved you, so thank her later. Ayden Smoot is married. Did you forget that being familiar with all the players, their position and team is part of my job?" she told me irritably before walking away.

I followed like a trained puppy all up on the back of her heels. I figured my next best bet was to ask her to make me a list of top potentials without wives, drama, and financial problems. Rachel stopped just as we made it to the elevators. She seemed angry about something.

"India, here's the key to the room. But let me just lay down a couple of ground rules." The winch had her finger pointed in my face like she was the boss of me. "There will be no guys in my room, I don't give a shit how much they make and who they are. Second, don't charge shit to my room that you can't pay for on Monday when we check out, and lastly do not throw my name around this hotel to gain you entrance into anything. This hotel will be filled with my colleagues and I have worked extremely hard to get this job. And I don't need any situations surrounding my name, got it? Oh yeah, and most importantly, Ayden Smoot is bisexual."

My jaw dropped low, showing off my veneers that hadn't been paid for yet.

"Yes, babe, so remember, I know all the players' business,

so before you think about boning anybody, check with me!"
Rachel said as she pressed the up button to go to the room. "Aren't
you coming to freshen up?" She hit me with the strangest look on
her face.

"Ahhhhh," I stuttered then looked over my shoulder. "Not
yet, I need about thirty more minutes to scout.

"Suit yourself, but I'm leaving here in forty-five minutes. I
can't be late. And without me, you can't get in the party."

"I swear I'll be up in thirty." My eyes began to beg her not
to say anymore as she stepped onto the elevator and began to judge
me without words. Her disapproving expression said it all.
"Chow," I told her with a royal wave and chin up as the doors shut.

As soon as I turned back around, Ayden Smoot was just
two inches away from my face. Sadly, with a chick on his arm. In
one quick desperate attempt, I pushed my bra up with both hands
causing one of my girls to peek just a bit. Just when I knew I had
Ayden's attention I licked my lips, stuck my tongue out and blew
kisses his way. *I had him. I just knew it.*

Just like that he stepped onto the elevator smiling, letting
the doors close leaving me standing looking stupid.

Chapter 5
India

I could tell Rachel would work my last nerve over the weekend. However, since she was the one with the connects and my ticket to the invite-only NFL party tonight, I had to stay on her good side. She'd made it perfectly clear before we left NYC that she only had one ticket to game day on Sunday so my goal was to find myself a ticket, quick. It seemed as if time flew purposely because before I knew it Rachel and I were in the towncar headed to the party. She never gave me a chance to do anything but apply a little more blush, some concealer, and fluff my hair a bit.

Meanwhile, she looked adorable in her black BCBG strapless dress that showed off her toned arms, and tiny, athletic looking body. Of course she had her cell phone glued to her hand. When we pulled up to the Miami Aquarium it was amazing to see how the venue was turned into a star-studded event. The location was perfect because it sat on the bay side of Miami, so the views from all angles were spectacular. The shit was so surreal and had me feeling like a queen. My adrenaline accelerated watching the limos backup along Bayside Street as a few notable players emerged.

"OMG! Girl, that's Eric Tatum from the Ravens, and Mark McGuire from Green Bay," I told my girl like a star struck kid.

"India, pull yourself together," Rachel instructed as our car stopped right in front of the place. "You'll see hundreds of players tonight so try not to act like a groupie." She gave me that look that

I hated so much just as the driver opened my door.

In just one full day with Rachel, I'd had enough of her tight-faced looks. She could keep lying all she wanted to, but I knew she'd gotten botox in her face by the way her skin closest to her cheeks had lost all elasticity.

"Have a good evening, Madam," my driver wished upon me as he bowed to the queen.

Red carpet lined the soles of my shoes as I stepped out of the car causing people to gasp. I knew the hater chicks on the sideline were whispering about me, my outfit, and wondering who I was married to. I just knew it. I could feel it. I simply smiled widely and gave off waves to no one in particular making sure my moves were perfect, Beyonce like. I'd watched she and Jay-Z on the carpet countless times and tried my best to mimic her positions as the cameras flashed, making sure my nine hundred dollar Bottega Veneta clutch bag got in the pictures. It had to be returned to Neiman Marcus for a refund next week so keeping it in good condition was important.

While Rachel stopped to talk to a few people she knew along the way, I began thinking about what it would feel like to be on the arm of a 300lb defensive lineman as he strutted alongside me smiling at the paparazzi. Or even a rookie who'd just signed a moderate contract with tons of media potential. Certainly he'd have every reporter in town begging for an interview and asking who the lovely lady was at his side. I couldn't wait.

Before I knew it, we'd made it inside the Aquarium as I drifted off into some other farfetched land every time I saw another player. My mouth remained wide open and my eyes were on alert with every strut taken. They were everywhere, lining the walls, dressed in the most expensive looking tuxedos my eyes had ever seen. Although the teams playing in Sunday's game would be the Giants and the Patriots, I saw guys from the Redskins, Lions, Saints and many more. My gut told me they were all watching, wanting me. Just the thought of the Giants directed my brain to reminisce about Chris Jackson, my number one target for the weekend. He was a tight end for the Giants, born and raised in Brooklyn, straight from my neighborhood.

Even though Chris probably wouldn't remember me from
when we were kids, I felt this unusual connection with him especially since he had just signed his second multimillion dollar contract. Chris was thirty-one, just five years older than me, but I liked
my men seasoned anyways. He would know exactly how to treat
me, giving me the finer things in life. I thought about his 6'2, dark
brown frame and body that would make you smack your momma
and prayed that I would run into him at the party.

"Chris will surely give me a ticket to the Super Bowl," I
told myself with confidence.

As we got closer to the food bar, Rachel stopped to talk to
one of the executives from the Giants. He was all over her, com-
mending her for having such a great staff put the party together.
My body cringed. The décor wasn't that great. I could've done better. I was sick of being her tag-along and decided to move away to
make things happen for myself. I took two steps away and surveyed the food waiting for Rachel to finish up her convo. Then I'd
give her the bad news. I was blowing her company for the night
because too many men were watching me, waiting for me to ride
solo so they could make their moves.

The sight of all the food had my stomach growling; lobster
tails, filet mignon, petite salmon sandwiches and all the ritzy hors
d'oeuvres only one would see on T.V. I hadn't eaten since early afternoon and was famished. I had my back turned to Rachel when I
saw the chocolate covered strawberries, my favorite. I took a deep
breath. I wanted one so badly but stuck to my rule. Never let a man
watch you eat unless it's the perfect item. Strawberries were too
messy and might've caused me to lose a good catch.

"Hey beautiful?" I heard someone say out of the blue.

I fixed my dress, pushed up my bra and grabbed a glass of
champagne off the tray before turning around. The shock of seeing
Calvin Barnett in front of me almost made me choke. The only
problem was that he was referring to Rachel as beautiful and not
me. Quickly, she'd ended her conversation with the exec and took
a few steps toward me to form a circle with Calvin and I.

"Wow, you never cease to amaze me, Rachel."

I seethed with envy as he lifted her right hand then kissed it lovingly. Damn, I knew dark dudes were in, but not women. Why was Rachel's black ass getting more play than me? I'd been wanting to nickname her darkie for years, but had always decided against it.

"The Football League always has one of the best parties during Super Bowl. Of course, that's because of you."

She blushed. Then blushed some more.

"And I'm her good friend, India," I interrupted, slipping my body in front of hers, blocking most of the view he'd previously had of Rachel. He was my catch, not hers. A cornerback from Dallas, been in the league for five years and had a yearly salary of 2.5 million. He was all me.

Unexpectedly, Rachel pushed me slightly by the arm making her way back into Calvin's face. "Yes, this is my friend India who still doesn't know how to behave."

Calvin laughed. Somehow he thought our little spat was funny.

"Nice to meet you, India," he told me then swiftly diverted his attention back to Rachel. "News travels fast in the locker rooms. I hear you're a hot commodity and every exec in the league is trying to offer you more money to leave the Big Apple and the Association."

"I'm New York for life," she cackled. "Plus, I don't want to work for a specific team."

Rachel was so plastic, it damn near killed me. She had zero game.

"Too bad for the rest of us. So, what about us hooking up some time over the weekend?" Calvin asked her.

What? With Rachel? What was the world coming to? I held my palm against my forehead.

The plastic kicked in again. "Now, you know I don't date players."

"That's too bad." He shook his head and stuck his hands deep into his pockets while staring into her eyes, like I didn't exist. "I've been with some beautiful women but most are shallow. After a while, in my line of business, you begin to think brains and beauty don't coexist. So, when I see an educated, professional black woman as beautiful as you, I get excited."

"I see somebody was listening in class the day they taught what women want to hear. Well anyway, Calvin, I hope you find your educated beautiful princess soon. In the meantime, I've got to go check up on few players. Good seeing you."

Rachel grabbed my arm and yanked me so hard I almost tripped. There wasn't any time for words as she pulled me into a crowd of four guys who were having a straight macho conversation while sipping on drinks that looked to be some type of vodka. I pulled myself together thinking of Jay-Z's song, *On To The Next One*. I attempted to fix my hair while scanning each face to see who I knew. At first I didn't get the reaction that I wanted. Once again, it was all about Rachel. I got quiet hoping not to show my frustration. Then a voice lifted my self esteem.

"So, Rachel, who's this?" the tallest of the three men asked.

"Oh, how rude. Forgive me. This is India. India, meet Charles, Kevin and Horace."

Jackpot! Horace Bass was a name that rung a bell. How much he made I wasn't sure, but more than I had for now. "Hel-loooooo, helloo…. Everyone." I grinned so hard I prayed my jaws wouldn't get stuck.

"India, what a pretty name," the guy Charles began. "You must be a model, so tall and slender."

"Nah. But my agent has me reviewing a few movie scripts at the moment."

"Oh, is that so?"

"Y.K.I."

A few wrinkles formed at the top of his head. Come again?"

"You know it," I said to him in a condescending manner.

It was crazy how I had to translate something so simple. After studying his teeth, it was clear he wasn't the one for me. He was too light and his swagger wasn't on point like Horace's. But it was unfortunate how Charles was the one who did most of the talking. The other two guys made small talk with me asking about who'd I'd come to Miami with, what plans I'd made for the rest of the weekend, and how long I'd known Rachel. As soon as Rachel stepped away to talk to a few females who were obviously Giant's players' wives, I lied and told them all we hadn't known each other long and were just rooming for the weekend. Rachel was known to be a snob and I didn't want them thinking of me that way.

Before long, Rachel had secured her place in another huddle not far from me while me and the three fellas chopped it up like long time friends. We laughed at the skanks who wore red lipstick, cheap, skimpy dresses, extra length extensions and beauty supply lashes that could be seen a mile away. After feeling extra comfortable, I was just about to ask the guys who had a Super Bowl ticket to give me when my eyes spotted the one person I didn't want to see.

Ironically, Rachel spotted him, too. I watched her back up a couple of steps cleverly, hoping not to alarm the two people in front of her. Anyone would notice the back of his head from anywhere. He was the only football player who still wore braids with beads at the end. Instantly, I wondered why Royce fell head over heels in love with this guy. Rachel's demeanor changed and I could tell she didn't know what to do. Royce was one of our best friends, and Rachel was the Godmother of their son.

I thought about busting him dead in his tracks when he turned showing the light blotches on his face, but I was busy, hoping to make my move with Horace. Little did he know, he would wake up beside me in the morning.

I thought back to the numerous times Royce had caught Trae cheating and still wanted to stay in the situation. So what was the point of me saying something just so she could be back with him the next week?

I figured Rachel felt the same way as she stood face to face with Trae's yellow ass and the thin, white bitch on his arm. She was probably weighing her career stability with her loyalty to Royce. Confidentiality in her business was a must. It was a golden rule to never reveal any information on a player, even if it was to his wife. Rachel worked hard for her position so she'd be stupid to lay it on the line for a friend.

"What's up, Trae," I heard one guy say as he slapped his hand and spoke to him as if he were a God.

"We're counting on you to take us all the way on Sunday,"

another, fair skinned guy commented as Trae gave up half-ass dap showing his arrogance.

They were all up in his spotty face; players, fans, execs and every nearby horny female. They worshipped the ground this nicca walked on.

"Aye, India," Horace said to me, bringing my attention back to our little party. "Charles, Kevin, and I want to know what you're doing the rest of the night?"

"You guys want to hang out?" I felt honored.

"Exactly." He grinned.

"What's the plan?" I questioned.

"Let's go back to Charles' room."

Female intuition kicked in. All three of us? What the hell were they trying to pull? I got up close in Horace's face. "I like hanging with you guys, but I sorta had something special planned for me and you." I grabbed him by the collar and allowed my 5 foot 8 frame to rest against his chest.

"Oh really. I'm paying two grand for all three of us."

My heart sank. Did they think I was a hooker? I was meant to be somebody's wife not somebody's hoe.

"Hell no!" I told them all sounding like I was on the verge of a break down.

"Oh, I'm sorry. I assumed that's what you wanted. I mean you were making it so clear," Horace replied.

"Wrong!" I shouted. I was furious. "I was being sociable, that's it!"

"So, you down," Charles butted in as if he still didn't get I wasn't a hooker.

"Absolutely not! I will be somebody's wife in the league one day. You watch," I told them all just after slamming my champagne glass onto a nearby table. I stomped off in Rachel and Trae's direction now ready to give Trae a piece of my mind. Tears flooded my face after not believing how badly I'd been humiliated.

"Trae, who is this trick?" I asked like I was the wife who'd come to whip some ass.

"India, what's up, girl?" He looked me up and down like he was hungry, ready to eat.

"Not you, nicca." I crossed my arms slightly below my chest.

"Let me check you out," he commented while leaning to look at my non- existent ass. "Has that thing gained any weight back there yet?"

That was it. I was tired of not having what they all wanted, a phat ass. I was pulling out the butt pads tomorrow, I told myself before going postal on Trae. "Does Royce know her?"

"Not exactly. But you and I need to talk. Give me a call to-morrow," Trae commented as he walked off still eyeballing me.

Rachel knew something bad had happened to me from the redness of my eyes. "Girl, I'm leaving," I told her. "I'll see you when you get back to the hotel."

"You okay?" Then her frown followed.

"I didn't do anything, darkie."

"What in the hell did you just say?" Rachel snapped.

"Nevermind. We'll talk later." I turned to leave and bumped right into Mr. Haskin who had some young, white broad on his arms. "Hello," I told him then rushed toward the door as the tears flowed.

Chapter 6

Royce

I threw back the cream, satin sheets that had been up to my neck throughout the night and jumped out of bed like the house was on fire. I searched for my phone like a crazed woman. Thoughts flooded my brain as I thought back to what Latrell was trying to do to me. It was so inhumane. So foul. So ruthless. But then again, those were all the memories I had of my husband. It was crazy how he'd just showed up out of the blue. Nobody knew I was married, not India, Rachel, Niecy, Lil Trae, and especially not Big Trae. Trae would never make me his wife if this ever got out.

I couldn't believe Latrell had found me after all these years. I thought I'd left his ass back in Atlanta high and dry. And I couldn't believe he'd hit me in front of my son. Who'd given him info on me? And how did he manage to find my exact address?

"Damn it!" I shouted.

The words he'd said to me last night stung hard as I reflected on each and every syllable. And I believed he'd do everything he threatened. He was more than capable considering his thuggish background. Each thought hit me like a whirlwind as I frantically tried to think of options to disappear. After I'd picked myself off the floor last night, he made me promise to meet him at his hotel this afternoon to discuss getting back what I took from him. Like an idiot, an agreement was made even though I had no intentions on following through.

A feeling of desperation washed over me while grabbing my iPhone to check for any calls that had possibly been missed throughout the night. It was 6:30 a.m., still nothing. Not one word from Trae. Something was wrong. I could feel it. Quickly, I punched in his digits, knowing I'd catch him before his early morning team meeting.

Of course another disappointment came. My blood boiled like lava when Trae's voicemail picked up on the first ring. Listening to his one minute greeting that I knew by heart gave me time to concoct another nasty message.

"Trae, it's me again, this is my twentieth message that has gone unanswered. This is crazy how when I need you, I can't get in touch with you! What if Lil Trae had a medical emergency and needed you? He'd be dead by now!" I paused and let a few tears trickle from my eyes. I fought to hold in the fact that I'd been raped. "And this shit about me not being in Miami with you is really starting to get me down. Yeah, I know that you made a lot of money selling your two free tickets that the team gave you, but since when have you been so concerned about money? Some shit, Trae is just priceless."

I stood up from my bed after seeing my son turn over a few times. I didn't want to wake him up while I continued with my marathon message so I walked toward my bedroom door. "Trae, I got a copy of the team schedule from Rachel, and your first meeting for today, Friday, isn't until 8:00 a.m., so there's no reason why your phone should be off and has been all night long. I swear if I don't get a call back, fast, I'm bringing my black ass to Miami, so play with me if you want!" I yelled, then pressed end feeling like I'd preached a sermon.

I knew our relationship was already on life support so I wanted to give Trae benefit of the doubt. But I wasn't stupid. Trae knew just like every other athlete the unwritten code of road trips. But my heart knew what was up.

I paced the floor for another ten minutes thinking about options for getting to Miami by sundown. It was almost impossible since my only babysitting option here in NY, was Niecy's crazy ass. She'd made it clear she didn't really want her own baby so leaving her with my seed for more than a day was a no-no. All of Trae's family lived in D.C. so who in the hell could watch my son? I power walked back over near the bed and took a close look at the only thing that kept the glue between Trae and I. It was crazy how Lil Trae had all my features and his father's nose. He was the spitting image of me with perfectly straight teeth, Indian colored skin and high cheek bones.

He had my eyes and naturally long lashes too but somehow ended up with curly hair. My guess, Trae's side of the family. It made us look as if we were meant to be together. I just prayed he didn't have my weak genes. I got up, rushed over to the mirror and thought about how I'd continuously allowed Trae to take advantage of me.

As I looked in the mirror, this pathetic being looked back at me. With the exception of the bruises on my face, physically, I was perfect so I'd been told; big ass, countless curves, beautiful jet black hair, and an inviting personality; but mentally I was batting zero. How could I have been so stupid to get left behind again? India and Rachel had invited me to go to the Super Bowl with them a month ago when the trip was first planned. Stupidly, I declined their offer hoping for the   chance of finally accompanying the other wives and families on the team's charter flight. Somehow I found myself staring in the mirror having a flashback of Trae's numerous lame excuses to leave me in New York.

"No wife of mine is going to the Super Bowl with her girl-friends. And if you going, it'll be under my watch," he told me. "Why don't you stay at home and look at some of those Bridal Magazines," he sang, in an attempt to fool me.

Somehow his talk game all worked since I was on my third year doing hard time, trying to be Mrs. Trae Harris. It wasn't until yesterday morning that I realized the entire team and their families were all going to Miami.

"Idiot!" I hit myself in the forehead and decided to call Trae one more time in hopes that his phone would finally be on and he would answer.

Maybe he forgot to charge his phone, I thought foolishly

trying to find some goodness in this fucked up situation. The phone rang but ironically this time it rang to the beat of my heart and it was uncontrollably loud. I inhaled and exhaled trying to blow out any negativity before he answered the phone.

"Hey baby, I've been calling you all night," I said, quickly forgetting all the pain I'd just endured the previous night.

"Trae, you there? Why aren't you saying anything? Trae?" I paused for about two seconds "Hello, hello," I continued before ceasing all words.

It dawned on me that I could hear sounds in the background. Somebody had mistakenly answered the phone. My heart began to beat as if I were running on a treadmill at the highest level. Adrenaline filled my soul. Then I began to perspire in a panic.

I got down on my knees holding the phone in my hand, still listening, waiting…for anyone to speak. I began to pray to my heavenly father that I didn't just hear another woman. Trae, Lil Trae and football had become my everything. There was nothing else for me but the bad life I'd left behind.

"Baby, you betta hurry up before you're late for your meeting, you don't wanna catch a fine do you?" a sweet sounding voice spoke from afar.

Just as the voices started coming in clearer, they began to fade out as if the phone was being moved around. I couldn't catch the male voice at all but the female began to speak again.

"You know you got me hooked, right? C'mere baby, c'mere."

Next I heard moans and groans. "Ummmmmm."

"Go 'head with that. Girl, you know I gotta go. Move back," the voice that I didn't want to hear said.

"So, you want some more, huh?"

The call faded again. But I knew I'd heard my man. I started breathing hard. Then I heard loud, kissing and sucking sounds. Then out of nowhere, the call was dropped.

My knees buckled. My stomach muscles tightened. I just knew I would throw up all over the floor. I kept looking back at the phone to make sure I'd dialed the correct number. Even though

Trae was programmed in my phone I wanted to believe in my heart that this wasn't happening. There was unbelievable pressure from the sides of my temples. My pain had gone from a headache to a migraine, to a possible low-grade tumor within minutes. I needed oxygen, could barely breathe.

I started pacing again, thinking about my next move. Nothing made sense other than to just kill myself.

Chapter 7
India

The next day rolled around and I couldn't believe Rachel had been gone all day after I told the chick I dreadfully needed to go with her. It was Friday evening and I had less than forty-eight hours before game time. I needed a Super Bowl ticket like the air I breathed to survive. I'd been out at the pool half the day hoping for a fresh start, but the pool, hotel lobby, and every crevice of the Loews was dryer than the Sahara desert.

I found myself back in the room refusing to give up only to remain a nobody the rest of my life. I deserved to be at the mall at this very moment, getting spoiled. Or even at a pre-show function for NFL wives and girlfriends. A thought entered my mind so I quickly picked up the receiver off the nightstand.

"Hello, this is Mrs. Shawn Grant in room #1228. I would like to get a car at 8:00 p.m. going to the Ruth's Chris Steakhouse, please." I used my professional voice since I truly believed that in order to be treated like V.I.P, you had to portray V.I.P.

"Sure, Mrs. Grant, we will be more than happy to have a town car here at 8:00 p.m., sharp. Will you be requiring a dining reservation at Ruth's Chris this evening?" the concierge asked.

"No, I believe my husband has already done so," I said in a sarcastic tone wishing that my lies would become reality.

I hung up then remembered to make that important call. I

grabbed my cell to call MBNA, Capital One, Discover, and all those other credit card companies to see which card would be picking up my tab at dinner if necessary. Friends always frowned upon my tactic, telling me I had no business dining in a restaurant that had high dollar prices. But taking financial risks like this was normal for me. It was an investment in my future.

"You've got to spend money to make money," I chanted to myself reaching to grab the tablet off the nightstand. I figured since the town was filled with players and ballers for the weekend, they had to eat, so what better place to catch a fish than Ruth's Chris.

"Please enter your sixteen digit account number followed by the pound sign," the Capital One recording stated.

"Please God, let there be at least $100 available and I'm in business." I sat on the edge of the bed waiting impatiently for the recording to reveal my fate.

"Your available credit as of January 30th, is $86.25. Your balance as of today is $9,913.75," the automated female recording said as if she knew it was a loser on the other end.

"You asshole!" I shouted like it was her fault that I'd been spending like crazy.

It didn't take me long to call every 1-800 number I had saved in my phone. Collectively, between my five credit cards, I had close to $220.00 for the entire weekend to spend.

"Oh, hell nawl," I told myself stumping toward the bathroom. "And I have to come up with Rachel's bread before she throws me out."

I stopped to glare in the full length mirror while my hand was used to flatten my stomach. It was time for that motivational talk that I'd have to have with myself on occasions.

I knew I was a professional at being broke but I had to be worth a million bucks to some lucky guy who needed eye candy, a loving wife and someone to take care of his kids. I wouldn't allow myself to think otherwise. "Okay, India, you know you're a hottie, right?" I shook my head up and down attempting to pump myself up. "And every guy wants you, right?" I nodded again. "And no matter what happens tonight, Mr. Right is coming along!"

I slipped out of my sexy stance and began pouncing, throwing jabs like a boxer. I had to remember to be a fighter, never giving up the fight of landing a man with money, preferably an athlete, one with lots of shine. It's all about location, location, location," I kept chanting, trying to convince myself that going to Ruth's Chris alone made sense. I thought back to a time when being in the right place made all the difference; it was when I'd made an appointment with Jennifer Lopez's hair colorist. I'd been on the waitlist for six months, because of course, regular clients had priority.

Luckily, someone cancelled and I was finally numero uno on the waitlist. It didn't matter that I had to take off work without pay. It was a part of the sacrifices that had to be made to land my hubby. Ted Gibson's salon catered to stars and getting hooked up was highly likely. I thought back to how my new blonde hair-color turned out fabulous and how I'd actually met Mary J. Blige in the salon. The downside… the stylist never revealed to me that my price would be $1500.00 until I was ready to leave. That shit really set me back, but at least I could say Mary and I were girls.

"That experience alone was well worth my money. And tonight would be worth spending my last, too," I told myself before jetting off to get dressed.

It took hours for me to get myself dolled up. Tonight was the night. I could feel it. After giving my eyelids a dark, smoky look with some new palettes and jet black eyeliner, I danced in front of the bathroom mirror admiring my beauty, especially my pointy nose. Growing up, I was always teased for that feature, but I would take a white girl nose over one that was spread clear across my face any day. With my hair and makeup finally done, I sprayed a few squirts of perfume in all the right places before grabbing my purse and heading out the door.

As I cruised down Bayside Avenue headed to the restaurant, I tried Rachel once again. Still, no answer. "They nerve of her," I mumbled, beginning to feel as if she were pulling the *disappearing act* on purpose. That's the type of shit I did to those beneath me.

I got teary eyed. How could I be in a town full of action, thousands of tourists, yet feel so alone? It seemed as if no one realized a star was in town, not even Rachel. This was beginning to be the story of my life. It reminded me so much of my childhood. As the car turned the corner passing a residential neighborhood, it immediately took me back to the house I grew up in, not the one where I'd spent my later teen years. The six bedroom Mediterranean, style home with the terracotta roof back in Potomac, Maryland where I'd grown up spoiled rotten, flashed in my mind, along with Raymond, my brother. He and I always had the finer things in life, clothes from Paris straight off the runway, and attended the best private schools money could buy. The problem was that my mother and father weren't home much, they traveled abroad frequently without us.

My best memories were with my housekeeper, Mimi. My face beamed a little thinking about her while I watched fancy cars fly by my window. She was responsible for making sure I had everything that a little girl could want from the age of ten all the way until I was seventeen. Between afternoons at Saks shopping for me, preparing meals, and cleaning our 10,000 square foot house, Mimi hardly ever had time to visit her own family, and had very little time to give me the love I desperately missed from my own parents.

Things turned for the worse and that wealthy lifestyle came to a complete stop when my father got busted for smuggling diamonds. At seventeen, I had no idea what was going on, nor did I want to know. All I knew was that the flow of money had stopped while my father waited for trial. Mom never talked much about it, so I assumed all was good until our cars were repossessed, including my convertible 3 series BMW.

Soon, my father was found guilty and sentenced to five years in prison. The federal agents seized the house, and what little money and jewelry were left. As a result, my mother, brother and I were forced to completely start new lives with only the clothes on our backs. I thought back to how we had to move in with my aunt Barbara in Brooklyn, NY, registering at the local high school. My heart hurt at the thought of how I'd gone from filet mignon to Ramen noodles within weeks. Sadly, two weeks later my father hung and killed himself putting extra grief on our family. It was a horrible transition. However, one positive thing I could say about the whole situation was that it taught me how to be a hustler. I'd been grinding, making shit happen without having to get a nine to five since the age of eighteen and didn't plan on stopping until I landed me a certified balla.

"Enough of the pity party," I told myself feeling the car come to a complete stop. I would continue to stay on my grind until I reclaimed my old life. The one fit for a queen.

My driver tilted his rearview mirror to get a good look at me as he pulled in front of the restaurant. As soon as he stepped out to open my door, my cell rang. It was a 704 number. I got excited, thinking about the guy I'd met in Charlotte weeks ago. I answered sexily.

"Chello."

"Ms. Grant, this is Mr. Douglas from Wells Fargo." The voice was a deep, authoritative one. "This is an attempt to collect a debt…"

I hung up, stepping out of the car, proudly, allowing the gentle breeze to brush against my face. I wasn't about to sit and listen to some bill collector tell me when to pay. That was the great part about being an American. Freedom. Besides, I was broke and they wouldn't get two cents from me if they tried.

I gracefully walked by two couples as they gave me the 'she must be somebody important' stare. My chin tilted upward and my head remained high as I gave up my Tyra Banks walk and headed straight for the bar area. The flattering French Connection dress that I'd chosen fit perfectly for someone tall like me. All eyes were on me; men, women, children, dishes and all. I'd decided on all white, determined to let some man see how his bride would look in the natural color. It was so sexy, yet demure. My confidence was back and a bit of sexy arrogance seeped through my pores. The moment I began to move the empty mahogany bar chair back slightly, a scent of Gucci Guilty daunted me from behind. It was an impressive smell, one that had to belong to a well kept man; most likely a paid brotha.

"Are you alone?" the deep voice asked me.

I pretended not to show interest at first, but once my eyes caught a glimpse of the major ice covering the entire first two inches of his wrist, I deviated from my plan.

I turned toward him swiftly with the perfect wide smile, then slightly pulled my right shoulder back to give him a snapshot of the pose I'd practiced daily.

"Ahhhhhh, yes, I was alone. But not anymore, since you're here now."

I patted the seat next to me with my horrible looking hands. A manicure was in order, but splurging on that didn't make sense until I could get a couple thousand outta somebody first.

I hit the mothafucking Powerball, I told myself as I studied the stats in front of me.

While he checked me out little did he know I did the same. From his broad shoulders to his thick, muscular thighs, it was clear he worked out regularly. He was super hairy from the top of his head to the sides of his face, something I didn't care for, but the pickiness had to end. I would fuck King Kong as long as he eventually put a ring on it. A pool of football faces began to race thru my mind. I tried to match a face with a name, but nothing came up.

"I'm Darrius Miller, and you are?"

"India Grant," I said seductively. I licked my lips and looked into his eyes as if I'd known him for years. The more I looked at him the more I could tell he still had a baby face. I think the hair had thrown me off at first. But it didn't matter, I'd gotten wet at the thought of him being someone important.

"It's a pleasure to meet you India. Can I buy you a drink?"

"Of course." I batted my eyes, but not too hard. My individual lashes were fake and hadn't been replenished in days. "Ah, bartender, bring me a bottle of Veuve Clicquot."

Darrius' eye diameter multiplied. I guess he wasn't used to a woman taking charge. And I didn't feel like playing the 'him ordering for me game'. I knew what I wanted…the best champagne Ruth's Chris sold. I deserved it.

"Wow, so what about dinner?" He chuckled a bit before I

realized what was so funny. "And you don't have to order right away."

"Funny." I slipped up and shot him a sarcastic smirk showing him a little of the real me. I was hungry as hell so I agreed to dinner and sucked down the first glass of champagne that the bartender placed in front of me.

Within minutes we started exchanging information about ourselves, where he was from, how long I'd been in town, and all the other bull that didn't matter. I was most interested in his occupation, how he made his moulah. And of course, how much? Strangely, Darrius didn't broadcast his player status which almost had me fearful that he wasn't even a player. Most players thrived off of their football status, and openly discussed it in the first two seconds of the conversation. So, I got straight to the point, even though the bartender stood in front of us asking for our order.

"What do you do for a living?" I had my hand in the bartender's face real disrespectful like. I didn't want to waste another minute on Darrius if he wasn't who I needed him to be. I'd even forgotten to disguise my tone.

"I play football for Cleveland."

I could tell he watched for my reaction closely. Yet I played things cool. My face silently said, "I'm not impressed", but my insides were jumping for joy that this guy was a good potential. The only thing that bothered me was that I wasn't familiar with his name, and that his face had such a youthful look.

"Are you guys ready to order?" the bartender asked again.

I blurted out about six items total including a lobster tail stuffed with crabmeat making Darrius think I hadn't eaten in days. Hell, I didn't know when I'd eat again if things didn't work out with him, so I ended with, "And after the petite filet and shrimp, you can bring me all those sides I asked for."

The moment Darrius finished ordering I got down to business. "Are you a franchise player?"

He laughed, but I was rock hard serious. My thin lips were pressed tightly together and I had my hands intertwined as if I were interviewing him. I needed to know his position, years played, and draft position which were all contributing factors to his negotiated salary. At twenty-seven, I couldn't get tied down with the wrong man. There weren't many years left for me to conceive and raise three kids as planned.

While I continued with question after question, Darrius' facial expressions changed for the worse. He no longer had that glow showing his excitement in me. He was either irritated with my questions or mad that he had a five hundred dollar dinner bill on the way soon. He had gotten to the point where he just changed the subject all together without my permission. How dare he? He began to talk about his family who were from Haiti and all the devastation his childhood community had endured. I didn't want to hear anything about Haiti. I needed his stats.

"Hey, don't mean to interrupt you, but by any chance do you have an extra ticket to the game?"

"What game?"

"The Super Bowl, darling. What else would I be talking about?" I frowned. "My girl needs a ticket badly. Can you produce?"

"Oh, naw. But I know this dude, he be scalping tickets."

I could tell he didn't study much in school by the way he conjugated verbs. I pretended to be in a good mood as I asked the biggie, "Can you do me a favor doll and call him? I really need to get this ticket for her."

"No doubt. I'll call. How much she wanna spend?"

"Oh, I thought a balla like you could handle that?" I showed all my pearly whites.

He laughed again, but I was certain he was mocking me. My body slouched a little from the disappointment. He didn't even have to say it, his facial expressions let me know he wasn't buying the ticket. At that moment, I got up and excused myself from the table with attitude. This dude was either broke, cheap, or not really a player. And if he couldn't buy me a Super Bowl ticket, I needed to reassess the situation. "I gotta go to the ladies room," I announced, grabbing my purse.

By the time I got into the stall, I felt like I'd taken a pay-cut already. I kicked off my shoes to give my toes some relief and whipped out my cell. After trying to get on the internet several times with no success, I began dialing, then paused; trying to wait until the young lady washing her hands exited the restroom. I didn't know if it was some money hungry tramp spying on me or not. As soon as the door closed, I finished pressing the digits then smiled when Tyesha answered.

"Yeah. What up?"

I hated the fact that she was so hood. "Hey girl, where you at?" I spoke rapidly. "I really need a favor."

"I'm at home, where you left my ass. Why, what's up?"

"My phone is acting up so I need you to get on the internet for me real quick. And I don't have a lot of time so I need you to move quickly. Look under my favorites and click on the website that says Players Salaries," I instructed eagerly.

"Damn, bitch. You still up to the same shit." She had the nerve to blow her breath like I was bothering her. My mind flipped through the countless times her scheming ass needed something from me. Besides, I was the only friend she had willing to room with her so whatever I requested, she needed to do.

"I'm there. What's his name?" she blurted knowing the routine.

"Darrius…" I revealed hesitantly. I felt as if the wheels of fate were spinning. "Darrius Miller," I added.

"Damn, he's fine," Tyesha exclaimed.

"Will you go to his salary history, girl? I know what the hell he looks like. He's been staring me in my face boring me to death with some shit I'm not even interested in."

"Okay, look he's a rookie, currently making $325,000 on a one year deal."

My foot barged against the door. "Damn!" I shouted. "I knew this was too good to be true. I shoulda known. I'm slipping," I said to no one in particular.

My face had begun to overheat. I knew if I graced the mirror, my fair skin would have turned a bright shade of red. I knew the horror stories about guys getting cut left and right after their first season. And I'd dated a few on their practice squads, too.

"Damnnnnnnnnnnnnnnnn, you're flying low baby," Tyesha commented letting me know she was still in research mode. "It says here he was a walk on." She laughed heartily.

"What? The nicca wasn't even drafted?"

"Nope."

"This is not happening to me," I cringed while slipping my shoes back on and exiting the handicap stall like it was the end of the world. "And just think, I couldn't even get a Super Bowl ticket from the broke bastard!"

"Ticket? You need a ticket?"

"Tyesha, you know I told you that before I left."

"Don't remember. But I got chu." I hated the way she always fast talked me. "See, I got this guy down there that will make it happen. Let me call 'em. How much you got?"

"Not much damn it. But get me that ticket, and cheap."

"On the job, baby." Tyesha hung up without even saying goodbye.

I smoothed my outfit out, picked at my hair a little bit, and peeped out the bathroom door. I spotted an extra short waiter who resembled a dwarf walking by.

"Hey, is there another way out of the restaurant?"

He looked at me suspiciously.

"Sir, my name is Mrs. Grant the wife of pro football player, Shawn Grant." I made sure to sound like a victim. "There are paparazzi posted up at the front of the restaurant trying to get a statement from me concerning my husband and his possible trade next season. I'm really not feeling well, nor am I in the mood for cameras in my face tonight. Is there a way you can get me out of here unnoticed?" I asked frantically.

"It would be my pleasure, Mrs. Grant. You can exit through our kitchen area." He held his arm out like a servant signaling for me to grab on. "Here at Ruth's Chris we are accustomed to the lifestyles of celebrities and we try and preserve any ounce of privacy we can for our clients," the man said as I bent slightly and grabbed a hold of his tiny arm.

He led me through the kitchen area causing all the workers to stare, mostly with envy. Even though I was pissed at the wasted evening, I ended it in first class by being escorted through a private entrance made especially for celebrities.

"Thanks so much, you're a lifesaver," I told the man gratefully as he held the door open for me to step out onto the street.

As soon as I broke free my cell rang. It was Tyesha. "Yeah, girl," I answered.

"I got the ticket."

My eyes lit up. "Front row? Somewhere near the players' families, right?"

"Bitch, you must be smoking. Look, dude said he'll call me tomorrow with the seat locations and different prices for each. But I told you I'd come thru. Don't I always?"

As usual, it sounded like my roommate had something up her sleeve. "Okay, girl, call me tomorrow or as soon as you find out something. But work your magic. Tell him I'm V.I.P, baby."

"Bet. You funny as hell, India. Aye, by the way, you talk to Royce?"

"Nope. Have you?"

"Long story. I'll get at' chu tomorrow."

Once again something seemed suspicious, but I didn't give a damn, I just wanted my ticket.

Chapter 8

Royce

It had gotten close to four o'clock by the time I made my move and threw our stuff in the car. I'd packed both Lil Trae's bag and mine in record time after Latrell showed up knocking on the door yelling rowdily like a wild animal from the outside. He'd even kicked the door in scaring my son to no end.

"Bitch, you told me you'd meet me at my hotel before two," he ranted. "I'm tired of your lies! But I'll tell you one thing, you won't keep lying to a nigga like me and getting away with it. You did me dirty and put me through too much, Royce!"

That's when I knew I wouldn't get rid of him as easily as planned. The more he ranted and kept talking about who he was, and what he would do to me, the more he reminded me that his personality was still similar to Suge Knight's. When he threatened to kill me saying he'd be back to shoot up everything in sight, I knew we had to jet.

I dodged in and out of the normal rush hour traffic headed north, attempting to regain my sanity. I was still nervous from the incident and could tell from the look in Lil Trae's eyes that he was, too.

"Honey, don't worry. Everything's fine," I assured him, glancing back into the back seat. He didn't respond, nor did he even look at me. Strangely, he wasn't interested in playing his Sony PSP, DSi or any of the other tons of games his father had gotten him either. My baby was shook.

As I turned each corner, I couldn't help but to focus on my rearview mirror. I kept thinking someone was following me. Nervously, I switched lanes, but none of the cars switched with me. I breathed a sigh of relief then focused entirely on trying to find out where Trae was staying in Miami. I whipped out my cell to call Rachel. She would know for sure. Seconds later her voicemail came on.

"Rachel, what's up girl? It's me, Royce." I blew breath into the phone so she could hear my frustration. "I need to know where Trae's staying. Some shit has kicked off, and I'm headed to Miami. Call me ASAP."

I hung up and called India next just as I was hopping off the exit headed to Trae's house in Westchester County. Scarsdale, New York was full of upscale homes, immaculate lawns and beautiful streets causing me to feel like I was committing a crime for driving so fast. I needed to get there before five o'clock for my plan to work. Another voicemail, another message… I mumbled as I gave India my quick sob story about what happened and how she needed to call me back immediately. I looked at the time on the dash realizing I only had fifteen minutes before Rosa got off causing me to step on it.

I thought back to how over the years, Rosa, Trae's housekeeper had grown to like me a lot. The feeling was mutual. Before Trae decided it was better for me and Lil Trae to have our own spot, Rosa and I enjoyed our days laughing together and watching movies, even when she was supposed to be cleaning. She confided in me about her relationships, career options and tips on American life. And even though I barely understood one complete sentence that she said, I thought of her as family.

Of course Rosa was disappointed, yet relieved when Trae finally got caught cheating. She'd tried to warn me many times. She even dangled a pair of thongs in my face once, asking if they belonged to me, knowing my plump backside couldn't fit into an extra small. The more I thought about Rosa, the more time ticked away. I knew I needed to call her so she wouldn't leave.

Within seconds, I called Trae's house. When Rosa picked

up I developed a cheesy grin. "Rosa, hi, it's me, Royce. I left some things at the house, please tell me you are still working," I said nervously.

"Hola, Royce. Yes, I still here. Five minutes, I leave."

"Cool. I'll be there in less than five minutes. Wait for me."

I hung up feeling like some crap for lying to Rosa. But my back was against the wall. I had no one else to trust. I'd finally had a feeling for the first time that things would work out for me as soon as I turned onto Sherbrooke Road. As the sun began to set once again, I had this eerie feeling. I looked into my rearview noticing a black Mustang. It wasn't directly on my tail but it wasn't too far behind either.

The neighborhood was for the well- to- do so I didn't have to fear being robbed or anything like that. Yet, it still seemed a little weird, almost as if I'd noticed the car earlier. I decided to slow down allowing the car to pass, but just as I slowed my pace, the vehicle turned into the driveway behind me, bringing my heart rate back to its normal speed. The fact that I was so paranoid had me on edge. Peace needed to come soon to keep me from slitting my wrist.

Moments later, I turned into Trae's long, circular driveway happy to see Rosa's Nissan Sentra parked on the side of the additional garage adjacent to the house. After letting out a big sigh of relief, and opening the back door for Lil Trae a comforting feeling welled up inside. The sophisticated, contemporary designed house made me feel at home. Like I belonged there.

"Daddy's home?" Lil Trae questioned as I grabbed his bag from the back seat then pulled his hat down close to his eyebrows so the wind chill wouldn't hit him in the face too much.

"No, but you're going to stay here a few days until he comes back."

He seemed sad as I told him the plan. "You're only going to stay with Rosa for a few days until Mommy and Daddy come back. Daddy is in trouble and he needs me."

One look into his cheerless eyes confirmed that I was repeating history by doing to him what my foster mom had done to me. I could remember being passed along from one family member, or friend of hers to the next. She never really took the time to make sure I was with her more than anyone else.

I grabbed my little man by the arms of his puffy coat and gazed into his cute little face. His smooth skin made me smile. "Look baby, Mommy loves you. I hate to leave you here, but I have to for now. I don't have any other choice. Do you understand that?"

He nodded, allowed a tear to trickle down his face, but never responded. I kissed him on the cheek and locked all the doors to my BMW X5. The moment we both turned around chill bumps flew up my arm. Fear filled my soul. There was nothing for me to do but stand and face the music.

"Latrell," I mouthed in a low tone.

He had obviously followed me. I turned to see the black Mustang toward the bottom of the driveway. How he'd snuck up on me I didn't understand? His hands were behind his back and his stomach moved back and forth confirming that he was breathing laboriously. I couldn't help but stare at the moles on his face.

"Still a grimy bitch!" he spat.

"No...I..."

I stopped when I heard the sound of a gun cocking. His hands were still behind his back so I knew what was going down.

"Yo, you playin' too many games. You promised to meet me at the hotel."

His face was so stern I wasn't sure what he would do next so I grabbed Lil Trae and pulled him close into my arms allowing his back to rest against my stomach.

"Latrell, don't do this. Not in front of my son. I was just dropping him off then coming to meet you."

"Stop lyin'," he shot back. "You think I don't know this is your man's house? I know exactly who you fuck with."

My eyes tripled in size. "Can we just talk after I get him inside? Please." I hated begging, it was a sign of being weak.

"No, Royce. No more passes for you. You know first-hand I've killed people, just because."

He wasn't lying. "C'mon Latrell, not here, not now."

"You fuckin' set me up! Wiped me clean of all my money

and you want more time?"

I saw Rosa tip toe outside stepping onto the front steps with a concerned look on her face. Quickly, I told Lil Trae to run over to her as I released him from my grip, praying Latrell would take his wrath out on me and not my baby. "I'm coming, Rosa. Just hold onto Lil Trae for me!" I yelled but the sound wasn't very loud considering the trembling in my voice.

"Senorita Royce, is everything okay?"

"Yes, I'm fine." I waved like all was good. But she knew I was lying. It was weird already that I'd showed up when Trae wasn't home and now I was having an altercation with an evil looking man she'd never seen in the driveway.

"Royce, forget the kid," Latrell said to me, causing me to face him again. He swiftly pulled his arms from behind his back, and stuffed the gun into the front of his pants. I shivered from both fear and not having on a thick enough coat. The fleece Northface pullover didn't do the job and the temperature had dropped to about thirty degrees so we were all shivering with the exception of Latrell who was wrapped up in a brown bomber jacket and skull cap.

"What do you want me to say or do?" My face had tightened and showed remorse. "I was twenty-one when all that happened. I'm sorry you went to jail, but I didn't set you up."

"You did!" Latrell shouted, causing Rosa to take a few more steps backwards closer to the house. She had a dreadful look on her face like she wanted to jet to her car.

"I didn't. I swear I didn't." My head swiveled from right to left repeatedly.

"Typical gold digger. You enjoyed the money and life we had when things were good, but folded when shit got rough." He paused before hitting me with unexpected words. "Did India have anything to do with it?"

"No, Latrell, she didn't," I answered strongly. "And for the last time, I didn't set you up."

"So, why didn't you come see me once I got locked up? Huh?"

"Fear, Latrell. I didn't know if I would get in trouble, too."

"Nah, what you were supposed to do was stand by your man." He took two intimidating steps my way causing me to press my back against the driver's door. "You weren't supposed to take my life savings from my safe. You ripped me the fuck off! And to make things worse, everyone told me you aborted my baby." His eyes darted over to Lil Trae. "Did you? How old is that boy?"

"Oh, no, Latrell. That's not your son. Leave him out of this. I'm begging you. Now we can talk later about the money I spent but that's it."

"Oh, we gonna talk more than you think, baby," he said, clutching a third of my hair into his calloused hand.

It hurt like hell giving me a feeling that each strand was being ripped from my scalp.

"After all, we're married." He grinned. "'Til death do us part! Now I know you don't want me to mess things up with you and yo' little boyfriend, Trae Harris."

A lump formed in my throat, He knew his full name and now knew where he lived.

I kept myself from tearing up since tears never worked in the past for Latrell. He was a rugged, no-nonsense kind of guy who took his business and his money serious. "Look, I'm sorry for the money, but I can't do anything about that now. I was just trying to handle our bills and take care of myself knowing you were going down for some years."

"Bullshit! You were spendin' like crazy."

He stepped back, released my hair and paced the ground in front of me.

"I got beat, Latrell," I yelled, pressing my hand against my scalp. "Some guy said he could help my career. I gave him $60,000 to produce my album. I trusted him hoping to make some money for me and you but he ripped me off. I never got my album made and he never gave me that money back. The rest really was spent on bills."

"Bullshit again," he responded harshly. "You set me up and cleaned me out before my lawyer knew how much time I would possibly do. You did me wrong, Royce. And now it's time for you to pay me back." He paused to look at the house thoroughly. "Your man got money."

I started shaking my head, knowing where he was going with things. "We're not even together like that. You gotta believe me."

"Oh, I believe you. I see that big ass ring on your finger."

Quickly, I put my hands behind my back. Why, I had no clue?

"Check this out. You took 250 grand from my safe over five years ago. That plus interest means you owe me a lot. And I want what's mine."

"I don't have $250,000!" I shouted, almost throwing a temper tantrum. "Are you crazy?"

"No, but you will be when I tell your boyfriend everything. And I'll tell him what you were involved in, too." He hit me with a devious grin again. "I'll give you ten days to come up with the first 20,000 and then we'll discuss a payment plan for the rest. I also need to know who helped you set me up. They gotta pay, too."

"Twenty grand!"

"Yeah. Ten days."

Before I could say anything else a police car drove by slowly near the bottom of the driveway, probably doing their normal run of the neighborhood. Suddenly, the cruiser stopped, then backed up. Even though the car didn't pull into the driveway, Latrell retreated instantly. Fright rose into his eyes but he remained frozen for several seconds until the cruiser pulled off slowly. Soon, he began backing away from me with ease, looking at me then over to my son, crazily.

"Don't fuck me again Royce 'cause this time you won't live."

As soon as he opened his car door, Rosa came running toward me pushing Lil Trae in the process.

"Senorita Royce, who that man?" Her face looked as if all the blood inside had washed away. "Me not know him. Him make me scared."

"Oh, don't worry, Rosa. He's an old friend. Just lost something, that's all."

My voice still trembled.

"Ohhhhhhhh. So good to see you, but me go now. Have to pick up son from band practice. You be safe," Rosa told me confirming that she didn't believe what I'd just said about Latrell being a friend.

"Oh Rosa, please take Lil Trae," I begged pushing him and his bag toward her car. "Mr. Harris hurt himself in Miami, so I need to go there now."

Rosa paused. She smiled at Trae lovingly. "Oh no, Senorita. Me no time to keep. I clean extra house tomorrow."

I clasped my hands together and shot her a look of desperation. "Pleaseeeee, Rosa. I have nowhere else for him to go. You're like family."

"Me can't…"

"Pleaseeeeeee."

"Her shoulders drooped. "Okay, Senorita Royce. But we not stay here. We stay my home."

"That's fine. That's fine." I kept repeating, rushing toward my car. "I'll pick him up here on Monday," I said, thinking about the long drive there and back."

"Yes, Senorita Royce."

"Oh and Rosa…" I paused after putting one foot into the car. "If that man comes back here or if you see him anywhere near Lil Trae, call the police. And definitely don't let Lil Trae talk to him."

She nodded and I closed the door unable to watch the tears falling from my son's eyes. I knew things would get crazy if Latrell found out that Lil Trae was really his son.

Chapter 9
India

As the evening approached, I'd just about given up on chances of rubbing elbows with the influential people in town. Tomorrow was game day, and I hadn't done much, scored anything, or even really had the fabulous time that I'd anticipated on. I sat in the lobby wearing some leather leggings, six inch heels and a sequin Michael Kors tunic waiting for something to pop off, someone to buy me a drink, or even for a ninety year old man to just talk to me. My love life had become hopeless. All thoughts of my legs up in the air and someone important getting me pregnant was null and void. Rachel had been invited to a private function that the NFL wives club threw at the Fontainebleau hotel. I almost fainted when she told me it was invite only and I, 'the show stopper', couldn't go.

I kept watching the entrance way into the hotel hoping someone special would enter when I felt my phone vibrate. Quickly, I grabbed it hoping for some good news. It wasn't a male like I'd wanted but it was Tyesha. Maybe she had something positive to say.

"Who the fuck am IIIIIIII?" she yelled like some loud rapper.

"Tyesha, I don't have time for games. What's up?"

"Look-a-here, babe, don't get shitty with me. You should

be kissing my ass right about now."

"And why is that?" I snapped

" 'Cause I got you the hook up. Dude with the tickets said meet him in front of a lounge called Setai. It's on Collins, so it shouldn't be hard to find."

My chest poked out a little and my cheeks perked up instantly. "When?"

"Now."

"Well, give me his number so I can call him."

"Nah, babe, shit don't work like that. Go meet 'em and talk then."

"But I need to know how much he wants, right?"

She laughed slightly. "I got chu a sweet deal," she sang. "Three fifty. No tax."

"Tyesha, are you crazy? You know I don't have $350.00 dollars."

"So, tell me this Barbie. How much did you think you would pay to go to the fucking Super Bowl? This ain't some bull-shit college game. These tickets are near the fifty yard line and near where the players' folks chill. Something like that woulda normally ran you about fifteen hundred."

As she continued to talk, I blocked out all her remaining words. I could only focus on the fact that I'd sit with the people who mattered most. All eyes would be on me. The wheels of my mind began to spin. Who could I get $350 from and fast? I thought about Jared who was just a friend, then Rachel popped into my head. She had the cash for sure, but I hadn't even given her money for the hotel yet. So, asking her seemed to be stupid. Then my mother popped into my head. I hadn't called her in over three months. But I knew if I called she'd send the money Western Union. She always tried her best to come through for me.

Finally, Tyesha had to get put on pause. "Tyesha, do me a favor. See if you can get in touch with the guy and tell him I'll meet him at the spot by eight. I gotta collect the loot first. What's his name?" I asked with concern.

"The ticket man. What else would it be?" she answered with sarcasm.

"But I need to know his name, don't I?"

"Just go with it, baby."

I hated when she used those words. I hung up on her, ran up to my room and commenced to calling my mother. I hated having to answer all the questions about where I'd been and why I hadn't been by to see her. I made up some crazy lie about how I'd come down with some rare kidney disease and had been going to see different doctors day in and day out. After she cried for about ten minutes, I told her I was in Miami and needed an expensive prescription that I had to have immediately. As expected, she fell for it and told me the $350.00 would be in Western Union within the hour.

Not long after picking up the money, I found myself standing outside of Setai waiting for *the ticket man*. I felt stupid in my Alexander McQueen bolero dress that I'd gotten on sale a few weeks ago. I was all dressed up with nowhere to go. Tons of looks, stares, and glares came my way as people passed me by on the streets, but none that were desirable or on my level. Quickly, I whipped out my gloss ready to replenish.

Before I could apply another layer, I noticed a nappy headed guy with way too much hair on his head approach me. I had to look twice just to make sure he appeared to be looking for someone and not just trying to get my number. His gym shorts straddled his knees and the oversized jersey he wore didn't even match the shorts.

"Yo, you India?" he asked sharply.

As soon as he said that the tension eased. "Yeah, that's me. You got the ticket?"

"You got the money?"

Damn, this wouldn't be as easy as I thought. I'd planned on teasing and flirting a bit to get some money taken off my bill. I'd purposely put $200.00 in the palm of my hand hoping to say I didn't have any more money and that we could date sometime in the near future. But ticket man was rough and rugged.

"Hey, I only got $200.00," I told him with batted eyes and puckered lips. "That won't be a problem, right?"

He turned and walked off never even responding. So, I

chased after him a few feet yelling like school aged kids chasing after a friend. When he finally stopped, I asked him to let me see the ticket.

"Let me see the money."

Letting out a huge sigh, I pulled the money from my palm and the other $150.00 from my purse. "Here's the three-fifty. Now, can I see the ticket?"

He handed it to me making me feel like I was getting a golden ticket to Willie Wonka's Chocolate Factory. I was going to the fucking Super Bowl and would be sitting on the fifty yard line —on the club level for everyone to see me noticeably. I would be the envy of everyone.

Before I could say thank you, dude was gone. I didn't really care though. His attitude stank and he was too arrogant for a salesman. I decided to go inside the lounge which sat just a few yards away. It wasn't exotic looking or anything, but reminded me of the old, prominent establishments we had back in New York.

I walked inside and took a seat in the back booth. The lights were dim which made it difficult for people to see one another clearly. There weren't many women inside which meant no one for me to outshine. I simply needed to look good for the twelve to fifteen or so men who weren't even looking my way. I ordered an Apple Martini to celebrate and told the waiter to start me a tab. One lucky patron would have to pay the bill no matter what. I was fresh out of loot.

While I patiently waited on my drink, I gazed out the window and slightly closed my eyes. Prayer was needed badly. I knew the Lord would send me the man I wanted. The one I needed to have…if I just prayed about it. Nothing else seemed to work so I thought about how I'd seen Rachel praying all the time. Two minutes into my prayer a voice was heard.

"Lord you're quick," I told the man above, tilting my head upward.

I opened my eyelids slowly, hoping to embrace my soul mate. I wanted him to be strong and chocolate. I quickly frowned as it was only a different waiter delivering my drink. I felt stupid wondering how long he'd been standing there, but never got a chance to say anything when an unexpected visitor appeared at the table behind him.

His diamond bracelet glistened and his Audemars Piguet watch got my attention, fast. This man just kept showing up. Why? Was this a sign from God?

"Hello, Mr. Haskin. It's good to see you again."

"Yes, this might be fate," he suggested in his domineering tone.

I liked that in a man.

"So, why are you here drinking when you're a top of the tier business man?"

He moved to the side and turned around slightly to point to a group of men sitting at a huge, round table on the opposite side of the bar. They were all dressed in expensive looking suits similar to Mr. Haskin. I wondered if someone over there actually owned the Dolphins. That's who I needed to meet.

"We're just here, relaxing and handling a little business. They're so many people in town tonight, we thought we'd do something a little different. Besides, I know the guy who owns this place."

I smiled. "Really? That's nice." Hell, I didn't know what else to say. He was obviously feeling me from the way he examined me from head to toe.

"I still can't figure out why a man like your husband would let such a beautiful woman travel alone, and hang out in bars alone." He took a seat allowing me to smell his cologne. It wasn't a familiar smell but one that I liked.

"Well, I have a confession to make." I shrugged my shoulders and gave off a half ass smile. It was my shameful, forgive me expression.

"And what's that, beautiful."

Damn, he had swagger for an old dude. "I'm not really married. I just told you that because it keeps the guys off of me. I don't like playing the dating game and having to meet different men. I'm content with being alone." I held my head downward to add to the performance. "My name is India Grant, but I didn't get it from Shawn Grant. It's my family surname."

He blew five quick kisses with his lips, then pointed his finger at me. "That's actually not a bad idea, and you know what. You shouldn't be alone. You should be getting spoiled right now, over at Bal Harbor Mall or something. Diamonds, pearls…you know, all the good stuff."

B.I.N.G.O! My insides bubbled and I got a little warm. I imagined myself laid next to him rubbing his freckled back in his oversized bed. I wanted to ask him how much he made, but didn't want to mess things up. He was a VP in the NBA so he had plenty of money. I'd be sure to Google him later.

"Look, I gotta get back to my meeting over here. But call me tomorrow so I can treat you to something nice. I wanna see a smile on your face. And oh, just in case you misplaced the card, here's another one."

My nipples hardened. The mall? Oh yes, things were looking up. *Prayer works*! I told myself as he laid yet another card in front of me.

"We can meet up after the Super Bowl before any parties begin, if that's okay with you?"

I nodded calmly, not wanting to appear to be a groupie.

"I'll have to stop by the Stephen Ross' party, the owner of the Dolphins, if that's okay with you?"

I nearly pissed in my pants. "Sure," My response came off in a nonchalant way as he moved slowly away from the table, continuing to look over his shoulder at me as he walked.

I couldn't believe how I'd just lucked up. Mr. Haskin was paid and all, but I knew right away that once he got me to the party I would find me a husband, my age, that everybody knew. I knew my sugar daddy had money, but I wanted more than that. I needed to feel prestigious in life. And I damn sure wanted every female who crossed my path to want to be in my shoes. Something told me I was real close to making that happen.

Quickly, I grabbed a napkin off the table and a pen from my purse. I began to jot down all the things Mr. Haskin would buy me from the mall. If I had to suck him off later for some extra loot then I would. My bills were way behind. Between rent, utilities, hair, make-up, past due credit card bills, dental bills and much more, my financial situation was headed for disaster. Mr. Haskin was now FEMA.

"Here is another apple martini for the lovely lady, compliments of the gentlemen at the end of the bar," the waiter said as he turned for me to see the purchaser. He grinned widely as if he'd just delivered a winning lotto ticket. "Enjoy."

A sense of hope spread across my face as my gift from God carefully approached my booth. I couldn't believe the good Lord worked that fast. From here on out I'd be on my knees every night, in church on Sundays and Bible Study on Wednesdays. My body began to shake as he got up close in my face. My mouth hung low in amazement. The charming 300 lb guy before me was none other than Xavier Simms, a middle linebacker for the Giants. He was well known by everyone and a hip, chic, favorite among the elite in NYC.

"Hope you didn't mind me buying you a drink."

"Oh, not at all." My voice needed to be perfect. "Have a seat," I said nonchalantly, "I'm just waiting for a friend."

"I hope not your boyfriend." He smiled giving me a chance to scan his perfectly trimmed goatee.

"Oh, noooooooo." Of course my words were elongated. I wanted to make sure he knew I could talk proper when need be; especially in front of his white co-workers that I'd have to meet soon. "I'm not into that right now. Just focusing on my career and all my charity work."

"Oh. That's cool. I'm impressed."

I gave him teeth for days hoping to steal a chance at slipping on some more gloss without giving off the wrong impression. I could tell the nicca had money by the way he was dressed. His jeans were simple, but the iced out Breitling watch on his wrist and diamond crucifix spoke volumes. We kept glancing at each other like the glares you give when you've got a high school crush. So the chemistry was there.

"I'm India." I extended my hand then sipped on my drink. "And you are?"

He hesitated then turned to scan the bar, almost as if he needed clearance before telling me his name. It made me think about Mr. Haskin. I really didn't want him to see me talking to Xavier just in case things didn't work out. So, I stood up searching for him like a mother trying to find her child. Luckily, he was gone. Nowhere to be found. At that point I knew I'd give Xavier every ounce of sex appeal I had.

"Cat got your tongue?" I asked seductively while sitting back down and pushing my boobs up high for him to see vividly. It was my best feature and Xavier needed to see what I had to offer. "I asked you your name. You don't know it?"

"My bad. You're so pretty, I can't even think. You got me all messed up inside. I'm Antonio. Antonio Carter," he lied.

"Nice to meet you, Antonio." Hell, if he wanted to play the game, I could too. Little did he know, I knew his stats. Out of the sixteen games he'd started in this season, he had a total of eighty-nine tackles, four sacks and had also forced three fumbles. He definitely wasn't one of those bench riders.

"So, what brings a lovely lady like you out and alone on a Saturday night?"

"I'm meeting some friends at 9:30." Xavier locked eyes with mine giving me the feeling that he wanted to eat me whole, right in front of everyone. "Why are you looking at me like that?" I laughed sexily.

He moved his lips slowly and spoke in a hushed tone. "Cause I think I'm in love."

"Damn, that fast?" I giggled then downed the rest of my drink.

"You think I'm playing. I haven't met anyone in a while that I liked as much as you."

One blush after another I'd become an emotional mess. I started thinking about how I would tell Tyesha I was moving out soon. Then about the engagement party that I would plan once he made things official. He kept smiling at me showing me he was hooked.

"Where are you from?" I questioned.

"New York."

"Oh wow." I placed my palm across my chest. "Me too. Are you in town to see the game?"

"Kinda sorta. What about you?"

The nicca lies good. I wondered if he did that in his every-day life. "I have a ticket but I may just hang out in my room tomor-row reviewing my latest proposal. I'm here working with one of the local homeless shelters."

"Word. I like that."

I blushed again.

"How old are you?" he asked me out of the blue.

"Why? Does age matter?"

"Ummm, not for tonight. But for the future, yes. I'm not gonna lie," he said, pouring his guts out, "I meet women all the time and things don't work out mostly because they're young and immature."

I laughed coyly. "I'm twenty-seven, far from immature. And if we start to date and things don't work out at least we tried. I'm not looking for any commitments, just so you know, Antonio. Been there done that."

"Oh really."

It seemed as if he was becoming more impressed with me by the minute. I felt gooey inside as he ordered me another drink.

"I say we just become friends, get to know each other bet-ter."

"I can deal with that." He shot me a gesture letting me know he liked my style.

All of a sudden my cell rang interrupting our little session. It was a 718# so it could've been important. I answered.

"Chello."

"India."

"Speaking." I had no idea who the male voice was on the other end but I had to make it look good in front of Xavier, maybe even make him a little jealous.

"Miss India Grant. This is Agent Miles from the F.B.I."

My back arched and I sat erect. "Yes, how can I help you?" I asked as fear shot through my veins.

"Ma'am I'd like to discuss Leah Vaughn with you. Can you meet me at our satellite office?"

"Uh, uh, uh," I stuttered. How'd they know. How could

they have found out? My heart fluttered. "Uhhhhhh," I kept repeating, "I'mmmm out of town right now."

"Ma'am, it's urgent that we speak in the next few days. When will you return?"

"Monday."

"Monday it is. I'll call you with the address." He paused. "And Mrs. Grant, just know that this is a federal investigation so make sure you are available."

"I sure will."

I hung up and shot Xavier a fake smile. All along I'd gotten nauseous. I knew this would one day come back to haunt me. I thought I had it all planned correctly. Now was not the time. And jail was not an option.

"So, what about this," Xavier announced bringing me back to reality. "I'm not into crowds. I'm expecting an important phone call back in my room. Don't take this the wrong way…"

Go ahead, say it! Fucking say it, my spirit urged. I had to forget about that troubling phone call.

"…But I'd love to have you come back to the room with me. No strings attached. Just a few drinks and good, mature conversation," Xavier ended making my night.

"Ummmmmm, I don't know about that." I pretended to contemplate the offer.

"I understand being careful and all. If not, maybe we can hook up tomorrow?"

I had to seize the moment. Little did he know I understood why he needed to get back to the room. It was the night before a game and every player had a curfew. I didn't want my money-maker- to-be to get fined so I put my pen and napkin into my purse preparing to get my lottery ticket to his room. "You know what, I trust you. Just drinks, right?"

"Just drinks," he confirmed.

Without delay, I swallowed any morals my mother had ever taught me along with downing the drink that just hit the table. I hadn't planned on having casual sex but if this was the first step in becoming Mrs. Simms, then the pussy was his.

Chapter 10
Royce

I found myself flying down I-95 South when my cell rang. It was on the seat next to me, still hot from all the calls I'd been making. I prayed it was Trae so he'd get my warning for what was about to happen, but when I saw Rachel's name pop up, I answered. Fast.

"Girl, I can't believe you just calling me back," I blared into phone. She should've been able to tell that something major was wrong.

"Royce, I do have a life, sweetheart." She paused and told the person I could hear in the background that she needed a minute to talk to me. "I just listened to your message. Tell me you're playing, right?"

Rachel sounded different, more relaxed than I'd heard her in years. It was obvious she was with a guy. Perhaps a date; one that would have to end soon considering there was only about forty minutes left on my drive.

"No, I'm not playing. I'm almost in Miami," I expressed in the most serious tone I could muster. "I'm dead serious. That muthafucka, Trae is with a bitch and he's getting busted tonight."

"So, you're telling me you really drove all the way to Miami like you said on the message?"

"Yep. Been driving all night, damn it. Eighteen hours."

"You're insane!"

"No, just in love. But the three, five-hour energy drinks and Rick Ross been keeping me company. But I think it's all beginning to wear off," I said while swerving. "I'll be at your hotel by nine."

"Look, crazy lady. First off, I'm not there. And secondly, I don't know where Trae is staying."

"You kidding me, right?" My voice changed showing my disappointment in my girl. We'd been friends for over seven years and this was the thanks I got for always being there for her? "I know you can find out. I know it," I uttered strongly. "The question is, have you even tried?"

Everything got quiet. I played back what I'd gone through to make the trip. I thought about Latrell and how he was trying to blackmail me, vowing to ruin my life. My body became weak and I was borderline ready to check into the hospital for exhaustion. Yet my girlfriend who knew everyone and everything about the NFL and its players was telling me she couldn't find out where Trae was staying. Suddenly, this emotional feeling shot through my body. It was a feeling of hopelessness.

"You're not trying to help me!" I shouted. I had this crazy feeling that she knew something deeper and wasn't telling me. "Oh my God! Why are you doing this?" I screamed while allowing the car to drift into the next lane. The person blew their horn loudly, but I didn't care, never even budged. Sadness filled my insides and instantly took over all of my emotions. Tears flowed and the sobbing began. "Rachel, pleaseeeeeee, help me!" I cried out between sniffling. "I need to know the truth about Trae. If he's cheating on me again, I need to know. I'm not going to keep going down this road with him."

"Whether you catch him in the act or not, you should already know. What does your gut say?"

My fist banged against the steering wheel. "You don't understand! I need to see for myself!"

"Why?"

My voice erupted like a cartoon villain. "Are you with me or against me, Rachel?"

It was clear that I was having an emotional meltdown. I cried some more like a toddler having a temper tantrum then screamed never giving Rachel a chance to get a word in for at least two minutes. My soul hurt deeply and my actions showed it. By the time I finished swerving again from not being able to see clearly from the tears, Rachel's voice registered with me again. I wiped my face hoping to regain my vision, quickly before I caused an accident.

"Royce, you've got to pull yourself together. And you gotta accept the truth," she warned. "Trae is no good for you." Rachel paused to catch her breath. "You probably did hear another woman's voice on the phone. And, yes, he most likely spent the night with someone last night. But instead of searching for him to argue all night, just leave him," she preached. "You can do better girl."

"I know…I know…I know," I finally chimed in.

"Men don't change, Royce. They are who they are and there are some good one's out there. But you can't meet them as long as you're with Trae."

Suddenly, I heard someone in the background say, "That's right, baby, some of us are good." Then Rachel laughed that school girl laugh that I used to do with Trae when we first met. Who was she with? I wondered.

"Rachel. You make good sense," I said calming myself slightly, "and I will move on if I have to. But right now, I need to see who he's with."

Her tone escalated. I knew she was fed up with me. "You heard a voice yesterday, right?"

"Yeah."

"So, what makes you think you're going to catch him with a girl the day after?"

"Let me worry about that. You just find out where he's staying. I know you can get the info. Please, Rachel, I'm counting on you," I expressed, hopping off 95 onto 195.

She huffed. "Girl, this is too much. I'm serious. So let me ask you this. If I do find out where he's staying how do you think we'll get the room number, or get into his room for that matter?"

"Leave that to me. You get the name of the hotel, and let me figure out the rest. I promise, I won't involve you in nothing crazy. I swear. I know how you are about your job. Just do this for me."

She hit me with another huff. "Alright," she said depressingly. "Pick me up from the Gansevoort. I'll text you the address. Just hit me when you get out front."

"Aye, who are you with, Rachel?"

Next thing I knew there was silence on the phone and then a dial tone. Rachel must've been pissed since there was no good-bye or anything. Nothing. No, I feel bad for you. No, I got your back. Zero.

I hung up and pressed on the gas even more as my mind flipped to what I would do if Trae was with a chick. I couldn't tell Rachel I'd plotted on the possibilities for hours of a premeditated ass whipping. Being caught in the room with another woman was grounds for murder, but I couldn't see myself locked up, unable to pursue my dreams, and not being with Lil Trae. I began to plan out my course of action, vowing not to cry no matter what. I just wanted the truth.

Suddenly my cell rang. I answered on the first ring.

"Hello."

"Ms. Pratt?"

"Yes. It's me. Who's this?"

"This is Ms. Campbell."

All I could do was pray that she'd found my birth mom.

"I see we keep missing each other . You're a busy woman," she said in a humorous way.

Little did she know I had nothing to smile about. "Did you find her?" I blurted.

"Ahhhh, as a matter of fact, I did."

My heart stopped. I had so many questions running through my head. Did she look like me? Did I have her features and of course why she did what she did. "When do I get to meet her?"

"That's where we have some problems, Ms. Pratt. I know where she lives but haven't been able to catch her. I've got to make sure she wants to meet you first. Legally, once she signs the paper agreeing to meet you, I can put the two of you in contact with one another."

I wanted to ask more questions but Ms. Campbell hit me with, "I've gotta run but will be in touch." Then the line went dead on me.

The whole conversation had me flustered yet anxious all at the same time. I kept drifting off wondering what it would be like to see my mother's face and just a chance to touch her. Time must've flown because I soon found myself out front of the Gansevoort applying some eyeliner and loads of foundation to my face hoping to cover the bruises. My eyes were super puffy between the crying and lack of sleep so there was nothing that could be done in that area. However, I had to try to fix myself up slightly since my Victoria's Secret Pink sweatsuit made me look so casual. My hair was easy. With a few quick strokes of the paddle brush, my jet black strands laid perfectly as if I'd just left salon.

When I spotted Rachel rushing over to the car I also got a glimpse of the good looking man behind her. She had a wide grin on her face as he kissed her all too passionately. We'd have to discuss as soon as possible. This was so different for her. When she hopped inside she immediately hugged me which made me feel one hundred percent better.

"Girlllllll, all I have to say is that you are a trooper. I don't know many women who would drive eighteen hours; straight."

I took that as a compliment while peeling off down the street. "So, where is he?"

"The Palms," she told me bluntly. "Just a few minutes down Collins Ave."

My gut said she'd known all along and just wanted to protect her job in case it was ever exposed that she'd given out the information. There was no way possible she could've found out that fast. "Thank you, Rachel. I appreciate it."

"It's cool."

"When we get there you don't have to go in," I told her as I dipped in and out of traffic hurriedly. "I don't want you to be seen with me just in case he got somebody in the room."

Rachel glared at me for much too long, I guess questioning my motives. I didn't expect her to understand. She'd never been deeply hurt by a man. All her relationships were short lived and she never even cared as long as her career was straight. At that moment I realized my girl had on stilettos and the sexiest off the shoulder dress she'd ever worn. This new guy must've really been putting it on her.

"Royce, what happened to your face?"

Damn, I didn't want to hear those words. I didn't think she'd notice.

"I'll tell you later," I blurted. "Nothing serious."

"Girl, you have flawless skin, so I can tell even with the foundation that something happened."

"I said, I'll explain later."

Out of the blue I got antsy when I saw the sign for the Palms. As soon as I pulled up in the front I began running down my plan to Rachel. "I'm going to get my room key from the front desk. Then I'm going inside Trae's room."

Rachel covered her face with her hands. "Whyyyyyy, Royce? Why are you doing this?"

"Look, it's already after nine so his curfew is near. If he's in there alone, everything's good and then we can discuss his whereabouts last night. If he's in there with a woman, one of us will be coming out in an ambulance."

"Royce," Rachel called to me as I opened the car door and jetted toward the entrance way.

Once inside, I inhaled taking in the serene feeling of the lobby. Candles were lit everywhere and people socialized all around. Most had drinks in hand and were dressed just as sophisticated as the lobby's décor. By the time I made it over to the hotel clerk, my lines had been rehearsed and memorized to a tee.

"Good evening." I whipped out my ID to make things seem legit. "My fiancé hasn't come back to the room yet and I left my key in the room so I can't get in. Can you be a sweetie and get me another key? It's Trae Harris' room."

She returned the smile and spoke just as warmly as me. "Sure," she said typing on her keypad faster than an experienced secretary. She glared into the computer for a few seconds then said the words I didn't want to hear. "Ahhhhh, unfortunately Miss Pratt, since your name isn't on the room, and your last name isn't the same, I won't be able to do that. I'm sorry."

I felt defeated. "Miss, I really need to get into my room." I got closer in her face, leaning over the counter.

"I'd like to help you but it's against hotel policy."

"But I'm Trae's fiancé."

"But your last name isn't Harris and your name isn't listed on the room."

"Where's your manager?" I asked angrily while turning to search for someone higher up.

Just as my eyes finished the virtual tour a feeling of despair hit me. I clenched at my heart when Trae hit the corner walking slowly toward the elevator. He and some short, skinny white girl strolled about three yards away from me as if they were a couple. Anger built up inside and I immediately began plotting out two homicides. With each step taken and the closer I got, I studied them as the chick kept laughing and looking into his eyes as if she loved his light, vanilla looking ass. It wouldn't have hurt as much if she'd been a hooker. At least I could've said there weren't any emotional ties. But the way she slipped her arm around his made my blood boil.

"Trae!" I shouted then charged toward him. My chest heaved up and down and an instant migraine developed inside my brain.

"Aweeeee man, c'mon. Royce, what are you doing here?" Slowly, he dropped his arms to his side so that they had no connection to the woman.

"No, what are you doing?"

"Know your role Royce...know your role."

He said the shit so calmly like I was supposed to just turn and walk away. "I know my role. That's why I'm here."

"Let's talk about this tomorrow. You know I got a game."

"I don't give a shit what you got tomorrow. Who is this woman?" I felt like Squeak from the Color Purple when she asked Harpo that same question, referring to Sophia. The only difference was that I wasn't about to get hit. They were.

I took a few more steps and got close up in Trae's face. "Who the fuck is she?" My tone with him was uncaring and cold, something he wasn't used to getting from me.

"What difference does it make? We're not married."

He said that shit so easily. It was as if he never cared anything for me. How could he have been so heartless? I refused to cry while thinking of my next move. I could see the spectators gathering just dying to find out what was going on. Then I saw two security guards rushing our way.

"I'll ask you one last time. Who is this bitch?"

"She's my girl," he shot back.

"Is everything okay, Mr. Harris?" one of the guards asked with concern the moment they rushed up on us.

"I think so," Trae responded.

He turned to look at me. "My friend was just leaving," he announced with ease.

I was already still in a state of shock from hearing him say the white chick was his girl. But now I'm a friend? "Oh no the hell I'm not!" I screamed hoping the entire lobby heard me.

"I'm warning you, Royce. This isn't a good look," Trae told me realizing people now knew who he was.

My finger pointed straight at him and moved fast like it was going through convulsions. "You got the nerve to warn me about something! I got a warning for you." My only hope was to play the only card I figured he cared about. My neck rolled and swiveled like a giraffe while I spilled my guts. "You better tell this bitch, I'm your woman, your fucking fiancé or you'll never see your son again!"

The white girl had a shocking expression on her face. But still, nobody moved. And Trae never claimed me. It made me sick to my stomach to know that he was that adamant about disrespecting me. And the fact that it was in front of this anorexic looking hoe had me about to blow my top.

"Miss, you're going to have to leave," the older security guard ordered directly to me.

"I'm not leaving! This bitch here is leaving!" I then turned to Trae. "She's not getting on that elevator with you. You hear me?"

He laughed at my comment. And so did she. That's when I

hauled off and swung like a wild woman. First, the windmill on Trae made me feel like there was some justice as he grabbed at my arms trying to pry me off of him. I kept swinging, biting at his chest, doing anything to cause him pain. I could see security coming for me, but Trae quickly told them he could handle me and to call the police. When I heard the anorexic chick laugh, I burst from Trae's grip and ambushed the bitch down to the floor. I grabbed her hair and yanked hard trying to mop the floor with her body.

We found ourselves sliding across the marble floor rumbling like two wrestlers. More people had gathered around and more officers were on their walkie-talkies calling for help. I kept punching, kicking and hitting her in the face as hard as I could. Every time I saw Trae's smirk from the corner of my eye more anger shot through my veins causing me to hurl to my feet and stomp the bitch in her face repeatedly.

Before I knew it, Rachel broke through the crowd, grabbed me by my arm and told me we had to leave before I ended up in jail. There were still no tears, only rage and deep, heavy breaths. I stood up, fixed my hoodie that had been yanked and pulled out of place and told Trae what I now meant for life.

"It's over, Trae!" I shouted, attempting to catch my breath. "This is the last time you'll ever do this to me! You can have your white bitch and any other tramp you want. I took my four carat ring off and slung it toward the elevator before following Rachel out to the car.

Chapter 11

India

By the time we pulled up to the Palms Hotel Xavier and I were laughing and kicking it like old friends. Even though he'd kept his hands on me the entire time in the cab, there was something special between us, something more than him wanting me sexually. It was that bond that only people who were meant to be had. I'd dated hundreds of men and knew all the signs. This connection came off far different than the others in the past.

"Yes, yes, yes!" I mouthed to myself as Xavier paid the Arabian cab driver.

When we hopped out of the cab, he held the door for me, when we made our way to the elevator, he grasped my hand ushering me inside, and when he stepped out the elevator before me and bowed, I thought damn, *what a gentleman*. We proceeded to walk down the hall arm in arm as he kissed me on the neck between all the many questions he threw at me. He wanted to know everything about me. Where I went to school? How many siblings I had? How many children I wanted?

Finally, when we reached room #2022, he stopped and pulled the key from his back pocket. My adrenaline rose as he gave me a sexy stare then plunged his tongue into my mouth. I latched on feeling myself moisten between my thighs.

Suddenly, he stopped to stare at me again. "You're so beautiful, where've you been all my life?"

"Ahhhh, Antonio, before we go in. Remember, we're just getting to know each other, right? I like you and don't want to mess things up between us. So, ride slow, okay?"

He opened the door and pulled me inside gently. "I feel you Miss Lady. I would never want to disrespect you." He let go of my hand and studied my model-like figure. "You're definitely the type of woman I would love to settle down with someday. Classy and not a gold digger," he told me sincerely.

I was speechless. That was exactly how I wanted him to feel. "So, where are the drinks?" I asked looking around the standard size room. I was expecting a lavish suite with all the bells and whistles I deserved. But I guess the team wasn't paying for all of that. That would come in due time, I told myself, when he and I took one of our many posh vacations during the off-season.

"I'm gonna order it from room service," he whispered in an even sexier tone than he'd been using throughout the night.

"Cool."

Instead of picking up the phone, he began coming out of his shoes, then his jeans, allowing his Burberry boxers to show off his cut thighs. The nicca was built and I enjoyed the sight, but I wanted to take things slow to ensure my spot in his life for later.

Quickly, I realized Xavier had different plans. He rushed up on me before I could say anything, allowing my head to connect with his chest. I got nervous as he swiped his hand beneath my dress, touching my clit slightly. We never said another word until he'd completely taken off all his clothes and asked me if I was okay.

"I wouldn't want to offend you or make you do anything you don't want to. I'm not that type of guy," he added genuinely. "We can just chill. I only wanna rub my body against yours. No penetration if you don't want it. I promise."

He was perfect for the father of my children. *A man with morals*, I thought deeply. I never officially agreed to anything but before I knew it he had gently undressed me causing my breast to sit erect from the sudden cool air. Xavier latched on, sucking like a hungry baby demolishing his bottle. My knees became weak from his touch and I could feel his stiffness against my abs. I got horny as hell while he began to grind like a buck against my skin. My juices flowed and body heat erupted. Xavier was obviously a pro at foreplay.

He whispered in my ear. "Stand here, don't move. I gotta get something."

He jetted toward the side of the bed grabbing something from a duffle bag off the floor. It appeared to be some sort of cosmetic bag. I had no idea what was inside, but those few seconds allowed me to see the rips in his naked body and his chiseled chest. His ass was tight, and fatter than mine. Luckily, my breast would keep his mind off what I lacked.

My muscle-bound lover returned within seconds after stopping to turn off the lights. Xavier rushed over to me holding his thick, rod in his hand. I'd become nervous all of a sudden like it was my first time. He leaned in and my instincts had my hands rubbing his chest vigorously within no time. The nicca got freaky, bending slightly to swipe his tongue across my midsection. He licked me like a soft serve of vanilla ice cream leaving not one piece of skin untouched.

"You're so freaky," I complimented, letting him know I enjoyed.

"You believe in fairy tales?" Xavier asked from down below. He'd gotten on his knees while I stood frozen waiting for him to hit the spot.

"I do. I do."

"What kind?"

"Any kind," I said quickly. I didn't want him to talk. I wanted him to lick. Immediately.

"You taste so good," he told me after gracing me with one, long, stroke.

I thought I had an orgasm that quick. It felt so good, nothing I'd ever experienced before. It must've been the tease. It didn't take long for him to plunge into me, clutching my ass like he was enjoyed a sweet piece of watermelon on a hot summer day.

"Oh, yes!" I moaned attempting to catch my balance. There was nothing to hold onto so I felt like a surfer on high tides as I got ate out by the best. "Got damnnnnnnnnnn. This- this- this- feels- soooooooooooo good!"

Suddenly, Xavier stopped. He stood quickly staring me in the face. "Hey, what are you doing?" I wanted to know.

"I got next, right? Then the fantasy begins."

What in the hell was he talking about? I wanted more of what he was giving. "I definitely want my fantasy to come true, but can that wait?" I begged with the tone in my voice.

"The question is can you handle my fantasy?"

"What's your fantasy?" My shit was pulsating. I hoped he wasn't talking about whips and chains. *Been there done that*, I thought to myself. I felt him kneel to grab his bag. No clues had come to mind about what lay inside, but my hormones had exploded so I was ready to get freaky right along with him.

"Well, for the first part of my fantasy, I'm going to blind fold you, if that's okay," he stopped to ask.

My reservations showed as I bit my lower lip. It took me a few minutes to even begin to talk. "Ahhhhh."

"Don't worry baby, if you don't want to, we can just chill."

"What in the hell was wrong with this fool? He'd gotten me all worked up with a fever that had to have reached 103 by now. Now, he was talking about chilling. This nicca played too many games.

"I just want to please you, India, giving you something to make you want to be with me forever."

"Damn. Okay, okay, go ahead." I'd caught a sensitive cat, most likely a momma's boy, I thought watching him pull the fabric from his bag.

"Don't take the blindfold off until I'm finish pleasing you," Xavier instructed while finishing his statement with a soft kiss and a tight knot to the back of my head.

I couldn't see at all, yet it added to the mystery of our experience.

"I promise everything will be okay. I want us to experience passionate love like we never have before," he whispered, caressing my shoulders and planting a soft, kiss on my forehead.

The sensual fabric felt like oversized sunshades leaving just enough room for my nose to peek from. I could feel him guiding me over to the bed, rubbing me sensually along the way. He meticulously placed me on the bed on all fours with my ass hanging close to the edge. Instantly, I got nervous again.

"Scoot back baby, and just relax. I promise you'll enjoy yourself. We both will."

"I don't want it in the ass," I blurted.

"Just relax," he repeated in that manipulative, whisper.

My heart fluttered. Then came the shortness of breath. There was only one thing I hated with a passion, and was afraid to do. That was dookey love. It was unnatural to me and nothing was sexy about it. Royce had often teased me saying that with the right man and the right lubricant, a pussy hole was no different from a butt hole. I never understood it, nor did I want to experience it.

"You the type of woman I want raising my babies," Xavier exclaimed in that voice that confirmed he meant it. "I just want to lick it for a while."

I never expected a big, famous jock to be so gentle, so loving. It didn't fit the profile. My girls would be so jealous after seeing who I snagged. I couldn't even think anymore as Xavier's tongue worked my asshole. Salvia dripped from my mouth since I couldn't control the muscles in my jaw, nor the feelings I developed down below. I never knew an ass licking could feel so good. Xavier kept making slurping sounds while I lifted my leg making sure he got in perfectly. Then he stopped right when I was about to squirt. He pulled my ass back ready to do what I feared. I told myself to relax and that everything would be okay. This was my time to shine and cop the life I'd been dreaming.

I began to fantasize what our life would be like together. I felt Xavier's dick against my ass but nothing prepared me for what happened next. My reflexes caused me to flinch and goose bumps popped up all over my entire body. He worked me slowly making sure I was still alright.

"Ride with me, India," he thrust and talked at the same time. "Don't be afraid to experience what you're not used to."

I obeyed then let out a loud squeal. It hurt like hell yet felt good all at the same time. It seemed like every body part began to swell as my back arched like a pro. Before long, he'd pulled out, flipped me over, and straddled me as if he was on the football field tackling the enemy.

His weight held me down as he pounded me like I'd stolen something from him. He was killing the pussy so hard I began to gyrate roughly, throwing it back at him. I wanted him to know this was just the beginning of our sex life and there would be more to come once we got back to New York.

"This is what you gonna get every night," I told him between breaths.

"Whose pussy is this?" he asked me.

"Yours."

"Whose?" he asked again as sweat dripped onto my already sweaty body. "Say my name!" he ordered.

"Xavier!" I shouted!

"You like that baby, does it feel good?" he said getting more buck wild.

"Yesssssss," I slurred feeling my orgasm coming. "It feeeeeeeeelssssss good," I moaned. I'd lost all control. In all my years, Xavier's lovemaking was in a class by itself. "Got dammm-mmnnnnnnnnnn, Xavier!" I shouted.

"Auh , auh, auh, " he panted, picking up the pace. I thought he was about to have a heart attack until I heard the loud yelp. "Aahhhhhhhhhhhh, shit! I, I, I'm cum, cuminnnnnnng," he yelled like Tarzan.

I laid flat, worn out for minutes while my mandingo kissed at my neck. He was hooked for life and I was too after that marathon. *That just may have been the best sex I'd ever had.*

When Xavier got up and grabbed a bottle of whip cream from the bathroom, I almost passed out. I just closed my eyes and smiled. I'd found a kinky one.

🎸 🎸 🎸

When morning rolled around, I woke up, sore asshole and all. It was completely silent in the room but the sunshine beamed through the partially opened sheers letting me know the day would be perfect. I stretched, looked around for Xavier then glanced at the clock. It read 10:00 a.m.

"Oh shit!" I shouted. I figured he'd gone to the stadium since the game started at three.

I hoped like hell he'd have some energy left after all we'd done. He needed to be the MVP during the game so the reporters would follow us immediately afterwards. I got all gooey inside just thinking about it so I got up feeling antsy about the game. As soon as my feet hit the floor I started to remember some of the not so pleasurable moments of the night. The pulsating ache that shot through my ass was probably from the forceful penetration. My thoughts were still a lil' fuzzy, but I knew some kinky shit had taken place. Xavier had turned me into every position possible and we'd climaxed at least five times throughout the night.

I'd already convinced myself there was no time to focus on the past while reaching for my clothes from the top of the dresser. It was time to plan for the future. The moment I picked up my panties, I noticed the sheet of paper with my name written across the top. A love note…how thoughtful. I picked it up only to realize it was folded, and five- one hundred dollar bills fell onto the dresser.

"Yes!" I shouted. "This man knows how to take care of a woman."

Quickly, my eyes scanned the writing. *Had to run out. Check out is at 11. I enjoyed last night. Now you enjoy the money. You worked for it. And just so you know, you called me Xavier last night so I know you know who I am. I'll call you later or maybe not.*

"Ahhh, shit!" And how would he call me later or tomorrow! Did he mean possibly Monday? What the hell? The parties were tonight!" I shrieked. And he didn't have my number. I got dressed fast and was out the door in less than ten minutes. Xavier and I had some things to get straight after the game.

Chapter 12

India

Rachel's red bottomed heels proudly exposed my newly pedicured feet and toes, compliments of Xavier. His money definitely came in handy allowing me to purchase the multi-colored Prada dress that showed off my firm breasts and brought attention to my ass that secretly had butt pads to thank for its boost. I knew Rachel would be pissed once she found out I had on her shit, but I didn't care. I needed to blend in with all the rest of the player's wives today.

Underneath the late afternoon Miami sun among crowds of people, I sashayed into the stadium to the seating section during the beginning of the first quarter. I knew the men lucky enough to be behind me were getting an enjoyable eyeful, making their wives or mistress' jealous. I didn't give a damn though. Attention was what the show was for; and increased my chances of leaving with what I came for.

As proudly as a Clydesdale horse I made my way down to the best seats in the house…The fifty yard line. Just short of the sky boxes, what better place was there for a boss chick like me? Just before I sat down, my eyes took a quick glance around and noticed Rachel about five rows up and one section over. They were decent seats, but much cheaper than mine. Just like I'd hoped, she was watching my entrance waving, trying to get my attention. I hadn't spoken to her all day and barely the whole time we'd arrived in Miami together. She'd called earlier, but I let her calls go to voice mail.

Too late!

Fuck her!

My avoidance was all for this particular moment right here. I wanted to surprise her with a grand entrance capped off with the crowning moment of me sitting down in seats she *couldn't* get for me. I gasped when I noticed Royce sitting two seats away from her.

"What the hell is she doing here?" I asked myself loudly.

It's crazy how Rachel couldn't seem to get me a ticket, but now Royce appeared out of nowhere and coincidently had a seat so close to her. *Bullshit!* I told myself. There would be more competition for me now that the bitch with the halo was in town. Royce and I had been friends since the twelfth grade, so I knew what to expect when men had to choose between two gorgeous women who rolled together.

Ignoring Rachel's waves and air kisses, I let her eat her heart out. I sat down, leaned comfortably back into my seat, and crossed my legs. From behind the darkness of my fake Chanel shades I nonchalantly let my eyes roam the stands while knowing people were most likely wondering what my occupation was or which player I was dating since I snagged a seat in the first row behind the railing. Although I didn't quite catch anyone's eyes on me, I knew they were there. They just didn't want to be so obvious about it.

As my eyes surveyed my surroundings I noticed Travis Freeman's wife and also Dominic Hardaway's wife. No doubt their multi-million dollar husbands had placed them in such excellent seats just several seats away from mine. They'd also laced them fabulously. Diamonds were literally dripping from the women's ears, necks, and wrists. Not only did Mrs. Freeman have an eight carat Harry Winston emerald cut diamond on her boney ass finger, but she watched the festivities from behind her limited edition, fifty-five hundred dollar Dolce & Gabbana shades.

Damn, I wanted those.

For a moment I couldn't help but picture myself playing the ladies' position. I could see my famous and heavily paid athlete of a husband spoiling me with the newest Maserati, fashions fresh off the runway, jewelry specially designed by Jacob, a mansion so big I would need three maids to clean that shit.

My eyes once again swung toward Rachel and Royce. This time Royce saw me. She smiled and waved. In all honesty I wanted to roll my eyes and pretend she was just as invisible as the air I breathed. But she was my so-called friend so I had to put up a front. My Mac covered lips reluctantly formed a smile. I then kissed the forefingers of my right hand and blew her a kiss.

Immediately afterwards, I turned my head and my body slightly. Looking at her any longer than I had to might've made me nauseous. Silently, I began to think of Chris Jackson again. I'd pulled him up on my phone just before the game and hoped like hell we'd meet tonight. Somehow. Some way. #36 would be a jersey to watch out for, I told myself devilishly.

Suddenly, the crowd roared loudly.

So busy checking for surrounding athletes, movie stars, rappers, etc, etc, I had no idea what had just occurred on the field. Suddenly, I felt a tap on my shoulder and sensed someone standing over me a lot closer than they should've been. My head swiveled to see two stadium security guards standing near my face.

"Can I help you?" I asked in a way that let them know I didn't appreciate their wanna-be cop asses all up in my damn circumference. Raising my shades, my eyes traveled from their eyes to their feet and back up again.

"Ma'am," one of them said. "We're going to need you to come with us."

"Excuse me?" I questioned, looking and sounding like he must've lost his mind.

"Please, ma'am," the other said, glancing around, hoping I wouldn't create a disturbance. "We'd really appreciate your cooperation in this matter. Please make this easy for all of us."

Embarrassment enveloped me as the clowns stood over me like I was some sort of a criminal. The crowd roared again at one of the plays but I focused on the dozens of eyes on me as if I was on display or something.

"Look, muthafuckas," I said with bass. My voice drenched with agitation and anger. "I don't know what the fuck y'all want or *who* sent you. But whatever or whoever it is, it's not me. So you need to take your little walkie talkies and flash lights and go find somebody else around here to harass."

I rolled my neck and eyes at them while shoeing their annoying souls away with my hand.

"Ma'am, we're trying to be polite."

"Fuck you. Go find someone else to harass. I'm with Xavier Simms."

People around me began to chatter among themselves.

"Ma'am, either come with us or we're gonna have to go get the police."

I folded my arms over my breasts. "Go get them then," I boldly challenged. "What are you waiting for? Maybe they'll help me get rid of you."

"Suit yourself, ma'am."

Both guards disappeared.

The nerve of those fucking flash light cops, I thought with anger.

The crowd cheered again.

This time I clapped.

Xavier's face appeared on the Jumbo Tron. He'd just made a big play for the Giants and his team mates were congratulating him. I clapped my hands for him and cheered right along with everyone else. I stood up proudly.

"Go baby! Go Baby!"

I kept thinking about how I would explain to him after the game why I never confessed to knowing who he really was. Seconds later, I looked to my left to see the two guards coming towards me again. This time they had two Miami uniformed cops with them.

"What the hell?" I whispered to myself. All I could think about was the phone call from Agent Miles yesterday. *Had my secret been discovered? Was I busted? Why at the game*?

"Miss," one of the officers said when he and his partner

reached me. "We're gonna need you to come with us."

"For what?" I asked in a less confrontational tone than before.

"Miss, we'll discuss that in a moment. But for right now we're gonna need you to be cooperative and do what we ask."

"I'm not going any damn where," I told them, folding my arms across my breasts again. I would play innocent to the end if this was about Olivia. They'd have to prove it first.

"Miss, if you don't do as I ask, my partner and I will be left with no other alternative but to use force."

Both cops positioned themselves in front of me. The sixty something year old with the salt and pepper beard scared me til no end. He looked as if he had it out for me.

"I haven't done anything wrong. I'm not going anywhere with you."

Both cops reached for my wrists.

"Get your hands off of me!" I demanded, jerking my wrists away from them.

Ignoring my demand, the older cop grabbed my forearms, pulled me from the seat, and forced me around. I immediately placed a heel into the seat and pressed into it with all the strength I could put into my legs. The force knocked the officers backwards and almost over the railing to the field. The sight must've looked ridiculous to everyone.

"Miss, stop resisting us!" they said, trying to control me.

"Fuck you!" I screamed, tussling with them as if my life depended on it. "I haven't done anything wrong."

All eyes were on us, even the Jumbo Tron had labeled me the wildest fan allowing everyone in the stadium to see me in despair. I felt my feet leave the ground as one of the cops lifted me. I started to kick, punch, and scratch like an alley cat fighting her way out of a corner. "Get the fuck off of me, damn it!"

"Miss, we can't do that," an officer said, trying to grab my wrist while ducking and dodging my wildly flailing fists and feet. "Would you just calm down?"

"No, not until you tell me what's going on!" I managed to dig my fingernails into a chair and hold on so the cops couldn't move me. Most of the fans near the struggle had gotten up and moved out of the way but were still watching and pointing, some even laughing.

"Miss, don't play stupid. You know what this is about."

"No, I don't."

"Yes, you do. That ticket you used to get in here was stolen. The scanner back at the ticket counter picked up on it."

"What?" I asked in disbelief. "There's got to be a mistake."

"Maybe there is, maybe there isn't," he said, placing his hand on the stun gun on his belt. "That will be determined later. But for right now, if you don't comply with our orders, I'm gonna be forced to stun you."

I wasn't stupid. The last thing I wanted was to be laid out on the ground with fifty-thousand volts of stinging hot electricity running through my ass. "Alright! Alright!" I said quickly. "I'll go with you, damn."

"That's greatly appreciated," the cop said, removing his hand from the stun gun.

"But I'm still telling you there's a mistake."

As the cops escorted me from my seat I looked at Rachel and Royce. Both were staring at me with worried looks on their faces. I rolled my eyes at them in both embarrassment and anger. Moments later, after walking through several mazes of hallways and down a couple sets of stairs, I found myself being led through a door into a white room. In it three jail cells lined one wall while the security offices lined the opposite wall.

I guess you really do learn something new every day, I thought to myself. I'd never known they actually kept jail cells in the bottom of stadiums.

One of the cops slid a key into the lock of one of the cells, turned it, and pulled the cell door open. "Please step inside, ma'am," he told me.

"How long am I going to be in here?" I asked.

"Until the game's over. Afterwards you'll most likely be transported."

"Transported where?" I panicked. "Xavier Simms will be waiting for me after the game. We've got interviews and parties to go to."

"Sounds good, lady," another officer responded.

"Not today," another shouted making me realize what was about to happen to me.

Chapter 13

India

Track of time got lost. I had no idea if it was still daylight outside or not. I knew people were still inside the stadium only because of the loud music that played above. Finally one of the cops stepped out of the security office with the keys in his hand. He opened the cell door.

"Alright, ma'am, you're free to go," he said, stepping to the side.

"Did you find out it was a damn mistake?" I asked, placing my hands on my hips and looking him directly in the eyes.

"No, ma'am. We just received a call from upstairs informing us to let you go. If anything else is to come about concerning this matter, I'm sure you'll be notified."

I shook my head. "I should sue you, you know that?"

"You're free to use whatever legal course of action you feel is necessary, ma'am," he said closing the cell and leading me to the door.

For about three minutes I was led through the same maze of hallways we'd taken to get to the cells in the first place. Finally we walked through a door which let us out by the concession stands. The game must've been over because the area was crowded with people headed towards the exits. It was dark outside when the officer and I reached the stadium entrance.

"You have a good evening, ma'am," he said then turned to walk off.

"Whatever," I replied.

"India!" someone shouted.

I saw Royce and Rachel rushing towards me from the gates. "Are you okay?" Royce asked when she and Rachel reached me. She looked me up and down, inspecting my body for bruises or cuts.

"I'm good," I said showing that I was still aggravated. Immediately my feet headed for the parking lot without having to be told.

"What did they arrest you for?" Rachel asked, walking beside me.

"They had the nerve to say my ticket was stolen. They made me miss the damn game."

"Stolen?" Royce gasped.

"Yeah, but those assholes knew they were wrong."

"India, think about it," Royce said strongly, "Rachel told me Tyesha hooked you up with the ticket guy so the ticket was probably stolen."

"No, it wasn't," I snapped.

"Okay, you keep believing in your tricky ass roommate. She's foul!" Royce added.

"The ticket wasn't stolen and those bastards knew they'd fucked up. They had no choice but to let me go 'cause I told them I was gonna sue their asses."

"Actually," Royce announced with hesitation, "Rachel got you out."

"What do you mean?"

"I pulled a few strings," Rachel chimed in. "You know I couldn't let you sit in there. And not with my Louboutins on, anyway." Her eyes darted down to my feet. "Next time, ask first. Don't floss in my shit to make yourself look good. Okay?"

My eyes rolled. The hoe was talking like she was a boss bitch or something, like she had pull. "Whatever," I said, never breaking stride. "I just want to get up out of this country ass city and get back to NY. I've never been so damned humiliated in my life. I'm out of here."

"Tonight?" Rachel asked with surprise.

"Hell yeah, tonight."

"But you can't," Royce whined.

"And why can't I?"

"Because we've got a Super Bowl party to go to tonight," Rachel sang holding three tickets.

"I don't care. I'm on the very first thing smoking up out of here back to New York."

"But you're always saying you want a football player," Rachel said. "Well, tonight's the only night you'll be able to make that happen."

Darkie was trying to play me again. "I had a player. Some-one I met last night and we made magic," I admitted proudly. "But he probably saw me getting arrested on the screen along with everyone else, so I'm sure that's ruined."

"Just explain to him what happened." Royce shrugged her shoulders.

The bitch did have a point. My pace slowed.

"Everybody's gonna be up in there. You can't miss it. You may never get a chance like this again in life," Royce continued like she had some newfound energy. "You could be missing out on your future husband, girl," she added. "Are you gonna let sitting in some fake ass jail for a few hours mess that up for you?"

Damn, they were right. What the fuck was I thinking about? This opportunity was what I'd come for. I couldn't walk away now. "Alright," I finally agreed with a conniving grin on my face.

Suddenly, my phone rang. With major paranoia, I took a deep breath. It wasn't a New York number again, so I exhaled. "Yeah," I answered.

"India?"

Instantly, I cupped my mouth with my free hand. I hadn't heard her voice in over seven years. This meant trouble. "Hey," I said slowly.

"Did they call you?" Her voice was filled with worry.

"Yeah. Yesterday. It was the F.B.I, right?"

"Yep. Some bonehead named Agent Miles. Look, I don't want to talk on this line. I'll be back in New York on Monday. I'll call you at the place we used to meet at. Okay?"

"Okay. But India…" she paused.

"I'm scared."

"Me too," I whispered. "But it's not like we killed anyone."

"In my eyes… it's worse," she told me before hanging up in my ear.

Later in the evening the three of us were making our way up a circular drive way to a humungous ocean side three-storied mansion. I'd put all my fears aside for the night ready to party. We passed countless Ferraris, Lambos, Aston Martins, and Bentley's. Benzes and BMWs meant nothing! There were absolutely none of those in sight. The ballas had brought out the *real* big boy shit tonight; hundred thousand dollar price tags and up. My skin throbbed at the potential.

Yo Gotti's, *Five Star Chick* banged loudly from the house as we approached the front door. When we walked inside there were wall to wall people. But not *just* people. Not just every day sort of folks you saw passing by on the street. Nah, these were the elite. These were rich people, America's trend setters.

Chad Johnson could be seen off in a not so far distance talking loudly, shrugging off the fact that he'd lost three hundred thousand dollars on the Giants today like it was nothing. Terrell Owens, Kellen Winslow, Plaxico Burress, and a host of other football players could also be seen as we made our way through the house. The Miami Heat was also in the spot. My mouth nearly dropped at the sight of Lebron, Dwayne Wade, and Kurt Frazier clutching Cristal bottles as they conversed with friends. Even a few rappers that I'd seen on 106&Park were in the house stunting out of control, ice all over their necks and wrists.

The experience seemed surreal. I couldn't believe it. I'd never been a part of something so big. The shit was breath taking. But I wasn't going to spend tonight star struck. I was here for a job. I was here to get me a balla.

As we began to sip champagne a few niccas tried to holla, but I shut them down quickly. No hanger ons, no members of a nicca's entourage, no bodyguards, no security. I was having none of that. Only a well known athlete, preferably handsome, was going to get a shot at this tonight. A part of me wanted Xavier to show up but another part said noooooooooooo, not tonight.

All of a sudden I saw Chris Jackson my soulmate come strolling toward me. My eyes couldn't believe it… #36- Giants tight end in the flesh. He was even finer in person than he was when I saw videos of him on the internet signing that new contract that sent him to the big leagues, nearly one hundred million dollars. I was absolutely sure he'd most likely seen me from across the room and felt he just *had* to come talk to me. I was glad he'd remembered me from back in the day. I smiled at his approach and rubbed my hands together swiftly thinking about my come up. My days in the hood were just about over. He smiled and extended his hand. I did the same.

"Rachel," he said, walking right past me and leaving my hand dangling. "I didn't know you could get any prettier."

He held her hand and spun her in a tiny circle getting a good look at her outfit. The dress was Christian Dior, but it wasn't nearly as cute as what I had on. Envy latched on to every cell in my body and I couldn't hide it; especially when the two hugged and kissed each other on the lips.

I damn near blew a fuse. What type of fuckery was this? He had to be joking. As the two began chatting and smiling, annoyance and aggravation boiled inside of me. What the fuck did he see in her black ass? Shit, I thought she said she didn't date players.

When Chris' cell phone rang, he answered it. After a few seconds he hung up. "Rachel, baby, I'll be right back," he said kissing her on the lips again. "Don't go anywhere. I've got to go handle something real quick."

"I'll be here," she assured him in some wack-ass wanna-be sexy tone.

As he walked away she smiled like a school girl. Jealous and unable to hold my tongue I asked, "How did you pull that off,

Darkie?"

Rachel looked at me like she'd just grown horns on her head. "That's it. I gave you a pass before. Don't hate me because I'm beautiful, India. Have you ever heard the saying, the darker the berry, the sweeter the juice?"

I just shrugged my shoulders. I could see Royce looking at me crazily so I was ready to lash out at her, too.

"You got that crazy, old school mentality that just because you're lighter, you think you're better," Rachel preached.

"Nah, but tell me, how did you pull that off? I need to know," I said, pulling out some gloss and applying another coat.

"India, contrary to what you believe, all men don't want you."

"What the fuck ever," I said shrugging her off.

"India, what's your problem?" Royce interjected. "Why can't you just be happy for Rachel?"

"I am," I lied. "If he wants your ass, he can have you. It's none of my business. Shit, I personally wouldn't be caught dead with an ugly nicca like him."

"That's foul," Royce commented. "Why are you being so disrespectful all of a sudden? We supposed to be girls."

"I'm not. I'm just pointing out her bad taste in men."

"My bad taste in men?" Rachel blared, placing her hands on her hips. "Chris is fine as hell."

I shrugged my shoulders. "If you say so."

Seeing Trae headed our way sorta got me off the hook. I'd listened in the car about how Trae disrespected Royce in front of everyone at the Palms, so as he approached things got a little tense. Rachel turned away immediately and left wanting no parts of any drama.

"What's up, Royce?" Trae asked wearing a somber expression.

Royce rolled her eyes and moved to my right side leaving Trae on my left. "Trae, me and you don't have shit to talk about."

"Royce, I know I fucked up, but I'm already having a bad evening. Don't make it worse, alright? I really want to spend some time with you right now."

Royce called herself making her man sweat. She pranced away showing off her curvaceous shape leaving him standing next to me. After only several steps I saw this well kempt looking dude with incredible swag pressed up on her. He had to be someone with the amount of jewels that draped his neck, arms and ears. The two began talking so I walked over to join the conversation since I hadn't quite figured out who he was yet. Trae watched us both like hawks attempting to hold back his anger.

"Hello, I'm India," I said, walking up on the beautiful, mocha colored brotha that had my attention.

"I'm Romello," he told me nicely showing off his perfectly straight, white teeth. "I was just telling your friend that her face looked familiar. I can't quite figure it out, but I'm sure we've met."

"Oh, Royce doesn't get out much," I boldly expressed with a smile.

He snapped his fingers a few times like it all came back then moved closer to Royce giving her way too much attention. I loved the fact that he had on shades at night and rocked a thick beard and goatee. Sexy.

"I knew I'd seen you before. My boy JR gave me your demo the other day. It had your picture on there and all your info. Damn, you're even more beautiful in person."

Ughhhhh. Boring, I thought.

"Wow. Who would've thought we'd meet like this. I've been hearing about you and your work for quite some time. Best producer around, so they say," Royce complimented.

Producer? Oh shit, that's royalties for life, baby. I looked over my shoulder mad that Trae was trapped in conversation with two men who appeared to be upset about something. I needed him to come get his woman so Romello and I could spend some time getting to know one another.

"Yo, your voice is unique, one of a kind," he uttered causing Royce to blush.

"You really think so?" she questioned.

"No doubt. I want us to do some things together."

Royce looked a little uneasy. I had no idea why and neither did Romello.

He pulled out his business card. "When you get back to the city, call me. I want to sign you to my label."

"Signed...just like that?" Royce questioned.

"No doubt. I heard your voice on all the songs. I told JR I wanted to meet up with you. You got the look and the voice. Besides, if you can hypnotize your audience with those eyes the way you're doing me right now, we'll have sold out crowds everywhere."

"You're too kind," Royce said almost in a whisper. "I'm definitely going to call though."

All too late Trae barged into our little circle eyeballing Romello like he was ready to brawl. Romello was no sucka. I could tell by the way he stood erect, chest out and tight abs in. The all black gave me a chance to explore his entire body. The nicca was fine.

"Royce, why would you walk away while I was talking to you?" Trae squealed.

Romello stood back calmly not wanting to interfere or overstep his boundaries. "You have a good evening, Miss Royce," he said showing that his words were done.

Chad Johnson happened to be strolling by us at that very moment. "The way you choked on the field today Trae, cost me three hundred thousand," he said spitefully.

"Fuck you, Chad," Trae shot back with annoyance in his voice. He shook his head.

"Choke artist," someone else said and laughed from behind us.

Trae held his head as if the constant comments had begun to affect him. I'd been hearing people in passing all night talking about how the Giants lost solely because of Trae. Mr. Big Shot Wide Receiver was now Mr. Loser. Apparently he'd fumbled a punt that immediately ended their chances at winning the game.

"Trae, I'm not done talking over business yet," Royce told him stepping back toward Romello. "He's a producer and someone I wanted to hear my demo. He likes it," she told Trae proudly.

"Oh yeah."

"Yep. He said I got talent."

Trae looked like a beaten man. He wasn't as cocky and confident as he usually was. The fact that he'd lost the game for The Giants on the country's biggest stage this afternoon was eating away at him terribly. And now his woman was beaming about some producer who looked like he had major paper.

"All I need is five minutes with you Royce," he damn near begged.

Royce sighed, then told Romello she'd be back. She walked off to the side to talk to Trae while I watched from the side-lines seething with jealously. We could all still hear; especially me since it was my goal. I even moved a few inches closer to them and crossed my arms while standing with a pitiful frown on my face.

"Oh, so that's how you doing it now?" Trae asked her in disbelief. "You're just going to talk to a nigga right in front of me?"

"Why not?" she asked boldly. "You had a bitch with you last night and didn't think about claiming me, apologizing, or even pretending that I meant anything to you."

"Man, I fucked up. I was drunk."

"You weren't drunk, Trae. But you did fuck up."

"Alright, Royce, I've been taking you for granted," he admitted in front of everyone. "But I want us to work things out."

I was glad Royce walked away 'cause that light bright nicca was lying through his teeth. When he grabbed her hand in front of everyone and damn near started weeping, I coulda bought him for two cents.

"I'm for real this time, Royce."

"And what would make me think you're ready to be monogamous, Trae?"

He pressed his body close to hers. "Because I love you," he said glancing back over his shoulder to stare at Romello. Trae made sure he saw him up close and personal with Royce.

Those words caught Royce by surprise and made her melt. I could tell. I knew her well.

"I'm ready to stop playing around, baby. I mean that. I want me you and Lil Trae to be a real family, all living under one roof and the whole nine."

I started walking away. The scene irked the hell out of me. Neither of my friends were even half as hot as me but yet Royce had a million dollar athlete practically begging for her attention and Rachel had gone off with the one I'd been wanting for the last five years. Nothing had come my way, not even a few scrubs. The night wasn't going at all like I'd envisioned it. I was pissed. Something had to give.

Then it happened. I spotted Xavier from across the room. With no hesitation I almost jumped hurdles trying to get close enough for him to hear me call his name. He moved so swiftly through the crowd there was nothing left for me to do but yell. I didn't know whether to call him Antonio or Xavier so I began with Antonio as I gained some yards on him.

"Antonio!" I kept yelling, pushing people out of my way.

When that didn't work, I switched gears, "Xavier!" I tried. Still no response. He wouldn't even look back at me.

Finally he rushed into a small room that held a magnificent view of Miami Beach. There were only four to five people chit-chatting inside, with one stopping Xavier dead in his tracks.

"Good game," the person commented, shaking his hand.

"Yeah, good game," I added, finally catching him. I placed my left hand on his shoulder. "You didn't hear me calling you?"

"Excuse me," he said politely. "Do I know you?"

"You gotta be kidding me, right?"

"Ahhh, no. I mean I meet lots of people. But I don't recall meeting you."

"Okay, Antonio, Xavier or whoever you want to be. This is not funny."

It seemed as though the room cleared magically as everyone could sense my mood swing. "You don't remember me or last night?"

He let out a huge laugh. "Maybe you were physically with me last night," he shrugged his shoulders," but I purposely forget those kind of nights."

"What! Don't do this shit to me! I'll tell everyone about us!"

"Yeah right, who do you think will believe you? You're a

gold digger and you know it. You knew who I was from the start. And you know how it goes. You're a big girl playing a big boy game, right?"

"You asshole!" I shouted.

"Look, enjoy your five hundred, learn from your mistakes and keep your goodies to yourself the next time."

My heart was now in my shoe. "What?" I was so humiliated.

"Get lost," he told me walking away like he didn't give a damn about me.

Embarrassment and agony reeked thru my pores. I'd never been treated so badly. I was going home on the first thing smoking.

Chapter 14

Royce

Six days passed since leaving the hood yet I still struggled to unpack everything from the boxes, even with Rosa's help. She was tickled to death that Lil Trae and I had moved back into the house causing her to slack on cleaning. I too should've been glad since my bills with Niecy had been whipped away in a flash. Trae cut her a three thousand dollar check to cover any set-backs I'd caused her. But strangely, I wasn't jumping out my boots like I thought I'd be.

Our home life was seemingly the same as it had been eight months ago before I left. I hated the fact that all the furniture I'd picked out had been tossed by Trae's mother the moment she heard I'd moved. Now the house had more of her touches than mine. Still in all it reeked luxury; a far cry from Niecy's place. All six bedrooms were lovely, contemporary décor in every room while wrought iron and marble adorned every corner of the house. Trae had dozens of sculptures and expensive football auction pieces but nothing compared to the Palladian windows and painted dome ceilings that I loved so much.

I hadn't really gotten settled yet since most of my time had been split between office visits with my newly hired entertainment lawyer and meetings with Romello's people. They were crazy about the details of my first release, who the producers of each track would be and what type of royalty percentages I would earn. There was so much to do on the business side. The thought of actually signing contracts, and getting big checks had me grinning to myself. When Trae walked in he caught me off guard causing me to jump away from the clothes being put onto the bed.

"Hey baby," he said blissfully, grabbing me from the back, wrapping his body cozily around mine.

"Hey." My response was real dry and low.

"What's my baby been doing all day?" He whispered directly into my ear but his attempt at trying to be romantic wasn't working.

"Just trying to get all my stuff unpacked, that's all." With extra strength, I managed to pull away from him and power walked to the opposite side of the bed. *Our* bed. "So, how'd the meetings go?" I asked only because it was the right thing to do.

"It was cool, but I missed you though," he told me coming out of his sweats and stripping down to just his boxers.

I hoped like hell Trae didn't want to have sex. I wasn't sure my spirit was ready for that since I knew in my heart he'd slept with someone when we were in Miami. Besides, he'd been gone for the last four days with his agent, strategizing on getting another worthy contract. He'd been traded so I didn't know if he'd worked in a few booty calls in between. Luckily, I moved in the first day he left so we never had to be in the room together until now.

"Look Trae, we need to talk," I said with authority in my tone. "We agreed that if I moved back you would add me and Trae on your health insurance. Did you do it?" I asked pointedly.

"Not yet, but I will," he added with extra charm headed straight to me, chest out and muscles bulging.

With a heavy breath, I held out my hands to keep him from standing face to face, body to body with me. He seemed to be extra touchy feely today letting me know me he was horny. I just wasn't feeling it. Sex with Trae was normally the bomb, but it was also what kept me in the stupid house with all his other tricks. That world was over for me. I wanted to be taken care of just long enough to become a star. Then I'd take care of myself and my son, leaving him behind if he didn't straighten up. I would then possibly even tell him that Lil Trae wasn't his.

"Trae, get back. You never want to handle business."

"I dooooooooo."

"You don't!"

Trae didn't say anything after that. Neither did I. As far as I was concerned we'd ironed out all the details of how things would change before we left Miami. Flaking out on me now wasn't about to happen.

"Trae, how many more years you plan on playing me?" Huh? Tell me that."

He stood in front of me, glaring into my eyes, giving me the look that always had the ability to make me weak. I felt myself giving in, wanting him even though I knew falling deeper in love with him wasn't good for me. I'd vowed to distance myself from him just in case he decided to do me wrong again. It would lessen the pain. Before I knew it, he kissed me slightly and held my shoulders firmly so I couldn't move. Our tongues were intertwined for several seconds causing me to moisten between the legs. When he pulled back slightly, he gave me that same loveable look as before.

"I told you that old life is over, it's just me and you now. I promise you that, baby."

"Why didn't you add us on the insurance yet?" My voice trembled with emotion.

"I was just busy. I promise I'll do it today," he said softly, "as soon as we get a lil' rest."

He stroked the length of my neck with his tongue causing my next words to release with a mild groan. "And what about adding me on the bank account?"

"I will Royce. Give me a few days. You know I've been gone trying to figure out who I'm playing with next season."

"How many days? And we're still keeping this house so I can remain in New York like you said, right?"

Shocked at my persistence his foreplay ended abruptly when he dropped his arms to his sides and developed a frown.

"You used to listen to me, without any questions. What's with the newness?"

"I told you when we were in Miami the way we did things before won't work anymore." My head shook back and forth violently. "I'm about to start working on this album and I can't do that with stress." He clutched my chin with his right hand sensing my building rage. "I need to feel secure, Trae. You told me not to worry about making money. You said you got me, just work on the album, and that you got the bills. You even said you'd step up to do Lil Trae, his homework and all. I can't do stress!"

"Shiiiit, some of Mary J's best music was made when she was stressed," he joked.

True, I thought to myself, but not funny. And that wouldn't be me. I needed to concentrate without drama-filled interruptions to make sure Romello liked my first few tracks. He was putting a lot of faith and energy into me by putting me in front of artists who had next.

"Trae, add my name on the bank accounts like you said."

"Royce, with all due respect. I want this to work," he said with a frustrated look on his face and his hands in the air, "but I'm not quite ready to put your name on everything yet? We'll be married soon enough."

He moved into my personal space again, this time with his dick, standing erect, and fighting to get out of his boxers. Without warning, he'd slipped my cotton, pajama shirt off my shoulders and began sucking on my nipples.

"I'm not quite ready to sleep with you yet either?" I announced even though my body really was ready.

He stopped licking immediately. "Oh, so that's how we playing now? We're exchanging money for sex?"

"No, security for real loving," I shot back. "I want my feelings to be genuine when I make love to you again. I'm tired of that same see saw, one week we in love, the next we not committed, bullshit!"

I must've hit a nerve because his entire disposition changed.

"You know what, you right," he told me kissing me in the mouth in between words. "I'ma be about my word. I'll get the insurance today. I'll pay all the bills, and I'll do Lil Trae one hundred percent so you can work hard at the studio." He paused to kiss me again, this time it was my inner ears, then my neck and then my nipples again. "And I'll add you to the household bank account for now."

I wanted to fight against being *only* on the household account and not on every account, but the way Trae's tongue had me feeling caused me to forget about arguing. He fell to his knees licking every crevice of my body. I wanted him. I could tell my pussy did too the way it pulsated. However, as good as it felt, I was also nervous since I hadn't been penetrated since the rape. I didn't even know if I would be able to cum after such a traumatic ordeal. Trae's hands were all over me, massaging me in places I never knew existed, making me think I was being touched by angels. One sensual rub after another sent me into a frenzy. He stood and our lips met again as he took my clothes completely off, me helping him, wanting him just as much as he wanted me.

Before I knew it we'd danced our way over to the bed, with Trae pushing me down, flat on my back, fondling me like an animal on attack. His thick piece was rock hard, and damn near punctured my skin as it charged up my thigh and stopped at my wetness.

"You miss me?" he teased.

"Uh huh," I said quickly, wanting him inside me.

"So tell me. Say it."

He kissed me passionately knowing I couldn't respond. Ferociously, I grabbed his dick, rubbing it against my clit slowly. "That feels sooooo good, Trae," I moaned. "I don't know why you keep treating me so bad."

He never responded, he simply dug in deep. I sighed at the incredible feel of him penetrating me just right. It was crazy how he knew the right speed, the right, angle, the right everything. He was even good at the art of spoken word. While I lay with my eyes closed and back arched, Trae ministered sweet words to me with each heavenly stroke.

"You know I love you, right?"

"Ahhh….Ahhh…huh," I attempted to say.

It felt so damn good. Then he paused.

"And you know you the only one for me, right?"

"Ah- huh, ah, huh," I said quickly. "Don't stop Trae, please don't stop."

I grabbed at his back, wrapping my arms around him tightly and yanked at him until he started drilling again. This time with more precision. The headboard got to rocking as the force from our bodies made it bang against the wall. Sparks flew from my pussy with every thrust he now threw at me. It felt like I'd won some sort of prize and was getting the reward of getting fucked royally by a race horse, a feeling I couldn't get anywhere else. I was quickly reminded that it was Trae's good love-making that had me strung out in the first place. He started hitting all my spots, grinding in and out, in circular motions, anything creative he could think of. Sweat poured while Trae hit all my spots.

"Ohhhhhhhhh- my-my-my- God!" I shouted.

"It feels good, don't it? Tell me you love it."

He pumped faster. Harder.

"Tell me you love it. And that you gotta have it, Royce?"

I didn't want to talk. I had begun to drool, spit sliding down the side of my mouth.

"Tell me," Trae begged, "tell me you love it."

I was on the verge of having an orgasm and Trae knew it.

Out of the blue, I pushed him off of me, wildly and straddled him like he was about to be arrested. It was the position that always sent him crazy. I needed him to know that I was the only woman he needed. I could make him happy if he just gave me the chance.

"I love it. I love the dick, Trae."

Quickly, he slipped it back in then I seethed through gritted teeth as he worked my walls once again for what seemed like an eternity.

"Damn!!!!!!!" I finally shouted. I'd lost control, riding him as if I were in a bull riding contest. Wildly, I pumped and grinded on top of him as he let out little female, cooing sounds. I had him where I wanted him. "Trae, tell me you're gonna change."

I grinded extra hard.

"I'ma- I'ma- I'ma change," he grunted.

His eyes rolled into the top of his head helplessly. Now, I was the artist of spoken word.

"Tell me, I'm the only woman for you."

Just like that, Trae lost control. I felt his dick going through a chemical change inside me. He pumped like a bull, while I pumped back. My insides raged, screaming with delight. Within seconds we both shook intensely, cumming together, ending with Trae's final words between breaths.

"You are the only one for me," he told me as we both fell onto our sides completely out of breath.

We lay flat on our backs, huffing and puffing like we'd just gotten off the track running a three mile relay. My cell rang from the dresser in reaching distance. I stretched, grabbed it, already telling myself not to answer. Seeing that it was Niecy I decided to pick up. Maybe the tax refund check I was waiting on had arrived. Or maybe the social worker had called over to Niecy's house instead of my cell phone. I'd called Ms. Campbell this morning to see if she'd contacted my birth mother yet. This process was taking way too long. Or maybe she just didn't want to see me. The realization changed my mood instantly.

"What's up, girl?" I answered half heartedly.

"You." She paused then silence followed.

All I could hear was Marlee, her baby screaming to the top of his lungs.

"Niecy, you there?"

"Yeah, I'm here. I just need this damn baby to shut up before I drop him off somewhere and never go back to get him."

That was Niecy, always talking about leaving her baby somewhere. It was sick but she meant it. Thank God I was out of her place, away from her drama.

"So, Royce," she began. Her voice filled with suspicion. "You got something you want to tell me?"

Little crinkles formed at the top of my forehead. I racked my brain wondering if I'd done something for her to be upset about. To be honest, I assumed we wouldn't talk much since I'd moved out; our relationship had been based mostly on me needing a place to stay.

"Uhhh, no. Did my check come?"

"No," she fired back with steam. "But somebody wants to speak to you."

"Didn't I tell you that you had until Tuesday!" the voice blared into the phone. "You think this a joke, don't you?"

Latrell's voice sent chills up my spine. Suddenly, I could hear the sound of my own heart beating. I glanced over my shoulder to see if Trae was watching me. I wasn't sure how to respond.

"Yeah. I got you," I spoke blandly.

"You got me! You got me! You got me!" he kept repeating. "What the fuck is that supposed to mean? I got you, bitch! It's Tuesday!"

"I'll have it tomorrow," I said meekly.

Trae must've sensed that something was wrong because he was now all up in my grill all of a sudden. I gave my best attempt at holding my composure as he began to ask me questions. He was hovering over me, close. Way too close.

"That's Niecy?" he questioned. "What she want? Tell'er you wit your man."

"Oh so that's your nigga in the background?" Latrell spat. "Does he want some of this?"

"No," I said softly.

"I tell you what," Latrell stated with fury. "If you don't have that twenty k by tomorrow and meet me on time at your spot, then kiss that son of yours goodbye!"

I got dizzy. Instantly. And every one of his words stung like bees on attack.

"Anddddddd," he added, "your NFL nigga will be next. I swear on everything you love, I'll kill everyone who ever meant anything to you until you pay me my money! You hear me?"

"Yeah. I hear you, girl."

"Oh, and gimme your mutha fuckin' cell number so I don't have to keep stalkin' your roommate."

I hesitated before rattling off the numbers but was soon answering to Trae when he wanted to know why I was giving Niecy my cell number when she already had it.

"Her friend is on the line asking for it," I told him swiftly, pushing him back a little with my hand.

"Stop talkin' to that bitch-ass non-football playin' nigga while I'm on the phone with you!" Latrell shouted through the receiver. "Meet me here at five p.m. tomorrow. And remember, your son's life depends on you comin' through," he told me sincerely before hanging up in my face.

For the next minute or so, I remained glossy-eyed deciding that I just needed to leave town. Latrell wasn't to be played with. And even though Trae was a football player and had money to hire protection, I knew of no one who could be a match for Latrell. Tears slid down my face as I buried my head into the pillow hoping Trae wouldn't notice I was crying my heart out.

Chapter 15

Royce

By the time the next day rolled around my insides were jumping. I had changed my mind about letting my husband run me away from my dreams. I kept looking over my shoulder with each swift step taken. I had to shake off as much of Latrell's threat as possible until mid-afternoon. His every looming word lingered inside my brain as horns blew from rushing cars just yards away. My appointment to meet Romello and the people I would be working with was at eleven sharp so I picked up the pace as I strutted down the busy, Manhattan side street, closing my coat tighter. The wind had picked up sharply since I'd left the house and the low-cut shirt didn't help keep the chill off my breast. Everything seemed to bother me; the clothes I'd chosen, the color of my lipstick, and even the Chai tea I stopped to pick up, hoping it would help coat my voice today.

When I finally made it to 4245, the address on the card, I breathed a heavy sigh of relief while grabbing onto the heavy glass door handle. Somehow, I made it on time. And without Latrell following me. Thank God! I told myself after doing a double take just to make sure he wasn't being slick before stepping inside.

Everything about the place made me feel superior all over. It was like stepping into a quaint penthouse. The lobby area reminded me of an upscale living room with plush carpet, unique furniture and dozens of frames arranged in several makeshift rows across the wall. I walked over for a closer look feeling privileged to be in the place where many legends had recorded. I didn't want to feel like a groupie but since no one else was around I took a closer look noticing plaques inside the frames that read platinum CD's for Rihanna, Lil' Wayne and tons of others who I admired. I jumped slightly, shocked that the door in the far end of the room opened and a scrawny gentleman emerged.

"You must be Royce," the man greeted me nicely.

I smiled then rushed over to extend my hand. "That's me."

"I'm Ray," the engineer. "C'mon inside. Romello's already here."

Just the mere mention of Romello's name had the inside of my mouth going dry. Especially when I stepped through the door which led into this amazing, cozy, state of the art studio about one fourth the size of a basketball court. Although I'd sung back-up for a few years actually being in a recording studio seemed foreign. My homework had been done though. I recognized a lot of the equipment; the Pro Tools LE system, a Mac G5 and twenty inch screen, reverb software and basic things like headphones, cables and amps. The décor of the studio was no different than the lobby area, plush.

Damn, I'd hit the big leagues.

Out of the blue, Romello emerged from another side door appearing in the snug sound booth. It seemed crazy that he wore shades even in the studio. He must've been searching for something since he was moving things around. Soon, we locked eyes, he mouthed a few words and my body went limp. By the time he came out the booth and made it over to me, my fingers were fidgeting with my purse and my legs were playing twist with one another. I was so nervous I didn't know what else to do.

"Hey Superstar," Romello greeted, kissing me on the cheek softly.

It wasn't one of those 'I'm ready to get in your pants' kisses either. It was genuine. "Hey, good to see you again." I blushed, hard.

"You ready to get things popping?" he asked then licked his

full lips.

His beard had grown even longer and thicker. I loved it.

"Yep." I started breathing heavy and my heart raced. He was that damn fine.

I'd already told myself that I had to keep things with him on a business level no matter what. His sexiness was off the chart and his smell was like no other. But all I wanted was this opportunity to record and to become a household name.

"Let's talk."

He grabbed one of the big, black leather chairs and pushed one my way. The moment he took a seat, I followed, not knowing he would scoot so close to me. I wasn't even able to look him in the eye as he began.

"So, you get how all of this is about to go down, right?"

His fist banged into one another just as I remembered them doing when we first met. It was crazy how he talked to me like a teacher to a student. But I was all ears, ready to learn.

"I think I do. Of course I'm new to all of this, but so many of your people have been telling me stuff all week." I fidgeted with my purse again then opened it to find a piece of gum hoping it would calm my nerves. Instead I got even more antsy when I spotted the 9mm gun I'd stolen from Trae's closet. It was my protection against Latrell. As Romello's eyes searched mine for more words, I continued, "All I know is today is supposed to be my light day, but after this my studio time will be in the evenings 'til the wee hours of the morning."

"You got that shit, right. Sometimes we sleep right on that couch ova there," he pointed proudly.

Suddenly music played on a low volume that filled the space. Obviously it was time to work. Ray had his headphones on and was now bobbing to some head-banging, body-shaking beat.

"Studio time cost me two fifty an hour. So we grinding. I got you scheduled for sixty hours off the break. You cool with that?"

"Yep. Like I said the other day, I'm willing to work hard to make this happen."

"Good. The most difficult part of all this is choosing a stage name. As I said the other day, we may not go with your real name."

"I understand. The name's not too marketable."

I hit him with my shifty eyes again, realizing I couldn't look at him more than thirty seconds straight. He'd been nothing but sweet to me, but had an intimidating demeanor all at the same time. I'd practiced all morning, having confidence without arrogance, yet none of it seemed to be working.

"I know the team will come up with something soon. They're working around the clock."

I grinned. "That's good to know."

"Also, I'm sure my Operations Manager told you that we got you on a fast track, something we don't normally do."

I nodded.

"Things are gon' jump off quick. That whole guitar thing is hot so we want to release your first single by Feb 22nd. He paused to bang his fist, one into another, again, "That's three weeks away."

A gasp escaped my lips. "That soon?"

"No doubt. I wanna get it some radio time. Get the people pumped about my new artist." He smiled. "You so damn beautiful they'll beat the doors down to see you perform."

My face turned beet red and I got hot instantly thinking about how fast things were moving. Yet Romello left no room for me to ponder on anything. He was all about business.

"That's why Whitney, our marketing director got you booked on a few radio shows as soon as the first single is released, And we got you opening up for D7 the first week in March."

I held my chest with my right hand and leaned far back in the chair. D7 was the hottest group out. Nothing could explain the joy I felt. All my life I'd dreamt of this moment. Music had my heart. And since the age of eighteen I had wanted to sing professionally. The countless hours spent on voice lessons, the money gone down the drain on bad deals, and the money spent on making the demo was all paying off. My dream of becoming famous would now become a reality. Everyone would know my name and I'd now be on V.I.P status.

"You still wit' me, Royce?" Romello asked while rubbing the tension out of my thigh. "Like I told you before, your sound is stupid. It's so unique. I just really believe in you," he told me sincerely. "My other sound guys are here, so let's get busy."

I'd blanked out until his sensual touch brought me back. Romello stood up eyeing me, letting me know our downtime was over. I'd enjoyed every moment of our time, especially when he licked his lips again. I truly needed him to stop doing that.

"Oh and they working fast to get the paperwork done for your advance."

Yes. I wanted to shout. "It's 30k, right?"

" No doubt. It's not much but you'll make millions sooner than you think."

Those words sent chills up my spine.

"You can put your purse over there next to the fridge. Nobody's gonna steal it." I promise you," he told me humorously.

I giggled slightly while I rushed to slide it in a corner on the floor near the couch. The moment I stood back up, Ray signaled for me to follow him into the recording booth. As I walked across the floor, Romello seemed extra pumped. He was talking to the chubby bald head guy at the mixing board asking to hear the beats he'd sent him the day before.

"Aye, Royce, I forgot to tell you about this hot ass collabo idea. The shit is dope and sure to give you a powerful start. We just need to get those folks to sign the papers and it's a wrap. It'll be the first or second track after your single."

"Anything you say," I shot back stepping into the booth.

Ray put my headphones on and I sat on the small black, stool close to the mic. I could still see Romello eye-balling me through the glass window. I loved the princess treatment that he gave me. It made me feel good. It was like a father watching over a daughter. Then I re-tracked my thoughts. Who was I kidding, more like a husband watching over a wife.

In less than three minutes, the sound in the booth must've turned on. I could now hear Romello, and the three guys talking loudly out near the mixing boards. He'd told me previously that my arrangements had been done and it was just about me laying down the vocals. Even though I knew all of that, hearing them made everything seem so surreal. The beats and tones that blared through were the sickest I'd ever heard. They had such good taste falling right in line with what I had in mind. My sound was Lauryn Hill slash Jill Scott unique, one of a kind, sure to be a hit.

The moment my voice began to flow I felt good inside. My sounds were sweet and I sang from deep below like I'd always done. I could tell Romello was pleased with the tones by the way he bobbed his head and tapped the floor with his foot. He stood back with his hands in his pockets as I let loose, giving it my all. The first track was the song I'd written, *Take Me Away*, which of course had me singing from the heart. The first two hours flew by like nothing, as if no one else existed. I'd only taken two breaks, one to listen to the re-play and one to take a piss. Just as I was getting back into the booth, two new guys entered the studio. Romello hit the intercom button that allowed him to talk to me inside.

"Hey Superstar, come out here for a minute. I want to introduce you to the dude you'll be doing the callobo with. I think you'll be pleasantly surprised."

Hopping off the stool, my thoughts were flooded. I could see everyone slapping hands and giving dap acting as if they'd known each other for years. The energy level in the room was soaring and some of my music began to play loudly.

"That's the shit," one dude applauded.

"And she hot, too," the other guy with the baseball cap pulled slightly over his head complimented.

Romello rushed over to me draping an arm across my shoulder.

"This the Superstar I was telling you about?"

My pupils dilated and I almost threw up.

"This is Royce. We'll have her stage name secured by to-morrow," Romello stated.

"What up, butterfly?" Tango said to me jokingly.

I remained quiet as fear spread across my face. I was certain Romello could feel my body quivering.

"This is Tango," he introduced then looked into my face. He frowned slightly not realizing what had gone on. I'd constantly wondered if anyone had told him about what happened when JR originally met me, but now I believed whole heartedly that he had no idea.

"You don't talk, butterfly?" Tango asked with that fucking smirk.

All I could think about was Romello changing his mind about working with me because I couldn't separate business from personal situations. But there was no way in hell I would sing with him. I could barely open my mouth to speak, but decided to give it a shot. I sucked it up, breathed heavily and spoke, "Oh, I'm good. Pleased to meet you again." My voice shook and was barely audible.

"Oh, y'all met before?" Romello asked suspiciously.

We sure did. Didn't we, butterfly?" Tango taunted.

Tears burst through. They cascaded down my face like an overactive waterfall. I couldn't hold the rage inside. I didn't give a damn if Romello dropped me from the label or not. If letting Tango degrade me in front of everyone meant losing my chance at stardom then so be it. Without delay, I darted half-way across the room, grabbed my purse and opened it. My hands shook at the thought of the gun. Seeing Tango's head split wide open sounded great.

I grabbed the 9mm tightly.

My hands shook uncontrollably.

Tango had to die. I kept chanting those words in my head. He had to die. He had to pay for what he did to me. But a small ounce of reason kicked in. I didn't want to spend the rest of my life in jail.

"Aye nah, what's wrong, Royce? Tell me what's up," I kept hearing Romello ask me as he rushed to my side.

"Nothing. You wouldn't understand." I sniveled a little, voice still trembling.

"Just tell me," he urged.

"Nah, it's okay. I just need to go."

"Go where?" Concern filled his voice.

"Home. I'll explain later."

"What…"

Before Romello could get his sentence out, I'd grabbed my coat and pounced through the lobby and then out onto the street.

My heart thumped and my vision remained blurry. All my dreams were most likely gone down the drain. Before I got my next thought out, my cell rang. I knew it was probably Romello calling to ask why I'd wasted his money. I just couldn't go back in there I told myself, answering with a weeping tone.

"Hello."

"Hello," the person shot back.

"Yeah. Who's this?"

"You know who the fuck it is! It's two o'clock. You got my money, right?"

The sound of his voice made bile rise up inside my gut. Vomit quickly filled the city sidewalk as Latrell reminded me that five o'clock was near. I knew I hadn't gotten the 20k he requested and didn't have any way of getting it. His last set of words made me realize that something had to be done.

"Kiss your lil man goodbye if you're not here at five o'clock sharp with my bread."

All I heard next was a dial tone.

Damn, I was fucked!

Chapter 16

India

Day six of my state of depression had me feeling like life was no longer worth living. I sat on my bed with six sharpies, a pack of white paper and dozens of magazines spread about all with the intention of polishing up my celebrity-like habits. *In Touch Magazine, Us Weekly, Juicy*, and *Hip Hop Weekly* had all in the past motivated me to live, eat, shop and talk like the rich and famous, the important, the elite.

Somehow today, nothing about the celebs that stared back at me from the pages made me feel important enough to continue with training. I felt worthless and my social life had been downgraded to zero since I'd gotten back from Miami. I couldn't even get one person to mention me on twitter or a like me on Facebook. And no dates in six days had to have been a record for me.

"I'ma has been," I mumbled to myself angrily, while blowing breath through my tightened lips and crossing my legs Indian style on top of the covers.

I whipped my matted hair up into a bun securing it with a long pendant. Quickly, I picked up another small stack of paper and began signing my name again on each sheet, meticulously one after another. I'd always been told that in order to be famous you had to know in your heart that you were meant to have fame. So, if practicing my autograph a thousand times would bring me out my funk, then I'd write all night, on every sheet, every hanger, every magazine, and anything that my sharpie would show up on.

India Grant… I wrote as fancy as my fingers would allow.

Suddenly, I heard loud sounds from my living room. Even though the bedroom door was shut, I knew it was Tyesha, but hoped like hell she didn't bother me. A part of me wanted to hop up and rush to turn off the lights before she walked past my room. Before I could even get my next thought out she burst through the door rowdily.

"What up chick?"

"Have you ever heard of knocking?" I shouted. "Uggghh!"

"You ever heard of cleaning this shit up. Or what about washing your ass?"

"Tyesha, I'm not in the mood." I pushed the palm of my hand flatly toward her as a sign to leave immediately.

"Bitch, you still in here signin' autographs for your lil' invisible fans!" She laughed heartily. "Man, you gotta stop this shit. Get out. Get a life."

"Mind your business."

"You have no business, bitch."

Something about the way she dipped her fork into the carton of shrimp fried rice made my skin crawl. It was disgusting the way she smacked and chewed between words, but even more degrading for a woman. It still amazed me that we were even friends; and now roommates. I knew I'd gotten desperate when that decision had been made. I watched Tyesha for moments as she watched me back. I knew she had something slick to say the way we eyeballed one another. Yet deep down inside, I wasn't prepared for a shouting match. I had no strength, no will. Lack of food would do that, so I heard. My last meal was a Hot Pocket a day ago.

"Aye, my homeboy got some food stamps he tryna sell. You wanna buy some?"

She could tell my answer from my scowl. I was still pissed at her for hooking me up with a broker who sold me stolen tickets. "Are you crazy," I blasted. "Didn't I just get locked up almost a week ago because you hooked me up with a con-artist?"

"Oh, so now it's my fault?"

"Hell yeah. You told me to meet the guy. I gave him the money on the strength of you! You shoulda known he wasn't legit. Do you understand what that did to my reputation?"

She shrugged her shoulders then hit me with a look that just didn't seem right.

"You ran game on me, Tyesha." I started nodding my head like I'd just discovered the news.

She gobbled some more food down her throat before speaking. "Get the fuck outta here. All I ever did was help yo' whack ass in life."

"Nah, it's cool though," I said, closing my magazines and gathering them into a stack. "I was blind for a while, but I now realize you were the reason I got messed up and embarrassed in front of all those people at the stadium."

"How in the hell are you gonna blame me? Dude was a broker. How was I supposed to know he had stolen tickets?"

"You shoulda warned me damn it, that it coulda possibly happened. I would have never bought the damn ticket."

"Oh, don't worry Ms. Ungrateful. No more hook-ups for you."

"Fine with me. Keep your fucked up hook-ups. You think we don't know you make money off of us when you so call hook us up?"

Her eyes widened. I had her attention.

"I now realize that what Royce told me about you is true."

"Royce?" she barked. "Miss Halo? What that bitch say?" she asked me defensively.

"She said you want a cut off everything you can get your hands on, even if it means seeing your friends go to jail."

"Man, whateva. Tell Royce to keep my name out her mouth," Tyesha said dropping rice on my carpet.

"I'm sure she will. She told me you almost messed her deal up with Romello from Indigo Records. But I hear she signed that contract anyway and started recording today."

"What?" Her nose flared and color disappeared from her face.

"Yep," I said pretending to be happy for Royce when deep

down inside I felt nothing but envy.

Why should she achieve all the fame? I wanted to now bury my head into the pillow. Just the thought of someone else's success had me in tears again. I didn't have to worry about feeling shameful in front of Tyesha 'cause she darted from my room the moment she realized what I'd said.

Next thing I knew, the house phone rang. A frown spread across my face after seeing Mercy Hospital come across the screen. Why would anyone call here from a hospital? Tyesha had no family or friends in New York; probably nowhere in the world. I was certain she'd snaked anyone who would've possibly claimed her. I knew no one who would call from there.

I picked up nervously.

"Hello."

"Ms. Grant."

"Yes. Who's this?" I responded with one brow now raised.

"You really need to get over to Mercy Hospital…"

Blah blah blah were all the words that followed. My mind blacked out followed by a set of knots in my gut. What had caused this to happen?

Why?

When?

The whole conversation with the nurse sent me into a frenzy. It didn't take long for me to throw a jacket over top of my sweats, apply some eyeliner and bronzer to may face before darting out the house. I made it to the hospital in forty minutes flat through city traffic and all.

When I walked over to the side of my mother's bed I noticed how frail she looked. Even though I was the spitting image of her, hair and all, her eyes bulged out like an alien making her look as if she were two steps from the grave. Instantly, my arms draped half her body. I couldn't believe she'd gotten sick and hadn't told me. I wondered how long she had been ill. The fact that my brother and aunts said nothing confirmed that they were all jealous of me.

"Mama, why didn't you mention to me anything about your health when I spoke to you last week?"

She simply shrugged then spoke softly as if it hurt her to

talk. "When you told me about your problems, I decided not to worry you. I've been praying for you." Instantly, she reached out to me. "Have you started dialysis yet?"

Her words made me feel sick to my stomach. My lies kept me from knowing the truth about my mother. "Yes, Mama. I have."

Her machines started beeping and going off like there was a problem, so I stepped back as a petite, male nurse rushed into the room. He wasn't friendly like the nurse I'd spoken to out front. He simply checked my mother's IV and stepped back out of the room. Quickly, I took a few steps closer so I could touch my mother's hand.

"You look nice," she complimented.

She ran her delicate hand up and down my hip I guess wondering when I'd developed the bump in the back. I hoped like hell she didn't notice I had on butt pads. I didn't want to hear one of her lectures. I wanted our visit to be peaceful unlike our past relationship. I needed to know how serious all of this was.

"The nurse said you've been sick for a while and you've been here for over four days now. You could've called and told me, or had Eric to call."

She stared at me with both love and frustration all at the same time.

"You know your brother refuses to call you. But don't worry. The blood clots on my lungs are doing a number on me but I'm a survivor. I might need another surgery but we'll see. And I pray day in and day out. Prayer changes things, India."

No tears flowed, but it hurt to see the woman who raised me in such bad health.

She grabbed my forefinger letting me know she had more to say. "Plus, I assumed you were busy, India. I hope working. You do have a job, right?"

I wouldn't dare tell her that I was completely broke. I simply smiled and posed like I'd seen in the magazines. "No, I don't have a job. But I do have a man. We'll be getting married soon so you get well so you can walk your baby girl down the aisle."

"Oh," was all she said. It caused me to simply rub her forehead.

"You should be happy for me." I grinned.

"India, you need to get your degree so you'll have something to fall back on. Look what happened to me when your father died."

"That's you, mother. I'm not wasting time on looking for a job. I'm going to be a housewife…like the ones you see on T.V. You watch *The Real Housewives of Atlanta*, right?"

She breathed a heavy, disappointing sigh.

"India, I'm not sure where I went wrong with you. Once upon a time people aspired to just do good in life, go to college, serve the community, have a career, you know, teachers, firemen, doctors, nurses, lawyers. Now everyone wants to be fucking important!"

My ears didn't believe what they'd heard. My mother cursed. Something she hadn't done in years. The fact that she attempted to scoot herself up on the bed told me she was angry with my way of thinking. Her eyes quickly saddened and rolled up into her head.

"You're not a celebrity, India. Do you realize that? Stop living this superficial life!"

Even though her last two words were delivered with stress and she was slightly out of breath, I had to respond.

"I am somebody, Mama!"

"Yes, you are. India Grant, an average Joe. There's nothing wrong with that. You are going to kill yourself trying to be something you are not!"

My voice roared. And words flew from my gut. "Oh yes! I want to be famous, mother! And I will be! What's wrong with that? I dream about what it would feel like to be chased by paparazzi and adoring fans. I'm certain it's the best feeling ever to be chased by people who adore me."

While I kept the words flowing about my hopes, dreams, and aspirations, my mother fell all the way back. She closed her eyes and bit her lip. She shook her head and tears flowed through closed eyes.

"Where did I go wrong, child?"

"You didn't, mother." I shed a few tears, too. Not because

of her pain, but because I wanted to get married soon. "I'm going to be a brand, Mama! I promise you."

Out of the blue my cell rang. It was the call that I knew was coming. I had to answer since I'd missed our appointment earlier in the week. Agent Miles made it clear that we had to meet before the end of the day.

"Hello," I answered nastily.

"Ahhh, Ms. Grant, are we ready?"

I huffed. "Actually Mr. Miles, my mother is ill, can we reschedule?"

"Yes, I know your mother is in the hospital. We've talked. Unless you want to get picked up, handcuffed and brought down here to talk, I suggest you make your way here within the hour."

My heart raced. *He'd talked to my mother? Pick me up in a car by the FBI?*

"I'll be there," I finally mumbled and hung up.

My heart wanted to ask my mother what questions the FBI had asked her and why she hadn't told me. Yet my gut told me not to. So many thoughts flooded my mind. Was she working against me? I attempted to kiss her on the cheek and told her I had a dialysis appointment. She quickly grabbed my hand and wouldn't let go.

"India, I can't believe you sold Olivia. I really thought she died at birth. I believed you," she cried. "And the thought of you being mixed up in a baby selling ring is ludicrous," she added.

My heart sank just hearing Olivia's name. "Mama…"

"Quiet, the agent told me everything," she belted as more tears flowed. "That was my grandbaby, damn it!"

Chapter 17

Royce

My steps were quick and controlled as I strolled out of the CitiBank branch on Somerset Avenue with my scarf wrapped tightly around my neck. Totally upset, my shades hid the tears and the pain visible from my eyes. I couldn't believe I'd forged and cashed one of Trae's personal checks. My actions were foul and I knew it. I wrote it for thirteen thousand with ease like it was mine to give. And to top things off, I'd stolen seven grand in cash from his emergency stash under the mattress.

I hopped back in my X5 and turned the heat on while sitting like a zombie staring out the window. The temperature had dropped into the twenties and my insides felt numb. I couldn't believe I was stealing from my fiancé, the man I would soon marry. My plan was to say Rosa stole the cash underneath the bed but bank records would eventually show that check was written to me and cashed by me. Criminal would be written all over me. I paused and threw my hands over my face as more tears flowed. Rosa was my girl. Throwing her into something she had nothing to do with was heartless. Then again, I did have a habit of constantly hurting the people I loved?

"Unlock the mothafuckin' door," I heard a stern voice shout.

With a quick inhale then an exhale, I hit the unlock button.

I really didn't want him inside my car but it was too cold to get out.

"You got that?" Latrell asked as soon as he shut the door.

I nodded, grabbed my purse and pulled out the envelope with the twenty thousand. "It's all hundreds," I told him with a few added sniffles.

"You wasn't fuckin' cryin' when you was spendin' my shit."

"I told you before…"

"Shut the fuck up! Don't nobody wanna hear them damn lies! You out for self, Royce."

"I'm not."

"You are!" he shot back.

Next thing I knew a glob of spit landed on my cheek. This muthufucka spit on me! I could tell he'd blown a fuse and didn't want things to escalate so I wiped the side of my face with my shirt gagging, almost throwing up in the process.

"People think 'cause you got that sweet voice and pretty face that you not the devious bitch that you are! No one would ever believe you were my partner in sellin' those babies. You did that shit without a conscience, but somehow I took the fall!"

His venom filled voice spread through the car quickly. Goose bumps rose up on my skin at the thought of his words. It was all true. We were partners in the business. Somehow I had lowered my standards and was his right hand in the illegal process of negotiating the sale and delivery of healthy babies to people who wanted children and for some reason couldn't have any.

At the same time I thought it was the right thing to do until Latrell took things a step further. The money was over the top. Good and plentiful. So much I couldn't count it at times. Hundreds of thousands of dollars, and everyone seemed happy from the birth mother to the new family. But soon things just blew up. Everything spiraled out of control. Latrell got sick with it. He escalated shit.

"Latrell, look I'm sorry for not coming…"

"Shut the hell up!"

I didn't want to give him the impression I was afraid of him but pleading my case wasn't going to work. But I did want him to know I wasn't gonna keep getting pimped like this. My whole life was ahead of me. It was my time to shine and he was now in my life fucking up my chances at success. I needed him gone, for good.

"How much will it take for you to just go away?" I asked meekly.

He laughed crazily, throwing his head back like I had said something uncontrollably funny.

"Count your blessings, Royce. Be glad I gave you a chance to pay me back."

"No, really. How much?"

"If you got bread like that then why do you need this installment plan. Your sneaky ass keep cryin' broke."

"My advance will be coming through soon. In less than a week. What if I give it all to you? It's seventy grand," I lied.

His eyes lit up. Then his entire disposition changed.

"I think I'd rather torture you. It feels good seein' you on edge, lookin' like you not gettin' no sleep." He attempted to touch my cheek until I yanked away. "You deserve all that's comin' your way," he added with spite. "Believe that."

"Oh my God! Are you serious?" I sighed with deep frustration and banged my head against the wheel.

"You got two weeks to have the next payment. And this time I want to know who helped you set me up. I know you didn't do it alone? You had help with that last deal and the way things went down. Shit gon' get crazy if you don't tell me."

The next thing I heard was the door slamming and my cell ringing all at the same time. I sat in a daze wondering what I would do about Latrell and wondered why Tyesha was calling me. I hated her and wanted nothing to do with her.

"Yeah. What is it?" I answered with hate in my tone.

"What's up, butterfly?"

Those words stung. They had meaning. A deep hurt and harsh pain for me. "What's up, Tyesha?" I responded dryly. My face frowned. Was that a coincidence or was she openly tryna tell me she knew about me and Tango?

"Haven't heard from you, baby."

"Whatever, Tyesha. Why the fuck did you leave me in that room with Tango?" I shouted.

"What?"

"Don't what me. You know what I'm talking about."

"You got the deal didn't you?"

My mouth opened wide. I couldn't believe her.

"Hello. Hello," she chanted like everything was cool. "You got my cut, right?"

"Fuck you, Tyesha!" My breathing intensified. My gut confirmed she knew. I was certain. "You set me up!"

"Now why would I do something like that, baby? How was I supposed to know the lil nicca Tango was horny," she laughed.

"He raped me, Tyesha!" I screamed loudly over the CD playing lightly. Tears streamed. My feelings were so hurt. No matter how scandalous she was I thought she was my girl. "He fucking raped me and you did nothing about it!"

"Hell, I thought the two of you were gettin' to know each other."

I heard a smirk and commenced to cursing her hard. But she didn't care. She had her own agenda.

"So, look-a-here, where's my money?"

"Tyesha, you didn't do anything, so there's no money for you. I met Romello on my own in Miami."

"Ahhhh so you into robbin' muthufuckas nowdays, huh? That's how you playing?"

"I gotta go," I said in between breaths. I was tired and had just gotten off the exit to the house.

"Know this, butterfly. I'm gon' get what's mine. Trust and believe."

The line went dead causing me to add one more thing to worry about to my list. Tyesha was shady. She played real dirty so I didn't know what to expect next from her.

I drove the rest of the way home in a daze. So much turmoil had come into my life over the last few years and now this year being the worse. All I ever wanted was a singing career, a loving man, and for my son to be happy. That wasn't too much to ask. Instead I got hooked up with a cheater for a man, back-stabbing friends, and once again my career had been put on pause. Romello had been texting me constantly wondering what was up with me. I didn't have the heart to tell him why I left nor did I commit to going back.

I wanted to call Rachel, spilling my guts about everything just to see what advice she had. The problem was that Rachel had gone back out of town with Chris, her new man, and wouldn't get back until the morning. I had no one with good, common sense to talk to. I mean, India was an option, but that was just a hollow ear if you asked me.

By the time I pulled into the driveway my head was spinning. Trae had taken Lil Trae to the movies, so I wasn't sure if they were back. The two of them had been really enjoying spending countless hours together, so much that my son didn't care whether I spent time out or not. The moment I walked up the walkway my heart began to pound. A black CLK darted up the driveway and parked like it owned the place.

My first thought was that Latrell or Tyesha had someone coming after me. But when the twenty-something year old girl stepped out her car with a short coat on, nothing else that could be seen, and tall thigh high boots, it seemed trouble was headed my way. I didn't know whether to stick my key in the door or not, so I waited for her to get closer. I kept wondering who she was and what she wanted.

"Can I help you?" I blurted with confusion spread across my face.

"Not really."

She brushed past me like I didn't exist, popping gum at forty miles per hour. Quickly, she rang the door bell and banged against the door three times.

"Who are you?" I asked sharply yet calmly.

"I'm here for Trae."

"That's obvious."

"Why'd you ask then?" She shot back and hit me with the nastiest look I'd seen in years.

One…two…three... four…I began to count to myself after

taking a deep breath. My mind swirled fast trying to figure out how to handle the situation without blowing a fuse. I wouldn't allow myself to fight another female over Trae. He wasn't worth it, but this bitch was still knocking on my door like she paid rent.

"Trae isn't home. But I am. I'm Royce, his fiancé."

She stopped knocking instantly then turned to look me up and down. "Bullshit, Trae ain't got no damn fiancé. Umph, I've been fucking up in here for the last six months. So, where you been if you the fiancé?"

Her hands draped her wide hips and her boobs sat perfectly in the air while she waited for my response. She was a cute girl, with dark brown skin and naturally wavy hair, but her speech made me wonder where she'd met Trae.

"Uhhhhhhh huh, like I thought," she said as if she had one up on me.

"Look, Trae's back with me now. I live here, so the party is over. Whatever you did with him you did. Consider it a gift."

I threw my hands in the air and asked her to step back so I could enter *my* home. Her eyes widened. Of course the hands went back on the hip.

"Ummm huh, ummm huh," she kept saying while rolling her eyes and gritting her teeth. "You think you doing sumthing real special. Well, you tell Trae I'll see him at the hospital in seven months. He's gon' be a father. Waaaaa waaaaaa waaaaa," she attempted to cry like a baby.

Chapter 18

India

Lost in my thoughts I stared into space while the background noise in the FBI field office continued to get louder. While phones rang one after another I could hear legal issues being discussed openly. I sat in what seemed like a waiting area in some fold-up chair making me feel like a criminal. Fear filled my bones as employees kept walking by swiftly discussing search warrants, judges' orders and undercover details that I never heard about. No one even looked my way.

"Ughhhhhh," I muttered to myself.

I didn't know how this meeting would go down. It was clear that if Agent Miles had already talked to my mother then he'd probably contacted other people in my family and possibly the person who Olivia was sold to. The thought worried me to the core. I glanced at my watch again while waiting for this stalker, agent guy to show up. The whole waiting game annoyed me. It had me sweating profusely underneath my arm pits and on the top of my eyelids. My damn lashes were falling off.

Just as I was about to sigh again a white man with average height appeared. There was nothing warm about the look on his face. Everything seemed business except his cheap looking suit. It screamed 'I don't make a lot of money'. I knew right off the bat this wouldn't be easy. We were from two different worlds; the young, and fabulous against the working Joe. Besides, those disapproving eyes of his proved that he didn't care for me too much either.

"Miss Grant?" he asked.

"That's me." I stood up and prepared to shake his hand.

"No need to be formal. You may be in cuffs soon."

I swallowed hard. Damn.

"Follow me."

He turned and headed down a long, narrow hallway while talking the entire time with me following unable to see his lips. I could only hear his words. None of them sounded promising.

"Of course you know I'm Agent Miles by now." He stopped abruptly and looked me in the eye. "But then again you're not that bright. Are you?"

My body and mind froze. I didn't know how to answer that. It was a deliberate attack on me, but I was afraid to get smart with him.

Next thing I knew, he opened the door to a room that had two small desks inside. Nothing was on top but a few note pads. "What is this all about?" I pretended not to know that this was about me selling Olivia. I had practiced the entire ride over on what I would say and what I wouldn't say.

"Oh, I think you know."

"No, I don't."

"Take a seat. You're not convincing," he instructed.

I turned my face away from him so he couldn't see right thru me as I sat down in one of the four available chairs. I kept quiet just watching him from the corner of my eye. He reminded me of Kevin Costner and I was sorta intimidated by his arrogance. Besides, he made me nervous from the constant pacing.

"Let's cut to the chase Miss Grant. We know that you sold your newborn baby to a complete stranger. What we don't know is for how much and all those who were involved."

His eyebrows crinkled and I remained frozen with a look that said 'CAUGHT'.

"I need names."

"Ughhhh..." I stuttered. "What?"

"You heard me. I want some names," Agent Miles spat. "Who was your middle man or woman?"

"Wait a minute. This is all moving too fast."

"What you did was sick and disgusting, Miss Grant! God knows who has your child!"

"I needed the money," I admitted shamefully. Then I attempted to let water build up in my eyes. I did feel bad but I needed to show him I could cry. "And I was too young to raise a baby?" I added with hope of sympathy.

"How old are you now?"

"Twenty-seven."

"And you still have the brain of a twelve year old, huh?"

"That's not true," I belted.

"No. You do! At twenty-seven you still can't see that your actions aren't normal?" He banged his fist against the desk and glared at me like a father scolding a daughter. "Only a sick woman could do such a thing."

"I'm not sick!" I shouted. "I had dreams. Goals! Something you obviously know nothing about!"

My emotions were starting to take over as I thought back to the day I gave birth. She was a beautiful baby with a head full of hair. So loving, so sweet, the spitting image of me. I remembered like it was yesterday how the mid-wife coached me the whole time in her home, through all the pain, sweating and times thinking I couldn't push her out. I wanted to keep her but my aspirations in life wouldn't allow it. I knew being a mom would hold me back, especially knowing that the father was some fake rapper who would never make it to Jay Z's status. Mr. Miles' voice brought me back.

"You could have legally signed the rights over to people who were checked out by proper authorities. You do know that, right?"

I nodded.

"Not get with a baby selling ring."

My eyes bulged. *He knew. Damn, I guess this is more serious than I thought. I guess it's not just about me. It's bigger than me, I concluded.*

149

Agent Miles backed himself against the wall folding his arms just above his waist. He gawked at me like I was an idiot. He despised me. I could tell. He seemed to be processing information in his head and thinking about how to handle me all at the same time.

I had to plead my case. "Look, Sir, I was young and dumb at the time. I fucked up but what's gonna happen to me now?"He could tell I was scared. A famous athlete's wife with a criminal record wouldn't fly well.

"Miss Grant, even sixteen year olds are now having and keeping their babies. Or giving the child up for adoption was another option. But selling a baby is not. It's foul. Disgusting. And despicable," he added while moving around the room.

He snatched one of the notepads off the table and commenced to telling me things I didn't even know. By the time he told me the story behind a major Baby Selling ring that ran mostly up and down the east coast for the past seven years, I had my hands covering my cheeks. Most of it I'd never heard, or knew anything about. Only a few people had been arrested on child selling charges so far. Most of those people had been caught just from isolated cases taken on by the state.

"For example, Miss Grant, you know Latrell Pratt, right?"

My eyes lit up. I breathed heavily like I had a bad case of asthma. Shit, he knew about Latrell.

"Of course you do." He grinned. "Latrell went to jail for five years for a specific case only because the mother of one of his clients had second thoughts and told the authorities. But this thing has gotten huge since then. More people have come forward. There are others. Lots of others. The cases from the states have flooded our office so we've got it now."

"I'm going to jail?"

"Maybe."

"But I wasn't involved with anybody else's baby. I just sold my own!"

"But it's illegal," he shot back.

"I can't go to jail. When I get married I'll be scheduled to be on one of those shows like *Basketball Wives*. You've seen it,

right?" My facial expression should have confirmed my seriousness.

"Ahhh, yeah." He frowned. "Sure."

"No, really."

"So, you don't know any of the sellers involved with the
ring? The master minds?"

"No."

"But you know Latrell, right?" He asked the questions so
quick I didn't have time to think. "You know he'll be facing new
charges soon. His other charges were minor compared to this."

Oh shit, I thought.

"Latrell and his people were getting up to a hundred grand
for each child they sold. And at least two hundred fifty infants that
we know about have been sold to date. And that's from the mothers who agreed to sell. There are many that he forced and kidnapped to give up their babies. So, we're charging the sellers,
mothers and all those involved."

Damn, that included me, obviously.

"So, who approached you? And who did you pay?"

I told one lie after another. And then another.

"Would you be willing to take a lie detector test?"

"No. Please no." I shook my head so fast it almost flew
from my shoulders.

"Quite honestly, Miss Grant, it's not you we're after." A
smile graced his face. "You play a small role in this young lady.
You shouldn't have sold your baby," he scolded with disapproving
eyes. "That's illegal. And jail time comes with that. But if you co-
operate and give up the other parties involved other than Latrell,
I'll grant you immunity. This is a serious crime that very few people in the U.S get into and pull off without getting caught. These
people are going down. And just because time has passed they
think they've gotten away."

My face was scrunched up into a knot which complimented
the knots in my stomach. I couldn't do ten to twenty years in the
Feds. Where would I get my hair done and how would I raise my
kids?

"Immunity?"

"Yes, immunity. And I'm a man of my word."

Somehow I didn't believe him. There was something about him that couldn't be trusted. Maybe it was the no-good smirk on his face but I thought about the text I'd gotten from Mr. Haskin just before I walked inside. He was flying into New York just to take me shopping and to dinner. It only took ten seconds more for me to think. I didn't have a conscience. And damn sure didn't have any loyalty.

To nobody.

All I could think about was that the agent told me the sellers were getting close to one hundred thousand for their babies. That bitch Royce only gave me twenty grand.

"Royce Pratt," I blurted. "She paid me for my baby."

Chapter 19

India

Chris Jackson's Manhattan penthouse screamed money; floor to ceiling windows, hand-made chandeliers, Italian made furniture and all the other stuff that I'd read about in the *Millionaire's Magazine* graced my eyes. By my calculations his interior designer had spent at least three hundred grand on furniture alone. The scene was like something out of a movie the way people lingered with champagne glasses in hand while grabbing tiny hors d'oruvres off passing trays. These niccas had money. Money I needed. There were only about thirty people in attendance but at least ten good potentials.

When the invite came from Rachel days ago, my first thought was to say hell no! Fuck her! She'd been distancing herself from me since the Miami trip, so I had mixed emotions. Then the more I thought about an exclusive request to attend Chris' party, even if it was Rachel's boyfriend, I got wet at the notion. She had been in out of town with him since we left Miami a month ago. Knowing that info, with each call I got from her, she got sent to voicemail until I heard who would be here.

Of course knowing how close they had become had me seething with envy, but she'd never know. I had two of my girls with me; the ones who cherished me, catering to my every need and made it seem like I was the star who they all just wanted to hang out with. The three of us laughed loudly in a mini circle while sitting back on one of the many white sectionals in the apartment. Secretly, I watched Rachel and Chris in the far right corner kissing, cuddling and fondling one another like two horny high school students while my girls chatted about a few good looking potentials they had seen mixing around.

Quickly, I stood up and asked the boney guy in the tux for another glass of Ace of Spade. Getting drunk was the only way to keep my feelings in check. Life had already been rough over the last two weeks since my meeting with Agent Miles. He'd scared the living shit out of me by saying I wasn't completely off the hook. Even though he didn't suspect me as being a part of the Baby Selling Ring, I had committed a crime and things had to work out for him in order for them to work out for me.

Such bullshit!

Not only did I have that weighing on my brain, but now I had to get tortured by watching Rachel cascade around in that skimpy, fabulous dress like she owned the place and they'd been married for years. The bitch hadn't even chilled with me since I arrived. She hit me with a fake "I miss you and we gotta do lunch soon". Afterwards, she greeted my girls snobbishly then vanished. Her newness had me fired up. I snapped back at the waiter after downing that glass and asked for another.

"Hey girl, sit down and sit back," Andrea instructed with a pocket sized video camera in my face. "I wanna get some footage of you to put on You Tube. You look hot."

"Really?" I smiled widely then did my Beyonce pose.

"Damn right. Sexiest bitch in the party."

Pleased with the thought I took a seat and crossed my legs sexily as she began asking me questions like I was being interviewed. As soon as that session ended my other girl handed me a stack of pictures that we brought with us. I knew what she wanted me to do so I whipped out my pen and started autographing a few. I would hand them out to people after we met and chopped it up a bit.

Just then a horrible feeling shot through me. When I saw her walk into the room I wanted to scream. Why did she have to come? Why couldn't she just stay away for just once? I wanted to shine for the night brightly above everyone else. Me, India, I wanted to be the show stopper. This time I grabbed two glasses of champagne from one of the four waiters nearby as Royce strutted my way. She was dressed in a cute, one shoulder dress that stopped right above her knee. Everything about her was perfect; hair, make-up, especially the five-inch ankle strap Giuseppe pumps she wore.

"Hey girl," I said happily when Royce approached with sadness in her eyes. We did the missed cheek on purpose kissy thing then I scrutinized her some more.

"What's up?" she returned.

Still gorgeous. *Damn!* I sipped on my drink.

"Royce, I'm glad you made it. I've been meaning to call you all week." I pointed to the ladies sitting with me. "You met Andrea and Mica, right?"

"No, I haven't. Nice to meet you both," she said to them then turned to me. "Can we go somewhere and talk for a few minutes?"

My first thought was to say no. It wasn't like I truly wanted to help Royce with whatever her issues were. I could tell by the way she moved around worriedly and with the troubled look on her face that something was up. I wondered if Agent Miles had contacted her yet? If so, she needed a lawyer and Dr. Phil, not me. Besides I was on the clock and needed to get my time in with Andrea and Mica.

"Sit down. Let's talk," I told her.

"No, not here," she shot back and grabbed my arm while looking over her shoulder. "This is serious. That's why I've been calling you like crazy. And you haven't even returned my calls."

"Sorry, sweetie. Mr. Haskin that I met in Florida has been giving me way too much attention. He flew down just to chill with me for a day and we've been kicking it on the phone like high school sweethearts."

"That's great, India," she spat cutting the rest of my fairy-tale short.

The girl was on pins and needles which I liked. I wanted to

see her sweat. Little did she know she wouldn't have to worry about anything soon other than washing that orange jumpsuit they give you in prison. Then out of the blue I got sidetracked when Chris brushed past us leaving the scent of his intoxicating cologne lingering in the air. Just the smell of it had me tingling between the legs. I now knew why he'd been voted one of *People's* sexiest men of the year.

"Let's go this way," I announced to Royce while grabbing her arm, pulling her down the hallway, hoping to see where Chris was headed. The back of his head was even sexier than the front of his chiseled body. His thickness made him look scrumptious in his jeans and unique button down shirt. When I saw him stop near a huge room that looked to be an office, that was my cue to stop, too.

"Right here is good," I told Royce, "nobody is close enough to hear us so spill it."

She gripped her purse and hit me with another distraught look.

"India, I haven't been too honest lately about a few things."

"O.R?" I crossed my arms. She had a puzzled look like she didn't know that meant, oh really, but I wasn't about to train no stupid hoes tonight. "I can see some shit really getting under your skin. So tell me what's up?" I turned slightly making sure my ear was pointed toward Chris' office. I heard some shit moving around every now and then, but wondered what he was doing in there. Even though the door was open I couldn't see inside from where we stood.

"Girl, it's Latrell."

"Oh word. I thought you and him were done. Finito."

"India, when all that illegal shit was going on, I ended up marrying him," I confessed.

"Bitch, you lying?" *Agent Miles must've definitely got at her*, I thought deceitfully.

"No, I'm not."

"So, why am I the last to know?" This bitch was sneakier than I thought. The way she shrugged her shoulders eluded that she wanted sympathy. I had none for her. I wanted to go see about Chris. I kept my eyes peeled that way until Royce grabbed me by the arm. The seriousness in her eyes had me worried.

"And I never told you that he got locked up for some of that same shit we were doing back then and went to prison because of it," she whispered while glancing from side to side.

I shook my head. "We were never true friends," I emitted. "Cause if we were I woulda known that he went to prison." I smacked my lips and realized how much I disliked Royce. She thought she was the shit, so she deserved to be on edge at the moment.

"So look, I gotta get back to the party. My friends out there don't know anyone but me."

"India, this is serious," she said clutching my elbow. "I got problems. Big problems. There's just one more thing."

"Spill it. Quick." I'd just about had enough of Little Red Riding Hood. I wanted some dick from Chris and she was messing up my chances.

"Me and Latrell had a son. Lil Trae," she added.

"Ain't this a bitch!" I said then pulled myself together. I just shook my head at her. That was her life. Her problems. "Okay listen, this info you giving me is too much. So even if Latrell went to jail and you married him and now you and him are the proud parents of Trae's son, what's all that got to do with me?"

"I just want you to watch your back. He's out now and wants revenge. He thinks you might've helped me set him up. He wants reparations from anyone who can give him some money, so just watch your back."

No, you watch yours bitch, was all I could think to myself. She had no idea that I had given her name to Agent Miles and that she'd be locked down soon.

"Look, I'm not worried about Latrell and you shouldn't be either. Just tell Trae." I threw my hands up letting her know to cry a river with someone else.

"Hell no! Besides, I never told him I was married either. Plus, I'm on the outs with him. He's still cheating."

"Well, your dumb ass still there." This was probably the perfect time to reveal to Royce that I'd slept with Trae, too. It was when we all first met him; that's when we were on even playing ground and everyone wanted to catch a big fish. She caught him and I didn't. So I hoped she was enjoying the grand prize.

"India, you don't understand. This time it's serious. I'm thinking about leaving him for good."

"Whatever, you wrote the book on stupid. I got problems of my own, you just don't know. Look, I gotta run and do another interview. Let's chop it up later in the night."

Without saying another word she walked off leaving me to do my thing. I fixed my hair, licked my lips and took about five steps more down toward the end of the hallway. Finally, my eyes landed on Chris. The diamond in his left ear glistened as he looked at some paper and took another sip of his mixed drink. All this time I could only hear him, but now I could see his perfectly crafted body. We locked eyes as he was pushing a piece of paper through the fax machine.

I smiled. "What's up? I see you're all alone." I grinned again.

I could tell he was just as intoxicated as I was by the way he slurred his words a bit.

"Just faxing a few papers that couldn't wait. You enjoying the party?"

"Now I am."

"Huh?"

"You do remember me, right?"

"Ahhh, India, right?"

"Yeah. But I mean don't you remember me from back in the day?"

"Can't say I do. Rachel was telling me that you said we grew up in the same area."

I shut the door, locked it and walked right up to him. His eyes bulged, but I caught him off guard. Within a millisecond I'd unbuttoned his jeans and slid them down in just enough time before he had a chance to reject me. Chris' facial expressions said no along with his "wait, uh, no, this is not good", but his body said something different. His rod hardened like a brick and stood stiffly in the air causing me to drool.

"Oh naw, we can't do this," he mumbled.

"Sounds good, Chris. It's what you're supposed to say," I told him stroking his dick with my hand.

Chris' dick only registered about nine inches long on my dickometer, nothing I wasn't used to, or nothing I couldn't handle. So I dropped down low as he tried to push my head back. One lick and I had his ass moaning with his back flat against the wall. He couldn't resist.

"Ahhhh shit," he groaned after about four long, sensual strokes.

"You like that shit, don't you?"

"Ssssssssssssss," he seethed between his teeth. "You gotta st- st- st- oppppppppp," was all he could say as I bobbed my head up and down like a hungry child sucking on a lollipop.

I knew I was getting the best of him the way he held onto the table nearby for dear life. Then out of the blue I squeezed his nuts with my cheekbones then licked him like nothing he'd ever experienced before.

Quickly, I hopped up. He had his chance to come to his senses if he wanted to. Of course he didn't. Like lightning, my dress was up and we were humping each other like two horny jack rabbits. First on the desk, then on the chair, then back against the wall.

"Got damn, got damn, got damn!" he chanted as sweat poured from all the physical action we made in the room. "Yo shit good baby."

His shit felt so good I couldn't speak. Our swift rhythm was perfect. I had to have this man in my life daily. Not with Rachel. Realizing I had him where I wanted him. I made my move. I threw it at him as hard as I could. I needed him to cum inside of me. We had to create a baby. A baby by Chris would secure my future. And this time I'd keep it I told myself firmly.

"Ahhhhh, Chrrrrrrrr...isssssss!"

"Oh yes. Ohhhhhhhh shit. Give it to me harder," he begged like a dog in heat. He lifted me off the floor. Then humped me mid air, wildly, crazily, feeling oh so good, grinding ferociously at the fastest pace he could muster.

He was close to busting one. And me, too.

"Uh, uh, uh, uh yessssss," I said.

"Ahhhhhhhhh… India, damnnnnnnn…"

In mid-sentence his speech became slurred. His facial expressions changed to one of undeniable pleasure. "Ahhhhhhhhhh. Ohhhhhh shit."

Those words escaped his lips again as his hips thrust rapidly back and forth pounding my insides like they'd done something to him personally. Next thing I knew, we both hit a series of low level groans, releasing all on the carpet.

I was still panting when Chris moved away from me. In between breaths he asked, "What the fuck was that about?"

How stupid. He knew what we'd just done. No sense in feeling guilty now I wanted to say. "It's about us."

All of a sudden he became paranoid, zipping his pants back up and smoothing out his clothes. "Aweee mannnnn, this shit was dead wrong. I can't do this to Rachel."

"Too late," I told him then attempted to kiss him.

"She's my woman."

Chris backed away with speed then reached for the door. "This shoulda never happened, India. Whatever I gotta do to keep this hushed, I will."

With that he opened the door and walked out. I also exited but not with a frown like Chris'. I beamed from ear to ear knowing that he would come to his senses until I got two yards down the hall and heard Andrea say, "Okay, times up. We off the clock and we need to get paid."

I became furious. This low budget bitch was tryna play me. I hired her agency to send two girls with me to the party to be my flunkies for the night. No one was supposed to ever know. They were supposed to cater to my every beck and call making me seem super important and here she was tryna collect in front of everyone. Her goal was to embarrass me.

Bitch!

Chapter 20

Royce

I sang my fucking heart out with my guitar in hand. No tension just pure emotion. I was in the sound booth damn near about to cry as my notes flowed high and flawless. I loved the fact that the guys trusted me enough to let me sing it live. So in return, I gave it my all. The pain in my voice reminded me of the way Beyonce sang Etta James' song in *Cadillac Records*. The only difference was that I was singing about Trae, a man who thought it was cool to be shared by multiple women. A man who just couldn't love me the way I wanted to be loved. The more I thought of him the more teary-eyed I became and the more my voice soared.

It was clear that every good song came from an artist who believed in what they were singing and no doubt the belief in "Our Man" was in me. It was a song I'd written in just eight hours flat and got the green light to add it to the album just a day ago. I'd been in the studio at least eight hours for the last three days, working and singing my heart out with Ray and Fat Cat, a hot producer that I'd been eager to work with. The only break taken was to attend Rachel and Chris' party. With three songs already recorded and completed, I only had two more to get under my belt by weeks end. When the song ended I smiled at Ray and Fat Cat before exiting the booth.

"That shit was dope," Ray announced with cheer.

"Yo, all that shit Mello said about you was right. You about biznesss," Fat Cat complimented.

"Thanks." I grinned even though I felt like I'd overdosed on music and fear all at the same time. I kept thinking Latrell would find me and walk through the door at any moment. It was past the two week mark and I hadn't heard from him. Strange. But my gut said the time would come soon. Unexpectedly.

"Yo, we gon' add a few vocal harmonies and one or two more instruments as overdubs and guess what, Ms. Royce?"

"What?" I answered Fat Cat slowly since my thoughts were on Latrell.

"We got ourselves another song."

"Yayyyyyy," I said like a little child, clapping my hands for added excitement. "You think Romello will like what we've done?"

Fat Cat's monstrous sized stomach jiggled as he laughed. He reminded me of a bald, dark chocolate Santa Claus.

"Hell yeah. You got at least two hits coming your way."

I smiled again.

Making Romello proud was my only goal. Thank God he hadn't been around and I hadn't had to face him yet. We talked on the phone a few times after I abruptly left the studio two and a half weeks ago, yet I never had the guts to tell him the real reason why all that happened. He chalked it up as stress, nervousness and any other cop out excuse that I gave. The point was, I'd held things up long enough with my bullshit and we were at least two weeks off target. There was no more room for error.

"Mello tells me we gon' drop the single next week? You ready for that?"

My eyes locked with Fat Cat's and my insides cramped a little. This shit was really happening. My voice would be on the radio. I would finally reach my goal. "Hell yeah, I'm ready."

Fat Cat laughed heartily again and started putting a few items into a bag. Within seconds Romello entered which changed the mood in the studio. Whenever he came around people scrambled to get in place making sure things were one hundred percent perfect and today was no different. He was on the phone arguing with someone raising his voice and using curse words as every other word. His venom filled voice let us all know he wasn't up for no games with the person on the line. I simply sat quietly watching his every move. The stories had been circling about how he could get but to see it gave me a different level of respect for him. When Romello ended the call he shot me a satisfactory look and hit Fat Cat and Ray with a few pounds.

"Tell me something good!" he shouted.

"Oh, we straight," Ray announced. "Didn't I tell you we'd get it done?"

Romello hit Ray with a quick, brotherly hug. He was happy as hell and it made me feel good that I'd finally done something right. "Where we at?"

"We just got a few final touches and we'll be ready to play shit back for you tomorrow," Fat Cat said proudly. "We out," he added, grabbing his 3x jacket off the stool.

"Good work, Royce," Ray told me with a pleasant glance. "And I'm glad you're keeping her real name," he said to Romello as he headed out the door.

"You know, I know what's best," Romello bragged as the door shut leaving the two of us alone. Just as I was about to comment on keeping my real name for my stage name Romello's cell rang.

"Mannn, c'mon," he answered harshly. "You gotta be kidding me."

I tried not to stare but the shock of seeing him go at the person on the line had my full attention.

"Look, I said what I said. You gotta problem with that?" he asked the caller.

I wondered who he was talking to and what the conversation was really about. I hadn't really seen that tough guy side of him until now.

"Yeah. You be there when I get there or you know what it is."

He ended the call abruptly and grinned my way just before waving me over to where he had taken a seat near the mixing board. I strutted toward him in my sexiest walk. It was something about him that had me aborting my promise not to get involved with him. It was either the power he possessed in the business area or just the mere fact that he was so fine that had me hot and horny.

"Everything a'a'ight?" he asked.

With just the sound of his voice goose bumps popped up all over my arms.

"Yeah. I'm good. Thanks for looking out."

"Awe, that ain't shit. You know you my number one girl, right? Sit down a minute," he ordered.

When Romello touched my thigh he caused all types of nasty thoughts to enter my mind. So I took a seat next to him with all the wrong intentions. His glare into my eyes made me think that he had the same thoughts that I did. I had just about given up on my relationship with Trae so if he tried his hand, I was willing and ready.

"So, I guess you know the single will drop next week."

I nodded.

"And we still on with interviews and everything so I want to make sure you're emotionally ready. When we last talked you seemed a lil' sad."

"Nah, I'm good now. I promise. It's all good when I'm with you," I added coyly letting him know I felt safe with him. "All I need is that advance. Will the check be ready soon?"

I prayed he would say yes. I had just written and cashed another check from Trae this morning for fifteen thousand so when Latrell showed up out of the blue I would be ready. The problem was that Latrell would be expecting twenty grand. I was five grand short. Fuck! I still didn't know why the first check I tried to cash for twenty thousand didn't go through. That was such an embarrassing moment when the teller told me the funds for the twenty thousand dollar check wasn't available. Luckily, I had Trae's checkbook with me and could run outside to forge another one for a lower amount. Thank God that one cashed.

"Nah, not yet," Romello finally said. "Next week for sure though."

I thought about asking him for the money as I searched his eyes. Desperation had kicked in. It would be a loan just until my advance came through. Then his damn cell phone rang again fucking up my chances.

"Really. Oh, really!" he shouted to the top of his lungs as he answered like an angry maniac. "So you just gon' keep calling a nigga? What the fuck?"

Damn- my only assumption was that it was a chick or a very weak man who let Romello chew into them that way.

"Like I said, the night's have been switched. Don't call back!" he roared.

When he first hung up the moment was awkward until I broke the ice. "Girlfriend problems?" I hit him with a sweet grin.

"Not exactly. This situation is more complicated."

Yes! I thought with excitement. Just to know that it probably dealt with business warmed my insides.

"But what about you and your boyfriend? That's the question," he commented catching me off guard. "I mean since we on the subject in all, I really want to know."

"Complicated," I said jokingly. Romello touched my thigh again. This time he held on a little longer. "That relationship is over as far as I'm concerned. But my son loves his father dearly so I gotta figure some things out first before leaving the house for good."

"Is that right?" Tyesha said, walking through the door. "He loves his father, but I hear Trae's not the father," she said in her animated Jerry Springer tone.

My expression revealed my shock. I wondered why she was there and why they never locked the doors in the studio. I also realized India was probably responsible for spreading my business around. "Tyesha, what do you want!"

She slapped hands with Romello as she stood beside him eyeballing me with tons of hate and jealousy all wrapped up into one. "What up playa?"

"You baby, what brings you around?"

"Oh, I'm here to collect. Your girl knows what's up. Fifteen percent."

I threw my hands up to cover my face. There was no way this was happening. There was never a dull moment in my life.

Drama always found me. No matter where I hid. With the most callous tone inside me I made my stance clear, "Tyesha, I told you before. You did nothing! So you get nothing! I met Romello on my own. I told you that a hundred times."

"Bitch, that shit won't fly." She jolted toward me with her fist balled up like she wanted to throw a punch. "I want what's mine."

Romello stood up quickly, as if to protect me. "Aye, you know the deal. No contract then no paper. Royce found me on her own, Tyesha. Go 'head with that bully shit."

"Nigga, if you hadn't listened to the demo from JR then none of this shit woulda happened so either you gon' pay me or she is." Her hand thrust outward. She waited. Then waited some more as Romello stood patiently thinking and typing something into his phone.

"I'm your agent, baby, whether you want me to be or not."

My eyes locked with Romello's. I didn't know what else to say. Just like kindred spirits he knew I needed him.

"Look, Tyesha, we cool and all, but you do know who the fuck I am, right?"

"Yeah. You the nigga who owe me fifteen percent. Big Balla Nigga…Wanna-be Puff Daddy, muthufucka."

Quickly, Romello pushed her toward the door with Tyesha talking big shit, taking backwards baby steps. "Man, you gotta go. Royce got music to make. And leave her the fuck alone," he blasted, " 'cause she don't have no paper for you. And you know I don't. You heard me?"

"Nigga, you not the only one who bringing heat," she challenged him as they made it out of my sight headed toward the exit.

I couldn't see them anymore but knew Tyesha was being thrown out. She made sure I heard her last words as the door was being opened.

"Game over, Royce!" she shouted. "No more passes, baby. Only time to regret."

Just like that, her voice disappeared and a male voice spoke replacing Tyesha's. Thank God he had thrown her out just in time. I knew how important his business deals were to him, so me bringing more problems wasn't good for our relationship. I threw my hand over my chest and sighed heavily knowing that we'd have to talk things over later after he finished up his conversation with his business associate. Everything that just happened hit me like a whirlwind. That was way too much.

I took several breaths and sat back down trying to calm my nerves. Unfortunately my problems were just beginning. When Romello hit the corner and his business associate became visible I stood up. Romello pressed his hand forward as a sign for me to freeze.

My heart damn near stopped.

A sense of numbness shot through me.

"Yes, hear me out! I just want to get to the bottom of this," Romello said worriedly. "There's money on the line Royce."

"What!" I screeched.

"I didn't know they cut Tango the check to do this track with you. So, let's talk…just the three of us to see what's the problem."

As usual, Tango wore his baggy jeans and malicious smirk. "What up butterfly?" he asked me sarcastically.

"Fuck you!" I shouted. "Don't say shit to me!"

I started backing up fearfully, one step at a time. The room started spinning closing in on me. I couldn't take no more. The world seemed to be against me. There was Latrell, Trae, Tyesha; and Tango just wouldn't go away. I started wailing, crying like a baby mumbling shit under my breath as the tears flowed. My chest heaved up and down and for some reason I couldn't catch my breath.

"No, no no," I chanted while snot pulsated from my nose as I made all kinds of whining sounds.

"Royce, calm down. I got you," Romello said trying to get close to me.

My head kept shaking back and forth and my nerves were completely shot.

Finally Romello grabbed me by the shoulders. "You gotta tell me what's up. Just calm down."

"He raped me," I shouted!

Romello's eyes tripled in size. At first they asked the question, was the news true? Then he turned to Tango to see his guilty, non-remorseful scoff.

"What? What? You did what?" Romello kept repeating. "Nigga you violated!" He kept throwing his fist, one into another with his face balled up in a knot.

"Man, it's just pussy," Tango responded removing his hands from his front pockets. "We gon' do this deal or what?" he asked with arrogance.

Before I could even say anything else Romello pushed me out the way. I winced a little when the first punch was thrown. The loud thumping sound of his fist connecting with Tango's jaw had my heart rate on blast. I never saw it coming. Neither did Tango obviously. Tango threw two quick punches to retaliate but missed with each throw. Romello responded with quick, powerful hits to his forehead, nose and chin knocking him down to the floor reminding me of a TKO in a professional boxing match. Before long Tango's nose looked like it had been cracked in three different places and blood flowed from both sides of his mouth. The beef had me shook.

"Stop! Stop! That's enough," I chimed in. "Look, I can't work with him, but don't kill him!"

Romello stood over Tango with his fist still balled up and lounging at his sides while I continued to whimper like some sucka who couldn't take a little quarrel. Silence filled the air as Tango looked up at Romello and Romello down at him. No words were spoken but a decision was made between the two of them.

I was still whimpering when Tango picked himself up off the floor telling Romello, "You got some shit comin' your way, dawg."

"Nigga walk. Walk nigga." Romello kept bucking at him along the way.

With blood dripping everywhere, Tango took off faster than I expected him to. I was certain he had some broken bones by the way he got beat down. Romello wasn't bothered by the words he shouted as he followed him to the door. When I heard it slam I figured his only concern was me by the way he rushed back over to the couch where I sat in a daze wiping tears with my right hand. Immediately, he took hold of my shoulders then held me tightly in his arms. It calmed me slightly even though I continued to cry from the trauma that I'd just witnessed.

"Don't feel sorry for that punk-ass nigga. He thinks it's cool to take pussy. So he got what he deserved. My job is to protect you. I told you you're my number one girl."

He grabbed the back of my head with his strong, firm hand making me feel more protected than I'd ever felt. Quickly, he pulled me close so our faces could meet perfectly. My hormones were raging like a youngster going through puberty. Partly because Romello was heaven sent and the other might've had something to do with the hard-on stabbing me in the leg.

He lifted my chin and slipped his delicious tongue into my mouth. I just knew he was what I needed in my life to pull it all to-gether; sexually, financially, emotionally and that man who would be there for me at all cost. Not a cheater or a liar, just a lover.

We took turns sucking each other's lips like the world was about to end and we needed as much time together as possible. Our moves quickened. My nipples hardened. Then it was happening. Romello released me then yanked my shirt above my head. He sucked my nipples so sensually causing my juices to flow down my leg. I pushed him back by the shoulders ready to help him get his pants down. Unfortunately for me, his cell rang.

I couldn't believe he reached over to answer it. I was like a little chihuahua in heat. I needed to get drilled badly. With a huge disappointing sigh, I slammed myself back on the couch waiting impatiently while he argued once again with the caller on the line. "Ugghhhhhhh," I muttered in an attempt to make myself known.

Obviously that childish move didn't work because within seconds Romello told me he had to go. It was an emergency. While I picked my feelings up off the ground, I attempted to ask when I would see him again. That wouldn't work because it took him all of thirty seconds to have me put my shirt back on, grab my shit, and make our way outside.

"I'm sorry, beautiful," he told me locking the door and rushing off to his car.

I couldn't understand why I was still standing outside the studio looking dumbfounded. I was alone, afraid, and knew things would only get worse when my phone vibrated and Trae's number popped up. I answered since I knew my son had been spending so much time with his father. Maybe he wanted me to come home.

"Hello," I huffed.

"Bitch, you got something you wanna tell me?" Trae spat into the phone.

Chapter 21

Royce

"Tell me why the fuck I gave a thief an engagement ring?"

My blank stare remained as it had been for the last twenty minutes. There was nothing for me to say.

"Huh? Tell me that, Royce. All I did was try to give you a better life!" Trae lectured like I was his child. "Giving you a chance to become a wife!"

I sat on our custom designed couch with my elbows on my thighs and my head resting between my hands. Guilty and defeated. Meanwhile, Trae paced the floor with his veins popping out the side of his neck cursing me out with words I didn't even know existed. It had only been three hours since leaving the studio and dealing with Tyesha and Tango all in one day so my head pounded like someone was inside hammering their way out.

"What else have you done, bitch? If it's that easy to forge my name and take my money, you might have some of my jewels tucked in your purse."

"Trae, that's ridiculous and you know it," I said meekly.

"Nah. Fuck that. What's ridiculous is how you come up in here talking about getting your family back and now you stealing from your man." He paused. "You know I could have you arrested, right?"

"Trae, c'mon. I know you're not serious," I stated sitting straight up to check his facial expression.

"I'm dead serious, damn it. My money been funny for a while now. I just never told you. So you taking thirty-five thousand from me hurts."

My mind spun like a windmill. I knew he'd been traded but that didn't mean no money was coming in. What was he talking about? I still had fifteen thousand of the money stuffed down at the bottom of my purse in all crisp hundreds but the meeting with Latrell was set for eight o'clock. He'd called just minutes before I walked in to meet Trae's wrath. I couldn't show up empty handed. Trae would just have to wait.

"I'll pay you back," I blurted. "I swear."

"Doesn't matter, Royce. You can't be trusted." His eyes hit me with a shameful disgusting look. "At all," he added along with some weird smacking sound of the lips. "Not as my fiancé and soon-to-be wife. We supposed to build together, not you steal from me."

"Look, it was a mistake!" I shouted. "You wouldn't understand why I did it if I told you."

"What? You on crack? That's the only reason I could see you blowing thirty-five grand. Or you giving it to some nigga? Is that it? You buying some nigga material shit with my bread?"

"Hell no!"

I wanted badly to tell him the truth. I just couldn't. Shit was too complicated. On one hand if I told him about Latrell it would possibly cost him his life. If I didn't, Trae would never know the truth and just never understood why I took the money. At least I'd decided against saying Rosa took it. I didn't really care about the relationship that much anymore but I didn't want it to get to the point where Trae believed I was a thief. I was just trying to pay Latrell back and get him out of my life for good.

Just then Lil Trae darted into the living room with his eyes filled with worry. I assumed he heard the commotion and wanted to see what was going on. I let a slight smile slip through the side of my frown as he took off running toward me in his newly bought Polo sweatsuit. It seemed as if Trae had been buying him new clothes weekly. His facial expression changed to more of a joyful one the closer he got to me. I opened my arms wide, ready to hug him tightly ready to pretend like everything was okay between his dad and me. Instead, he bypassed me jumping straight into Trae's lap.

"Daddy, are you gonna play games with me again tonight?"

"You bet, big head. Just me and you," he told him, while they tussled and played roughly on the couch opposite me. "How do you feel about your mom going away for a little while?"

I gasped. What in the hell was he trying to pull?

"And me and you can spend some time together just having fun? And I can help you with your school work like we've been doing, okay?"

I started to object to Trae's manipulation but my son was all for it.

"Oh, mommy has to go sing again?" he asked his fake father looking into his eyes lovingly like he was the one who gave him life.

Mommy is going to go away for a while," he said throwing his shifty eyes over at me. "But you'll be here with Daddy."

"Yayyyyyyyyy," Lil Trae chimed.

I had already stood up with my arms across my chest once Trae said I was going away. When Trae told him to go to his room I shut shit down. "No, son! You stay here with me." My voice was firm but I didn't want to scare him. Even though he kept looking up at his father for approval I continued, "I'm not going away honey. Don't you worry."

"I'm not worried," Lil Trae answered in his usual sweet voice.

Trae smiled broadly. "See he's cool with it and so am I. So, it's settled. You go ahead and go away for a while. Go focus on your lil' singing career or whatever that shit is that you do at the studio. We'll be fine." He clutched Lil Trae's hand tighter.

My heart began to beat faster and faster. I could see what was going down. "Oh, hell no. Come over here Lil Trae. We gotta run out for a minute."

"No, you stay right beside me, son," he stated with authority.

Nobody moved. We all remained frozen. I looked into my

son's eyes, the little boy I cherished with all my heart. I could tell he didn't want to go with me. It hurt like hell to know that I was the one who raised him and I was his mother, but he really wanted to be with that jerk. Someone who wasn't even blood.

Without warning, I darted over to where they both stood hand in hand and snatched Trae into my tight embrace. His back was pressed against my stomach as my entire body wrapped him up like a blanket. I began to walk backwards putting distance between Trae, and me and my child.

"He doesn't want to go with you!" Trae shouted making the situation even more chaotic.

"Let me go mommy, let me go!"

Knots formed in my gut to even hear those words. While my son kept screaming Trae kept taking steps toward me. "Honey, we just need to go talk. I'll bring you back to stay with your father after that," I lied. "Is that okay?" I prayed my words would calm his nerves.

"Uh…uh…uh…huh," he answered with short sobs.

As snot trickled from his nose his wild movements ceased. I turned his body toward mine and kissed him on the cheek. "We'll be back," I told him before heading toward the door.

Twenty minutes later, I found myself still in rage driving wildly while keeping my eyes on Lil Trae from my rearview mirror. We had been driving in silence with him just watching me never even asking where we were going. I hated dragging him along with me to meet Latrell but my hands were tied. Trae's action had me nervous with all the talk about me *going away* as he so called it. It sounded like he wanted me to leave, but without my son.

I turned slightly, ready to talk to Trae when I realized I'd a missed call on my phone. Quickly, I pressed the button to check my messages. The moment I heard Ms. Campbell's voice chills ran up my spine. The second her words registered, I wanted to cry. She said my birth mother said she wasn't ready to face me. I wanted to shout from the dejected feelings that shot through me but the more I looked into my son's eyes I couldn't focus on myself.

"Honey, you alright?" I asked with hurt in my soft voice.

He looked down at the floor. "No," he replied still whimpering.

"What's wrong, baby?"

He remained silent for about thirty seconds. I was about to repeat my question until his little squeaky voice muttered, "I want my daddy."

I damn near slammed on brakes. How humiliating for a mother who's given her child her all to be getting this type of treatment?

"Trae, we'll be back with him soon. Mommy just has to make a stop," I told him pulling into the parking lot of a bagel spot. I studied my surroundings not liking the chosen meet-up spot at all. It was dark, cold and deserted.

I saw Latrell's car parked toward the end of the lot but I wasn't about to pull into a trap. I sat idly waiting, tapping my fingers on the steering wheel and hoping he would hop out soon. I had something he wanted so he needed to come to me. My mind hadn't gotten off overload the entire ride over. The lies I would tell for not having the whole twenty grand hadn't popped into my head yet. Hopefully something would come to mind soon. Several more minutes passed with me still waiting and unable to see any movement in Latrell's front seat. Then finally, Latrell appeared out of nowhere scaring me half to death. He stood outside his car about ten yards away waving for me sharply and telling me to get out of the car.

"Trae, climb up here," I whispered to my boy.

Quickly he took his seatbelt off and hopped up front with me. His face still had a frown but at least he had his arm around my neck. "I want my daddy, mommy."

"I know, baby, I know," I said grabbing the envelope with the cash from my purse.

It didn't take long for the both of us to walk toward Latrell. Both my hands shook severely with one clutching Lil Trae's hand ever so tightly. His body trembled crazily with me feeling every inch of his fear. I needed to keep my baby close so he would know everything would be okay. "Everything will be alright," I announced out of the blue just before stopping in front of Latrell.

"Here," I said, handing him the envelope. For some reason I thought it was best to be honest just in case he counted it. "It's only 15k," I added, making sure we didn't make direct eye contact. The black bandana that he wore along with the nasty snar made me uneasy.

"Where the rest of the money, Royce?"

"Um…um…um…look," I stammered.

"Oh, so you up to the bullshit again?" he questioned with frustration.

"No, really… I got it. I just had a set-back but I didn't want to be late."

He lifted his shirt displaying what looked to be a Desert Eagle. It was difficult to be sure in the darkness but my pupils tripled in size just knowing it shot bullets. Even in the cold I began to sweat. I didn't know much about guns but I knew from the years spent with Latrell what his guns of choice looked like. My first thought was to keep him calm and ask why he thought a gun was needed, but I didn't want to mention the word gun in front of my child. Before I could say another word, Latrell reached swiftly for Lil Trae clutching the bottom half of his tiny arm.

"C'mere, lil faggot," he said, yanking his body toward his and wrapping his chiseled arm around his neck securely. "Your mama thinks this shit is a game," he said roughly as if he were talking to someone from the streets.

Trae yelled instantly. "Mommy, nooooooo. Help me, mommy!" His hands were stretched outward as water welled up into his eyes.

He kept screaming and shouting to the top of his lungs as he scrambled to escape in mid-air. His sobbing and crying sent me into panic mode. Quickly, I clasped my hands together as my tears trickled down my face. That moment sent me into a frenzy; seeing my baby held securely by someone he feared. Someone with a gun.

"Shut up, lil nigga."

"Mommmmmmmmmmmmy!" he screamed more and more.

The look in his eyes begged for me to do something. I could only stand by pleading and praying inside with little hope in my voice. "Latrell, please. I swear I'll get the rest of the money by tonight. Just let me make a call."

"Yeah, you do that," he firmly agreed. "You got three hours to get it."

"Three hours?"

"You heard what the fuck I said!"

"Okay…okay…okay," I repeated. "Just let my lil man go. Pleaseeeeee, I'm begging you."

"Nah, I think my son will stay with me so we can get to know each other a little better. I'll decide if and when you get him back when you bring my money. And I want thirty grand now…just for the lies you tell."

My entire face became flushed. All color disappeared and I felt like fainting on the spot. Had I heard him correctly? "What did you say?"

"You heard me. My son. And bring me thirty."

Lil Trae's eyes grew to the size of balloons. "Let me go," he shouted while kicking madly.

"Where'd you get that from? Who told you that?" Thoughts flipped through my brain like a roledex. "Was it India?" I asked with speed. "Who was it? You gotta tell me."

"Tell me why you never told me the kid was mine?" At that point he yanked the gun from inside his jeans.

I calmed myself as fast as I could. "Ummmmm...ummm-mmm…to be honest, Latrell, I don't know. I guess because you were going to jail."

"Go get in your car! Now!" he shouted pointing the gun at me and still gripping Lil Trae helplessly by the neck. "Call me when you got my money ready."

I backed up thinking suicidal thoughts. The first was to rush Latrell fighting him for the release of my son. The second was to just get shot and die as opposed to leaving my baby with a murderer. Then reality hit. I needed to call the person I knew I could count on. He would give me the money and make sure I got Trae back.

Like an Olympic track star I jetted to my car with tears streaming along the way. "Mommy will be right back," I shouted out loud opening my car door. Once inside my fingers hit the digits hard and quick. I could barely talk when Romello answered. "I need help!" I wailed into the phone.

Chapter 22

India

The aroma of the soft leather interior had me intoxicated. All I could smell was money, money, money. The old school sounds of The Stylistics' *Stop, Look, & Listen* played softly from the state of the art stereo system, serenading me like a pampered princess.

Underneath the Brookyln street lights the tires of the Maybach spun slowly as it turned onto my street and approached my building. I sat in the back seat leaning into Mr. Haskin's body staring out the window as he held me tightly in his arms. He was dressed in a crispy white button down shirt, sharply creased black slacks, and a pair of suede Gucci loafers. On his wrist was a Jacob, but not one of those big gawky ones you see rappers rocking. It was more subtle, but never the less, pricey. On his right pinky finger was a gorgeous mid-sized five carat diamond ring that sparkled nonstop.

Mr. Haskin had flown in from a business venture just to spend a few days with me. He pampered me with his attention and a few high-priced shopping sprees. He would be leaving today in just a few hours to head out to Los Angeles to close some big multi-million dollar deal I'd heard him talking about on the phone several times over the past few days.

Traveling, brokering business deals, and getting money was pretty much what nearly every second of my new boo's life consisted of. Although he was from Miami he was rarely there. He was far too busy to stay in one spot too long, let alone his own home. Plenty of times when I would call him, in the background I would be able to hear people talking in French, Italian, Spanish, and other countless exotic languages. The only thing that bothered me was that he spoke of his twin thirty-five year old daughters way too much and talked on his phone constantly.

I liked when he spoke of money; how much he had and how much more he was trying to acquire. Today though, since he would be leaving me to catch his charter jet to L.A., he only answered his phone a few times, choosing to give me his time and undivided focus.

"Did you enjoy yourself?" he asked me as the Maybach made its way down the street.

"Yes," I answered, while still staring off into space somewhere. My answer was halfhearted. My body was in his arms but my mind was someplace much, much farther away. I couldn't really enjoy the moment knowing how stressful shit was about to get for me.

Gerald was what I now called him since we'd been on a first name basis and he'd had taken me on a breathtaking helicopter ride up the Hudson River to the Harvest Restaurant. It was one of those types of spots where you only got in by reservation, and you only got in if you had *major* paper. Shit, the cheapest thing on the menu was a few hundred dollars.

While there, I saw Tiger Woods sitting with a beautiful white woman. I also saw Jack Nicholson's old decrepit ass sitting with some woman who looked like she could be his daughter. When we were leaving, Magic Johnson was climbing out of a limo with his wife.

Each of them wore expensive suits, while their dates wore expensive gowns. They talked quietly, surrounded by countless businessmen who conversed at their own tables and never batted an eye as if having a famous actor or sport's star sitting only a few feet away from them was an everyday thing, nothing out of the ordinary. But the weird thing about it was that *I* didn't even gawk. I was just way too stressed to.

Noticing how far away I seemed, Gerald asked in the back seat, "Princess, what's wrong?"

I always loved when he called me that. It made me blush.

"I'm fine," I lied.

"You're lying."

"How do you know?" I asked softly.

"Because you haven't been your usually jovial self at all today. Your beautiful body and angelic face has been with me. And I'm grateful for that. But your mind hasn't. You didn't like the restaurant?"

His voice had a hint of worry in it.

"It's not that, baby," I said, quickly rising from his arms to face him and not wanting him to think I was being unappreciative. "I loved the restaurant."

"Was it the shopping sprees? Am I giving you too much attention?"

Looking him in his eyes I placed a hand softly on the side of his face. "Gerald, I loved the shopping sprees. I love spending time with you."

"Then what's the problem?"

I couldn't answer. Allowing him in my personal business wasn't something I was sure I wanted to do.

The Maybach pulled to the curb in front of my building and stopped.

Gerald softly took one of my hands into his own and squeezed gently. "Talk to me," he said, not quite ready to let me go, although knowing his personal learjet was waiting at the airport as we spoke. Looking me directly in the eyes he said, "Maybe I can help."

My eyes dropped to the floor.

Placing a hand underneath my chin and raising my face to his he said, "Please, tell me what's wrong."

Shame enveloped me. I didn't want him to know that I was a fraud, that I wasn't the princess he treated me like. He'd probably treat me differently if I told him. As a matter of fact, he'd probably want nothing else to do with me. He'd see me as ghetto trash.

"I can't let you go until you tell me," he said with my chin still in his hand and his eyes directly on my face.

Sighing, I finally answered. "Sweetheart, I did something bad when I was younger."

"What did you do?" he asked worriedly, releasing my chin.

"I can't tell you right now. All I can say is it was bad and I'm definitely not proud of it. It was a stupid mistake. And I really wish I could change it but I can't."

Gerald stared at me intently. The look of worry had faded. It was difficult to make out exactly what he was thinking. I recognized that as his business face. He rocked it whenever he didn't want opposing businessmen to know exactly what way he was leaning towards during business deals. I really didn't want to go on but something wouldn't let me shut up.

"The FBI is trying to tie me up into something big. I don't know what to do or where to turn."

His face now showed concern.

"They keep calling me and badgering me," I continued, the stress and worry of the situation evident in my voice. "Now I may have to testify. I could possibly go to jail."

Tears started to form in my eyes. My vision began to grow blurry. Just the thought of having to go to prison scared the shit out of me. It made my body tremble. Visions of tiny jail cells and walks around the yard filled my head. I'd seen enough History Channel specials about female prisons to know it wasn't the place for me.

Seeing my fear and developing tears, he took both of my hands into his own. "Don't worry."

"I can't help it. I'm scared to death. Oh, God, I don't want to go to jail." The first tear fell.

"Don't be. No lady of mine will be going to jail. Money cures everything. What's the agent's name whom you've been speaking to?"

"Agent Miles."

He nodded. "Okay, I'll have my lawyers get right on it immediately."

"Baby, I don't want to get you in the middle of my problems."

He wiped away my tears. "Nonsense, that's what I'm here for. From this point forward, don't say anything else to the agent. If he wants answers, refer him to your attorney. Don't speak to the authorities period. Understand?"

I nodded. My world brightened.

"Then smile for me."

I did. His reaction to my confession surprised me. Damn, he really was feeling me. I mean, powerful men like him had countless mistresses on the side. I wasn't naive enough to think he was any different. They spoiled their mistresses with shopping sprees and dinner in five star restaurants. But getting involved in serious criminal matters was something all together different. That was some shit they didn't want their names associated with or mixed up in.

He smiled approvingly. "That's my princess. I love that smile. If you only knew how much I miss it and think about it when we're apart."

After wiping away my tears he leaned forward to kiss me. As his lips approached mine, my stomach turned slightly. It always reacted that way when he kissed me. It couldn't be helped. The fact that Gerald Haskin was a seventy-four year old white man was still a small issue for me. Although he wasn't all that bad looking, he was old enough to be my father. Every time I kissed him my mind somehow conjured nauseating thoughts of Ben Gay, Viagra, and caregivers. My body was also still getting used to his touch. I was coming along though. If I was going to hook his old ass perfectly, age would have to be thrown to the wind. The end justified the means.

It is what it is. I loved being pampered and spoiled. I loved the shopping sprees. And in time those things would become a permanent part of my life. I just had to stay reeling him in.

Reluctantly my lips allowed his to press against mine. His tongue, although pepper minted, sent nauseating tremors through my stomach as it slid in between my glossed lips. Ignoring the feeling, my mouth allowed his tongue's entrance. It was only for a brief moment though. Going too long would possibly cause me to puke.

The chauffeur opened the door and I stepped my red bottoms out and onto the sidewalk.

"The attorney will be calling you tomorrow," he said.

"Alright," I said smiling. "I.L.Y."

"Back at you. And no more worrying. You're too beautiful for such trivial things."

The worry had subsided but not fully. A great attorney wasn't always a guarantee of beating a case but it eased my mind somewhat to know that I now had a fighting chance. After saying good bye I headed up the walkway to the front door of my building as the Maybach pulled away from the curb and headed up the street. My heels clicked loudly as I finally reached the door and sashayed through it. Suddenly in just a blink of an eye I saw a fist coming full speed at my face. It connected before I could react, causing me to see stars. My legs grew wobbly.

"You shady, bitch!" Rachel screamed as she grabbed me by my ponytail and sent another punch straight into my mouth. "You think you can just fuck my man and get away with it?"

Immediately, I could taste blood. I spit a huge glob of it onto the floor. My mouth filled with pain. Since I hadn't quite recovered from the first punch, my hands reached out by instinct to try and block the next punch.

"I should kill your sneaky ass, India!"

From the darkness behind my eyelids I quickly charged my right shoulder into her stomach as hard as I could. I had to fight back even though I knew she must've found out about me and Chris. Quickly, I gave her a gut shot that sent her curling over.

"Bitch," I gasped, tiring from the struggle, but didn't let up. "He never really wanted you for real, Rachel. You don't know this game. Who could want your dark ass for their eye candy?" I watched her eyes grow redder while I went in for the kill. "If… he really wanted you he wouldn't have been all up in this pussy calling my name over and over again."

My eyes were clearing enough to see my target. Seeing her hunched over and holding her stomach, I bum rushed her hard, sending her to the floor. I wanted Rachel to know that I could fight. Well.

"It's not my fault that you couldn't hold on to your man."

Rachel peeled herself off the floor with tears in her eyes. I thought it was over until she charged me eventually pressing my back to the wall.

"You low down tramp!" she screamed, squeezing my neck as hard as she could. "You don't care about nobody but your damn self! No loyalty! To anyone!"

As I struggled to breathe she squeezed even tighter while repeatedly slamming the back of my head against the wall. My girl had gone bananas. Didn't our friendship mean anything? With the years we'd known each other, she should've cut me some slack.

"You fucked with the wrong bitch's man this time, India!" she screamed.

Since I could see her emotional breakdown getting worse, I gave her a strong rib shot that loosened her grip. And another one to the stomach made her let go completely. I followed up with a punch to her right eye that made her grab it immediately. She'd underestimated me. She thought she was coming here tonight to whip my ass for fucking her man.

WRONG!

Chris wanted me. He loved all the juices I gave him. She should've been fighting him.

Rachel staggered still holding her eye with one hand and trying to fend off the upcoming blow with her free hand. I hit her again.

"Owwww!" she yelled in pain.

"Look, Rachel, I'm willing to forget all of this if you are," I spoke sincerely. "You my girl and I just don't think we should be fighting over no dude."

"You really do have mental problems, don't you?" she asked grabbing her stomach again.

"Look, I don't want to keep doing this with you. Let's just talk it out," I said softly letting her know I was done. "No more hitting, okay."

Rachel never agreed to my plea she just kept huffing and puffing, attempting to catch her breath.

"But just so you know the rules. Don't ever come at the

chick in a case like this," I told her bluntly. "Next time check yo' nicca. Don't try to check the bitch. If your man wanted you, he wouldn't have been with me."

Rachel locked eyes with me. For a moment it was as if she couldn't believe what I was saying. Then her disbelief turned to fury. As snot fell from her nose and tears from her eyes she eye balled me like I was the most despicable person she'd ever seen.

"Last chance to squash this Rachel," I told her with my hands on my hips. "Chris is up for grabs until he actually marries you. So until then we should just forget it ever happened."

"India," she finally opened her mouth to say, "I will never forgive you. And if it's the last thing I do on earth, I will pay you back, bitch!"

"Whatever Rachel, whatever," I responded and turned to go to my apartment, leaving her looking like a hurt, brainless woman.

Chapter 23

Royce

As I quickly bent the corner my tires squealed. It was a little after seven p.m. and the sun had called it a day leaving me driving in the darkness. Over and over my car darted in and out of traffic at a high speed. Visions of my baby sitting in a basement or dark garage terrified out of his mind and missing me wouldn't show my nerves any mercy. They were past frazzled. They were shot. I was scared to death for him and felt like I'd let him down.

"Latrell, I'm on my way to meet you now!" I said into my cell frantically. My hand was trembling so badly it was a wonder it could even hold the phone without dropping it on the floor.

"You got my muthafuckin' money?" he asked from the other end of the line. There was no hint of compassion in his voice. Separating a mother from her child meant nothing to him. For a grimy person like Latrell, it was nothing but business as usual.

"Yeah, I got you."

"You sure?"

"Yeah."

"Real talk, Royce. No more games. If I you don't got every single penny of my damn money, I'll kill this lil muthafucka."

"Even though you now know that's your son!" I cried.

"You never thought that shit was important for me to know before, so why now!"

"Oh my God!" was all I could mutter. Visions of my baby dying appeared in my head. The sight made my heart drop and also sent shivers throughout my entire body. If something ever happened to my baby, I couldn't live with myself. I couldn't go on. His death would cause my own suicide.

"I swear, Latrell," I said quickly. "I'm not playing games. I've got all your money."

"That better be the truth. If you're lyin', his funeral will be on *your* hands."

My hand gripped the steering wheel. My eyes closed tightly for a brief moment. The sound of those words echoed through my mind over and over again loudly.

"Please, Latrell," I pleaded, opening my eyes to the dark street ahead of me. "Don't hurt my son."

"Shut the fuck up, Royce!"

I didn't respond. Everything inside of me wanted to curse his ass out. If he cared about *our* son at all, he would spare his life. I hated him but I held my tongue. I couldn't take the slightest chance on pissing him off. If I did, he'd possibly kill my baby.

"I'll be waitin'," he said. "You got thirty more minutes to get here."

The line went dead.

Sitting the phone on the passenger seat, my eyes began to shed tears, making the traffic ahead of me look fuzzy and blurred. Quickly, I ran the back of my wrist across my eyes to dry them. My heart was already aching terribly enough. Crying would only make me feel a million times worse. I had to keep my composure.

Ten minutes later, I turned down a side street immediately searching for Romello. With all my heart I was hoping he was there like he said he would be. I was hoping he hadn't let me down. He was my only hope at the moment. As my BMW passed car after car parked at the curb my heart raced. Finally I could see the tail end of Romello's black Phantom parked just up ahead.

"Thank God," I whispered in heavy relief.

Seeing the back of his head in the driver's seat I swerved behind him and parked alongside the curb. After shutting off the engine I opened the door and slid out of my seat into the night. Just as I was closing the door, my cell phone rang. Thinking it might be Latrell again I hopped back inside and answered.

"Hello?"

"Where the hell is you at?" Trae asked angrily.

There was both an air of relief and disappointment inside me at the sound of his voice.

"Trae, I'm busy," I told him as I climbed out of the car and shut the door.

"Too busy to answer the phone. Too busy for me after you ruined our relationship?"

I sighed with annoyance as I made my way from my car towards the Phantom. "No Trae, you ruined our relationship years ago before the whole taking your money thing happened. And what about the girl that's having your baby?"

"Mannnnn, fuck that, she lying!"

"Okay, well whatever, I can't talk right now!"

"I've been calling your ass for the last three hours," he said.

Without breaking stride I mumbled through gritted teeth, "Look, you don't understand what I'm going through right now. I just need a minute."

"Royce, to be honest, I don't give a damn about what you're going through. Where's my son?"

I opened the door of the Phantom and slid inside. Obviously I couldn't tell him that my baby had been kidnapped. "He's not here right now."

"Look, damn it!" he shouted ferociously. "Don't play games with me about my son. It's over between me and you, Royce. I want you and all your shit out of my house tonight. But I want my damn son. Do you hear me?"

Right now wasn't the time to argue.

Romello was staring at me from the driver's seat.

"I gotta go."

"I'm not playing with your ass, Royce. I want my…"

Click.

I pressed the end button.

"You alright?" Romello asked, looking at me worriedly.

"No." I breathed heavily. "This shit has got me going crazy."

"How much does this nigga want?"

"Fifty thousand," I said, knowing damn well it was only thirty that Latrell requested. The deceitful answer rolled off of my tongue with a straight face.

Lying had always come easy to me. Even a situation like this one couldn't hold me back from trying to get something extra for myself. Knowing it was wrong, I just couldn't help myself. I felt terrible about my actions but it is what it is. Maybe it was always feeling like I grew up with not enough. *Never enough*, I thought.

"Alright, I got you," he said, softly placing a hand on my thigh. "I told you I would bring the money."

The words eased my nerves but worry for my son was still heavy.

"I got that on me," he told me plainly.

"Yes," I said excitedly. "Thank you. Thank you so much."

"Here, stick this in your purse." He handed me five bundles of money. I assumed ten thousand in each stack.

He leaned in for a kiss. With all that was going on, I didn't care. His timing seemed perfect as we kissed passionately. His lips and tongue had never tasted better. As we released and I looked into his eyes a car slowly pulled alongside of us. It stopped directly beside the Phantom. Its tinted driver's side window slowly came down revealing a buffed man in the driver's seat.

I panicked. Oh Shit!

The man locked eyes with me.

I simply cringed in my seat.

Then he and Romello nodded to each other.

"Who is that?" I asked Romello frantically.

"My bodyguard, Moe," he answered as the car pulled in front of us and parked. "I felt it would be best if we had a little back up."

Company didn't make me feel totally at ease but it helped.

After telling Romello where the meeting spot was he started the ignition and pulled away from the curb. The body guard's car pulled away from the curb also and followed closely behind us.

The trip was completely silent. I really wasn't in the mood to speak. All I could do was stare out of the window thinking endlessly about my son and wished that I hadn't gotten him into this. Lord, if anything happens to him this evening, I'll never forgive myself, I thought over and over again.

The drive seemed like it was taking an eternity. The closer we got to the meeting spot, the further away it seemed. Finally we pulled into the parking lot of an abandoned factory. The sight of it made me nervous. I had arrived to get my baby but couldn't help being overwhelmed with dread. I had a bad feeling something would jump off. After all, this was the type of spot perfect for killing someone without witnesses around to see anything. Latrell had said he wanted to meet here instead of someplace crowded simply so he could see me coming from a distance. He didn't want to take a chance on being cornered by the cops. Shutting off the engine, Romello looked over at me and asked if I was alright.

Nodding, I said, "Yeah," although knowing it was a lie. In all actuality I was a nervous wreck. I just couldn't help believing something terrible was about to happen.

Seeing my uneasiness he spoke to me with confidence, "Don't worry. I'm going inside with you. I won't let anything happen to you or your son."

The two of us gave each other a gentle smile. I wanted to stick my tongue down his throat. I desperately wanted to feel him inside me.

We climbed out of the car.

Big Moe climbed out of his, too.

"Stay close behind us," Romello called out to him.

The three of us headed into the factory. Inside we were greeted by darkness and a heavy stench of mildew. Slight rays of moonlight burst through several broken windows, giving the large room only a slight illumination. Rats could be heard scurrying in its dark corners.

"Hold up right there," Latrell said from overhead in the distance.

We each did what he said and looked up to see him coming down a set of old stairs. In front of him was Lil Trae. Unsure, he looked to have a gun to his back. The sight broke my heart. Knowing that my baby was so close to something that could kill him was the scariest thing I'd ever seen in my life.

"Mommy!" my son screamed, happy to see me.

"Shut up, lil'nigga," Latrell ordered, grabbing a hold of his shoulder from behind.

Latrell walked towards us with suspicion written all over his face. His eyes glanced at Romello, who was standing beside me. They also glanced at Moe, who was directly behind us.

"Man, who the fuck are y'all niggas?" Latrell asked my company, while keeping a strong grip on Lil Trae's shoulder.

"Friends," Romello answered with no emotion from behind his dark shades.

Not liking the answer, Latrell looked at me. "What the fuck you bring them with you for? I told your ass no games."

"I'm not playing any games," I spat. "I'm not. I just didn't feel comfortable coming alone."

He squinted his eyes. "Bitch, don't let this be no damn set up."

"It's not. I swear it's not."

"You know what the fuck I told you over the phone."

"I know. That's why I'm here with your money. All I want to do is get my baby and go."

"Where's the money?"

I slid my purse from my shoulder and reached inside to get the cash.

"Slow, bitch!" he demanded.

My body tensed in surprise. My hand froze inside the purse.

"Do that shit slowly!"

"Alright," I agreed.

My hand gripped the money and began to pull it out.

Suddenly, my ears popped at the loud sound. It was the sound of gunfire. The surprising and sudden explosion from beside me made me scream. Before I even knew what it was, Latrell dropped to the floor. Immediately, I looked beside me to see Romello standing next to me with his gun drawn. My eyes darted back to Latrell as he lay on the floor flat on his back with his arms stretched out widely. With a gun in his hand he gasped for air. There were two holes in his chest as it heaved up and down repeatedly. Blood soaked his t-shirt causing me to gag. The scene was surreal.

My son dashed to me and wrapped his arms around me, screaming like crazy.

"We don't have time to waste," Romello ordered. "Get the boy out of here and take him some place safe," he instructed Moe.

Lil Trae looked up at me as Moe stepped towards us. "It's okay, baby," I assured him. "I'm right behind you. This man is here to help us."

He hugged me tighter than before, then did as he was told.

When he was out of sight, Romello walked over to Latrell's dying body, stood over it with the gun pointed.

Latrell was wide eyed and attempting to say something. His words couldn't be understood. Each one he tried to speak was met with choking and gasping sounds as blood and torn inner tissue clogged his wind pipes. The crimson liquid spewed from his mouth.

With no hesitation Romello squeezed the trigger again.

The loud exploding sounds of the gun echoed off the walls then faded.

Seeing Latrell lying in his own blood dead, had me frozen. I didn't know how to react; what to do or what to say. My eyes could only stare.

"We got to jet, Royce," Romello said, quickly turning and heading towards me.

I didn't hear him. The moment had me in shock.

"Royce!" he called out just before grabbing my hand.

I finally broke out of my trance and gazed into his eyes.

"We can't stay," he said. "We've got to go."

Moments later, we were back in the car. The factory was being placed farther and farther behind us but my mind wouldn't let go of what had just happened. I couldn't forget what I'd just seen. My body wouldn't stop shaking. My heart wouldn't stop pounding. I kept wiping away tears over and over again

I'd worked so hard to get to where I was in life. My career was at its peak. Now, here I was an accessory to murder. The thought was driving me crazy. I could lose everything.

"You alright, beautiful?" Romello asked as he drove.

I shook my head.

"What's wrong?"

I looked at him like he was a nut case. "What the hell do you mean, what's wrong? Romello, I didn't want him dead. I just wanted him out of my life. If the police find out about this, my career is over. My life is over. They'll lock my ass up forever."

"Relax, sweetheart. They'll never find out. No one saw anything."

"How do you know that?" I asked, unconvinced and partially angry. All my mind could picture was a life sentence in prison.

"Because I do," he said. "Don't worry about anything. I got this."

"Damn it. I can't believe you did that. The police are going to lock our asses up and throw away the key."

Immediately, I turned around to see if the cops were behind us. They weren't but visions of them surrounding us eventually wouldn't cease or fade.

The Phantom pulled out of traffic, and pulled into the parking lot of a dark elementary school. Romello pulled it behind the school and parked. He turned towards me. "Royce, baby, I need you to relax."

I leaned back in my seat and shook my head. "I can't relax. We left a dead body back there, Romello."

He softly grabbed my hand. "Look at me."

I couldn't.

"Royce." He squeezed my hand but only slightly.

My eyes slowly met his.

He looked at me tenderly. "Do you think I would ever let anything bad happen to you?"

Something about the way he looked at me calmed me.

"Do you?" he asked again.

"No," I answered slowly. Inside I knew he was only pro-
tecting me just as he had done with Tyesha and Tango.

"Then trust me when I say I got you."

My eyes fell to his thick, full lips.

"Alright?" he asked.

I nodded. The sight of his lips made something inside me
awaken, something between my legs come alive. Knowing that he
was down for me enough to kill a nigga had turned me on. Unable
to help myself, unable to even want to help myself, my upper body
quickly leaned over the center console. Our lips met so hard our
teeth nearly clanked together. My hands were all over his chest.
Moments later I was out of my seat and sharing the driver's seat
with him while ripping and tearing at his shirt. Our faces touched
one another as I sat on top of him squished between his body and
the steering wheel.

"Damn, Royce," he moaned as my lips began to plant
kisses all over his chest. He moaned even harder as they wrapped
around his nipple and sucked softly.

I loved the feel of his hands running through my hair. He
surprised me by grabbing a handful and jerking my head back to
gain control of the situation. He was now planting kisses all over
my neck.

"Oh, baby," I muttered.

He reached his hands underneath my shirt, lifted it, and
began to kiss my breasts. I took off my shirt and bra like a savage
to give him better access. He immediately began to devour my
breasts and nipples. I placed my hands on the back of his head,
forcing him to get every inch of my breasts, not wanting him to
come up for air.

The both of us grabbed and tore at each other for minutes.
The moment was intense. My body had never wanted anyone
more. I knew he felt the same. Moments later, my jeans were off
and I was back in position on top of him. Romello's pants were
down to his ankles and his ripped shirt was off. Within seconds I
was riding him like an energetic jockey. Our rhythm was wild and
crazy.

"Fuck me, baby!" I demanded as he pounded his hips upward into my gushing pussy. His strokes were so hard that the top of my head kept banging against the roof.

"Shit, girl," he said, loving the feel of sweet cave.

As I rode him the muscles in my pussy tightened like a vice grip around him. I didn't want him to come up out of it. My arms were also wrapped around his body just as tightly. I was holding on for dear life as he fucked me the way I needed to be.

A feeling arose inside of me. The feeling I'd been welcoming. The feeling my body needed. My moans grew louder and heavier. Finally my pussy came so hard all over his dick my body almost went limp. He showed no mercy though. He squeezed me tighter and pounded harder. Seconds later, I was releasing again. But even though my body was drained, his rhythm and stamina inspired me to keep going. I wanted to give him the same pleasure he'd given me. I began to grind on his dick like a savage, making him groan louder than before. I took over his dick and refused to give it back.

"Shiiiiiit," he grunted through gritted teeth. His body grew weak as an orgasm built.

I grinded even harder and faster. "Cum in this pussy, baby," I told him. "It's all yours."

Romello leaned back into the seat. His body tensed. As I worked him, I stared into his face, loving the expressions he was making. At that moment, he finally let loose inside of me. My body collapsed on top of him.

Romello wrapped his arms around me. I loved the way they felt. I felt safe and protected. We sat in each other's arms silently, our bodies recovering from what we'd just done to each other. Neither of us wanted to move or let the other go.

"Royce," Romello finally said.

"Yes," I answered.

"I've got something to tell you."

I raised my breasts from his chest and leaned backwards to see his face. What he'd just said made me nervous. Those words were never good. The two of us looked into each other's eyes.

"What's up?"

He paused for a moment.

Thinking the worst, I said, "Oh, shit, Romello, don't tell me you've got something."

"Nah. It's not like that."

"Then what is it?"

He sighed.

"What, baby?"

"Royce, I'm sorta married."

The news took me totally by surprise.

He looked at me intently and said, "Royce, I'm feeling you, so I hope this doesn't mean we can't chill together."

I still had a distraught deer look on my face. I was speechless.

"The news isn't to hurt you. I just feel you need to know everything about me before we move on."

I could only sit in his lap in silence. But I think I'd fallen in love with this dude.

Chapter 24

Royce

Two weeks later

Thank God my life had turned around. It all happened so quickly. There was no more worrying about Trae cheating on me or stressing about money. The world seemed to be at my fingertips and the best part of it all was that I'd survived Latrell's wrath. For once his death was completely out of my mind as the crowd chanted.

"More! More! More! More!"

"Thank you for coming out. I love you guys!" I shouted back to the crowd.

"Royce, Royce, Royce, Royce!" they cheered.

I blew out a few kisses then winked at Romello for approval to end my set. Once he nodded from the side of the stage, I dropped the mic with the greatest feeling ever that swiftly spread through my bones like fire. *They loved my performance*, I thought to myself; overjoyed with the feeling as I walked off the stage feeling giddy inside.

I headed to my dressing room with my head held high after being wanted and talked about by so many people throughout the night. Some just wanted to touch my hand, others wanted autographs, and some just nodded.

"You sounded damn good tonight," Marcus, one of the

group members from D7 said as I strutted by.

I beamed inside but kept walking thinking about how I'd come up out of nowhere. It was the moment I'd been waiting for all my life. I'd just opened up for D7 and had the #5 single on the radio for the week that was quickly climbing the charts toward #1. I had to pinch myself at how my life had gotten so much better in just weeks. Lil Trae and I had been staying at the Gramercy Park Hotel in Manhattan for the last two weeks, compliments of Romello. It had been a strain for me trying to keep my son away from phones, away from calling his father, and attempting to erase my visions of seeing Latrell die in front of me. But now none of that mattered.

I'd just gotten a standing ovation at the Z club, the hottest spot in Manhattan known for hosting celebrity events and star-studded performances. Tickets ran one to two hundred a pop and only the best got booked at the Z. That made me realize the buzz about me and my single were real.

"Yo, Royce, that last song was hot," someone from Romello's label shouted just as I opened the door to my dressing room.

"Thanks!" I replied then shut the door.

I expected my son to jump from the chair to hug me, congratulating me. After all there were over two hundred people out there still cheering for me. He didn't. Instead, Rachel put a bright smile on her face while Lil Trae kept playing his PSP like I didn't exist.

"Girl, you were fabulous," she commented then reached to wrap her arms around me. "They loved you out there."

"I know, I know, I know," I kept repeating, almost unable to believe it myself.

Lacey, my vocal coach knocked twice then entered the room carrying a cup of hot tea with honey and my cell phone in the other hand. "Here, drink this," she told me firmly, "not champagne."

After glancing over my shoulder I realized that Romello must've had those five bottles added to my rider, my list of demands for the evening. There were loads of fruit, Skittles and all the little things that made me happy in life. The only thing that could've made me feel any better was just a little eye contact from Lil Trae. He hadn't been himself since we'd been staying at the hotel. At first I thought the newness of my success would excite him, like the visits to the radio stations to promote my single or the numerous celebrities he'd met over the last week. Yet none of it moved him.

"So, tell me what's next?" Rachel asked interrupting my thoughts about my son.

I shrugged with a wide grin.

"C'mon girl, you must know. They've been playing your song on the radio like crazy!" She clapped her hands together tightly. "Can your good friend at least get a promo copy before the album drops so I can say I knew you before all of this?"

We both laughed then Lacey told me to stop talking and take a few sips. "That Trae guy was calling you back to back," she revealed as I kept drinking.

"I know. He won't stop calling," I explained to Rachel as Lacey left the room. "We'll discuss him another time when my son isn't around." I grinned like everything was under control then hit Rachel with a question. "Ahhhhh, now, I need to get some details from you, Rachel, Miss V.P."

She smiled modestly.

"You're talking about my success but you downplayed your new job lady. But I know all about it." I patted her back with a congratulatory hit." "Vice President of Player Personnel is huge!"

I reached to hug her realizing that she even looked like an executive. Her stance, the way she crossed her arms all said *I'm in charge.*

"It's not that serious, Royce. You're the super star."

"You make over six hundred thousand a year now. That's V.I.P status. I just got my advance yesterday and believe me I have a long way to go to get to your status."

"You'll get there. Trust me. Just keep singing."

"Listen, on another note, you feeling any better about the Chris and India situation?" I hated to bring that up but I needed to know since India told me she'd be at my show. I didn't know if she was out in the audience or not.

"Oh, I'm over it now. Her loss. And Chris', too," she said like she really meant it. It could've been her poker face that led me to believe her.

Unexpectedly, Romello entered with flowers and commenced to kissing me on both cheeks. He smelled good enough to eat and complimented me well in his all black attire and shades of course. We were the perfect couple.

"You know that performance just made you a star, right?' He kissed me again.

"You think they like me?" I asked like an excited little kid.

"You damn, right. Didn't you hear them cheering for you?"

I simply nodded followed by a wide grin. The feeling was unexplainable. Just to be on stage fulfilling my life-long fantasy and hearing my man and musical guide tell me I was great still seemed like a dream. All I needed for him to do was tell me what he would do with his wife. She obviously had to go if he was serious about me. He kept saying we'd talk about it later. Now was the perfect time if you asked me.

"Good to see you again, Rachel. I heard about your job offer," Romello said to her.

"Thanks, Romello. I appreciate that. And thanks for looking after my girl."

"You mean, my girl," he responded then pulled me close. "What's up, Lil Trae?"

We all turned to see that my son still had his head down and wouldn't even look up.

"Aye, I told you maybe we should let him go stay with his father."

"No," I snapped. "I want him with me. And I hope you still have security out there in case his father tries to come here to take him."

"I told you I got that covered. But just think about what I'm saying, that's all. We need your boy smiling again."

As bad as I didn't want to admit it, Romello made sense. He always did. I guess that's why I'd fallen hard for him. I thought about how the days I had the privilege to spend with him were spent heavenly. He had me on cloud nine. He worked a lot day in and day out, but he'd set aside Tuesdays and Wednesdays just for me. Those days we laid up sexing each other to death, eating, and enjoying each other's company. It amazed me how everywhere we traveled we were treated like celebrities, no lines, fast service, straight V.I.P treatment. New York City showed Romello lots of love and now that my single was on the air, I seemed to be getting the same. I wasn't sure where I would be without him and owed him my life.

I felt the need to show him some gratitude for everything he'd done. I jumped up, wrapping my arms around him tightly kissing him all over his face. "You're not leaving me tonight," I said with conviction in my voice. We have some things to settle."

"Royce, I wear the pants. You know this, right?" He grabbed me by the shoulders even though we were still attached.

"I like you with no pants," I told him seductively. I wanted him to put aside his tight work schedule and just chill with me.

"You keep talking like that, you gon' make me put everybody out this dressing room." He grinned then let me go.

"Just stay with me tonight, Romello. C'mon, pleaseeeee. Let's celebrate. We have all this champagne."

"I told you, I can't baby. It's Saturday," he said flatly. "You got Tuesdays and Wednesdays."

He kissed me once again this time on the lips then turned and walked out. I looked at Romello's backside feeling neglected, all the way until he left the room. I was ready to go after him telling him our relationship wasn't going to go like this when someone knocked on the door.

I quickly opened noticing Lacey again. This time she had a woman with her wearing a backstage pass. I glared into her eyes for seconds wondering if it was really her. We had the same nose, eyes, and mouth. I just kept staring, not even asking her to step inside the room. Then finally her voice spoke.

"Hello, Royce. I'm here."

"Ummmm, ummmm, well," I stuttered.

"I'm your mother."

Even though Ms. Campbell told me my mother had a

change of heart and wanted to meet me I never truly realized what the moment would be like. I'd called my mother and told her to come to my show and that I would leave a backstage pass for her. Somehow, now that the moment was here I wasn't sure if it was a good idea.

Immediately, Rachel grabbed Lil Trae by the arm and pulled him toward the door. "We'll give you guys about ten to fifteen minutes alone. We'll be back."

"I want my daddy," Lil Trae shouted.

"You'll see your father soon," Rachel responded pulling him closer to the door.

"Can you take me to him now?"

He sounded so pitiful but there was nothing I could do. His father wasn't getting him. Besides, I had the woman who gave me life standing before me. She was now priority.

I smiled at Rachel then mouthed a thank you to her. She knew how important this moment was for me. As soon as the door shut my body tensed up. It was such an awkward moment. The feeling was unexplainable. Seeing your mother for the first time at the age of twenty-six spoke volumes. I felt like all the missing pieces to my puzzle were found without even saying a word.

"So, I'm glad you tried to find me," she finally said. Her arms were crossed over her chest and she stood like she was afraid to move from her spot in the middle of the floor.

"Yeah, me, too. I've been researching for about two years now. Just finding out bits and pieces about you along the way. I guess the question is why you never attempted to find me."

My mother's mood changed instantly. "I knew that question would come. This is all too complicated, but I think we should take things slow. Maybe talk in a different setting. I just wanted to see your face," she added.

"The setting won't change the fact that all I really know about you is that you sold me at birth."

Tears welled up in her eyes. "I knew coming here was a bad idea."

She began shaking her head, hyperventilating. I had to remain strong. I kept telling myself not to get emotional, but I wanted her to know that her actions made me do some horrible things in life. "Did you know that I came up with this wild hair schemed idea of making a living off selling babies because that's what you did to me?" My voice became stronger and my anger showed.

My mother's hands were in the air. "Hey, I'm leaving," she told me. "Maybe we need a mediator. I didn't expect all of this."

"To mediate what? What did you expect?"

"I expected to come meet my daughter and have a civilized meeting."

"You ruined my life! And in return I ruined others. I got my man mixed up in that coldhearted business of selling babies for big money. It was my idea. He went to jail and is now dead. I'm incapable of loving someone for all the right reasons because I'm so accustomed to doing wrong. But it's you...all because of you."

My mother was in tears then a knock sounded at the door. She turned ready to leave but I wanted her to stay. I had an earful of stories and lost dreams to tell her about. I swung the door open to ask what the person knocking wanted when my worst nightmare stood at the door.

"We made it baby! You got my loot?" Tyesha asked me with a devious grin.

Chapter 25
India

The moment we stepped into the owner's suite my haters showed their true colors. There were about ten people prancing around, mostly white folk. Some whispered, some pointed, while others balled up their faces at me; especially the chick with the long, blonde hair dressed in the tight leopard jumpsuit that must've come from Forever 21.

Surely my blue, twelve hundred dollar Jason Wu sheath dress had both the women and the men slobbering from the mouth, so I understood why the nasty looks were shot my way. I looked good and so did my man. I'd gotten his old ass to dress a little more casual, not always suited up like he was about to sign his name on the dotted line.

I'd been in Miami for over two weeks trying to school him on how l liked things done. Time seemed to fly as we spent countless days shopping, dating, more shopping, making out, and more shopping. I loved showboating and flossing like I'd come from money; had access to it all my life. His house was fabulous similar to the homes I'd seen on T.V. which I now acted like I owned along with Gerald. The feeling was amazing to wake up to maids, butlers and incalculable people calling to make sure I was straight. As far as I was concerned, I didn't ever want to go back to New York.

The basketball game was in the second quarter and our

grand entrance had people talking about *my man* instead of what was going on down on the court. Some lady hung onto his every word as he chatted with a few people in a mini-circle. Even being out-dated, and old as hell, he was a superstar in his own right. The President and owner weren't around so we were the head honchos in charge as far as I was concerned. Gerald and I were just like Bonnie and Clyde.

I started snapping my fingers like I'd been doing all week at my new mansion. "Ah, excuse me guys." They got hit with my phony smile. "I just need to borrow my man," I told them breaking up their little party. "And can someone snag me a drink? Chop chop!" I snapped my fingers again.

"So, this is India?" one of the men in a suit said allowing his eyes to explore my breast.

"Yes, this is her. This is my baby," Gerald said, pulling me close.

"Wow, she's beautiful, Haskin. I see why you've been missing in action these past two weeks."

"Are you going to introduce us?" a woman who looked to be in her forties announced, walking up on us like she had a problem.

"Ahhhh, yes sweetie, I was getting to that." He kissed the chick on the cheek and rested his hand on the lower part of her back. Their bodies were close, way too close. I didn't want anybody trying to press up on my coins so I frowned. "Elise, this is India. India, Elise."

Aw shit, I thought to myself.

This was his oldest daughter that he'd been talking to and about way too much. Before my thoughts could even get right, another bitch walked up on us. It was the chick in the leopard jumpsuit who deserved the *Hoochie Mama of the Year* award.

"And this is Eliza."

What the fuck?

Eliza had about six piercings in her ear and one in her nose. I stared her down while she did me the same way. The question in her eyes asked why I was there with her father. Maybe it was because I was one of the few blacks in the suite and the cutest, of course. The few times he'd put me on the phone with her the conversation didn't go too well. She always seemed cold unable to find anything for us to talk about. Of course now seeing them both, her and her sister in person, I understood why.

Gerald left me standing in the middle of the room speechless. I had nothing to say to these rich, white women who had no class or sense of fashion. I wanted to follow him or at least grab a seat close to the glass so I could watch the game. Strangely, Gerald kept walking around nervously unable to contain himself. He patted his pockets then walked over to the counter where the food sat. I wanted him with me.

"Honey, come over here," I called out to him while snapping my fingers. Damn, the finger thing had become a habit. And the pitch of my voice had changed, too. I was now more Hollywood than I'd ever been in my life.

"No, I need you over here sweetheart," he ordered, becoming more and more antsy by the minute.

"What do you need, baby?" I asked, making sure everyone in the room heard me call him baby. I made my way over to him, swaying my hips royally along the way.

"This is a good night to ask you for your hand."

"For my hand?" What are you talking about?"

Before I knew it, Gerald had slowly gotten down on one knee and was now glaring up into my eyes. We were in the middle of the floor for all to see.

"For your hand in marriage. Will you marry me, India?"

My body instantly froze.

Joy erupted throughout my entire soul. It was the moment I had been waiting for since high school. A filthy rich husband to take care of me, love me, and spend every penny he made on me. It was happening. I couldn't believe it.

"No, he didn't," I heard his oldest drag queen looking daughter say from behind.

The other one remained silent but held a sour face for minutes. It was clear that neither of them liked me. But the feeling was mutual. The moment I officially moved into his house the phone number would be changed. The locks, too.

"She just wants his money," I heard one of them say.

"Bitch," I mumbled to myself then turned to my knight and shining armor. This was obviously the man the Good Lord wanted me to have. "Yes, yes, yes, I'll marry you."

Gerald pulled out a platinum ring that looked to be all of ten carats, a rock that looked like it came straight from the mines of South Africa. The DeBeers' mines were the ones I'd read about in my *Millionaire's Magazine*. He slipped it on my finger letting me know this moment was real. I knew I was now envied by all that watched. I wanted those muthufuckas to eat their hearts out.

I gripped Gerald's wrinkled body as soon as he stood up. We hugged like real lovers and maintained our tight embrace for several minutes. I wanted everyone in the suite to gloat. This should've been posted on the big screen for the entire arena to see. I would be Mrs. India Haskins in little or no time telling all these clowns what to do and how to do it. I would even rule Gerald's secretary. Things would be changing for the better soon.

"I love you, India," he whispered in my ear.

"Me too, baby. I'm so excited!"

I kissed him lovingly, dismissing the smell of Bengay and mothballs from my mind. Those scents were now replaced with the smell of money and fame.

"India, I need to hear you say it. Do you love me?" he asked me calmly and with the most serious expression I'd seen from him since I had known him.

"Of course I do, Gerald." I kissed him again. "Of course," I repeated dismissing any second thoughts he was having. "I need to call my family and friends," I exclaimed, throwing my hands in the air so all eyes could remain glued to my ring.

"Someone hand me my phone." My fingers snapped quickly.

No one moved so I rushed to grab it myself. With my cell in hand, I attempted to make everyone jealous. I punched the digits into the phone fast, waiting for my mother to answer while everyone else began to mingle and talk louder than before.

"Hey Ma!" I shouted the minute she answered. "I have

such great news."

"I'm sure," she responded blandly.

I refused to get smart with her since she'd been home from the hospital for only a week. The doctors said she needed lots of recovery time with no stress. "I told you I would be married soon. I got engaged to a man who loves me, Ma. He really does."

Her words weren't too encouraging and before I could get out more words she told me she'd have to call me back. I hung up feeling like my own mother had to be added to my list of haters. My next call was to Royce. The call to her was to simply shit on her success. She thought she was doing big shit back in New York, becoming a singer. I had heard her single on the radio but wasn't impressed at all.

Who cares? I thought to myself. It reminded me of one of those corny cruise ship performances anyways.

"Hey Royce, what's up girl?" I sang into the phone as soon as she answered. "I heard your song on the radio. You are doing big things girl."

I listened to her ramble on about how good things were going for her and how she and Romello were now a couple. So I hit her with my news. "Girl, I'm getting married!" I started doing the fast, victory dance the football players do on the field showing my excitement.

"That's so wonderful, India. Quick, but wonderful," she commented.

The bitch was just jealous. I added fuel to the fire. "I did tell you he's the V.P of the Heat, right?"

"Yes, you told me, India. I know," she said real snobbish-like. "You know Rachel is a V.P now too, right? The Giants…"

"Anyway, gotta run girl. Will let you know when the wedding is. It'll be soon. TTYL," I ended with a devious look on my face.

There was no way in hell I would let Rachel's promotion upstage me. I was the most important person in our group and I would show them all. I didn't want to wait another minute to be Mrs. India Haskin. "Gerald," I called over to my fiancé who was chatting it up with another executive in the corner near the bathroom.

He walked over fast. "Yeah. What's up, beautiful?"

I wrapped my arms around his neck and slobbed him down. It was the wettest sexiest kiss he'd gotten from me since knowing me. "Honey, let's go to the Justice of the Peace tomorrow. I don't want to wait to be your wife another day. I love you."

"Tomorrow? That's soon."

"I now, but I love you."

Suddenly, I noticed a buildup of rage brewing in his youngest daughter's eyes. She pounced over to me ready to say a few harsh words obviously.

"Can I ask you a question?"

"Ah, yeah. Shoot."

"What do you want with my father besides his money? He's old enough to be your father."

I pointed in her face. "Your father and I love each other. And age doesn't matter when love is involved."

"Get real, lady. He's almost fifty years older than you."

"I'm timeless, bitch! We're getting married tomorrow whether you like it or not."

Gerald remained quiet but his friend interrupted. "That won't work," he said with a crinkled brow. "You need time to have the prenup drawn up."

"Prenup?" I could barely say the word.

"Yes, prenuptial agreement," the guy said to me as if that was standard in their world.

Within seconds I began sweating, feeling faint. There was no way in hell I would sign a prenup. His money would be my money. All of it.

"There's no prenup, right honey?"

I watched my fiancé crawl in a shell ignoring us all when a woman walked in trying to get his attention. After hearing someone call her Mrs. Haskin, I became ill. "I gotta throw up," I told Gerald then rushed off to the bathroom.

Chapter 26

Royce

I sat on my plush couch that had just been delivered thinking about how great things had turned out for me, mostly good. My publicist had just left telling me about all the interviews and performances I had lined up for the rest of the month. The ink was already dry on the Essence magazine interview. My album dropped just yesterday and the listeners loved me. I'd decided to turn my radio on so I could hear myself once again, when I heard a knock at the door.

"Ugh," I sighed. Since it was Tuesday morning, I knew it was Romello. That had been his pattern to show up on Tuesdays and chill with me for two days straight then bounce. Maybe it was selfish but I wanted more. Today was the day I would tell him and it didn't matter that he'd gotten me a fancy apartment in Manhattan. That was material. I needed him to love me seven days in a row.

I unlocked the door, pulled on the knob, then walked away as I began my 'I'm pissed off' performance. When I didn't hear Romello's voice I turned to look over my shoulder. My heart raced at the sight. Why was he here? How did he find me? Trae stood in my doorway with his fist clinched, down to his sides.

"What the hell are you doing here?" I shouted, rushing back toward the front door. My intent was to shove him out into the hallway and lock my door. Sadly, Trae was already inside and his body stiff as a board when I pushed at him.

"I came for my son!"

"Fuck you, Trae," I barked. "I told you we don't want anything else to do with you."

His voice warned me that he was in a harsh state of rage. "Why did my son call me then? And for the record, I'm not here for you."

My nose flared at the thought. I had forbidden Lil Trae from calling him but I knew how much he missed his father so maybe he'd really snuck and called him. "Look Trae, even if he did call you, it doesn't matter. That's my son and I want him with me."

"He's my son too, Royce. And guess what?" he uttered taking a few steps closer to me. "He wants to be with me."

"Doesn't matter what you say!" I shouted. "He's staying with me. Now get out!"

"Don't go, Daddy," my son's voice cried out. "I wanna go with you. Please don't leave."

The sound seemed so pitiful it broke my heart. It hurt me to the core though. Lil Trae peeped from behind the hall closet door. I wasn't sure how long he'd been standing there or how much he heard but the sadness in his face was clear. "C'mere, baby." I spread my arms widely so he could come to me. Even from a distance the water that welled up in his eyes was clear.

My insides seemed to be jumping around as he walked toward us. I prayed he would come to me and not Trae. I had to prove that I was what he wanted more than anything. When I felt his embrace I immediately began to cry. His little arms hugged me so tightly reminding me that I'd given him life, not Trae. The thought made me realize it was probably a good time to tell Trae that he was not the father.

"Mommy," Lil Trae whispered into my ear with his sweet sounding voice, "Please let me go stay with Daddy. I love you Mommy but I can't sleep anymore. I just wanna live with Daddy so I can sleep."

My heart skipped several beats. My head lowered with guilt. How could he feel that way? How could he want to be with him and not me? Tears flowed more and more as we continued our embrace.

My son pulled back slightly to look me in the eye. "Please don't be mad at Daddy. I called him. I asked him to come. Maybe you can come live with us, too?"

He turned to look at the man he thought was his father, pleading and begging with his eyes to allow me to live with them. The scene was so awkward even though I knew the relationship was completely over. I didn't want Trae anymore and he didn't want me either. A part of me wanted to tell the truth about Latrell being his father but I couldn't, my heart wouldn't allow it. My son loved Trae and that's who he thought was his father. How could I hurt him like that?

"Listen Trae," I said standing. "I'm sorry about all that's happened between us. I just can't understand why I'm the one feeling guilty about all this shit." I placed both hands at the sides of my head massaging my temples aggressively. I felt as if my head was about to explode. "It was you, Trae who ruined our family and now my son can only be with one of us."

"Royce, cut the performance. Get his stuff."

"Mommy, please get my stuff," Lil Trae said latching onto my jeans. "We gotta go."

"No, you hear me out, Trae. It was you who never truly treated me the way I needed to be treated. You never had time for me, at all. It was always about other women, traveling, and whatever made you feel good." I paused to give him the most sincere look I could. "You were never really there for me when I needed you. Never."

"Relationships and loyalty go both ways," he shot back. "Did you forget you stole from me?"

"I stole from you to pay a man who was extorting me. A man who is Lil Trae's…"

"Save it Royce. Not interested," he belted.

"Bye, Mommy," Lil Trae said abruptly, running into Trae's arms.

After taking a few steps in their direction, I froze at the sight of my son's eyes. He clearly didn't want to be with me. Fear that I'd remove him from Trae's arms filled his eyes. I loved him too much to keep the war going on. It would only hurt him in the future.

"Give mommy a hug?" I said with tears streaming. I walked right up on him just close enough for him to lean down from Trae's arms to hug me slightly. "You call me, okay?" I ordered with a fake smile.

"I will, Mommy. Don't cry. Right, Daddy? Tell her not to cry," he said to Trae.

Within seconds, Trae shot me a dirty look and turned to leave my apartment. He didn't even ask me to get his clothes or games. Nothing. When the door slammed, I fell apart. There was nothing that had ever caused me so much hurt and sorrow. My child had been my life ever since I gave birth. The fact that I'd gained so much success in the eyes of people who knew me but couldn't get my own blood to want to be with me sent me hurling onto the couch and burying my head into the pillow.

When my phone rang, I hopped up thinking maybe Lil Trae had a change of heart. I jetted across the living room into the kitchen snatching the phone up as quickly as possible. "Yeah. Hello, hello."

"Royce, hi."

"Yeah."

"Royce?"

The voice wasn't the one I wanted to hear at the moment. "Yeah," I repeated.

"It's your mother."

"I know," I said blandly.

"Look, it doesn't sound like you're in a good mood. I was just calling to see if I could take you to lunch next week? Last night didn't go too well, so I wanted to give us another shot."

Suddenly, the doorbell rang. This time I was certain Lil Trae had a change of heart. I spoke rapidly. "Okay. Sound's good. Give me a call tomorrow. We can set the time and place," I said, hanging up without giving her a chance to say anything else.

I rushed to the door like an aggressive sprinter in a track meet. It slung open and my eyes did the whole big as paper plate thingy once again. Too many surprises in one day would give me a heart attack soon. The man stood before me with his badge showing. Why would the FBI be at my door, I wondered? Anxiety ripped through my veins.

"Yes, can I help you?" I asked with my right hand still attached to the door, ready to slam it shut at any moment. All I could think about was Latrell lying in a pool a blood and now I was going to jail for it.

"Royce Pratt?"

"That's me. What's wrong? Why are you here?" My words were fast and precise.

"I'm Agent Miles, can I come in?" he asked, already stepping foot inside.

I shut the door and turned to see him looking around, scruffy hair and all.

"What's this about?"

"Can we sit down?" His hand gestured toward my new couch. He never waited for an answer, he just plopped down quickly then flipped open a small notepad.

"I'll stand. What's this about?" I repeated nervously with my arms intertwined across my chest.

"This is about a crime committed. You know anything about the illegal sale of babies."

My head shook back and forth violently. My entire soul shook at the thought of being busted after all this time. "No, I don't. Whose baby? And why would I do something like that?"

The agent snickered. He simply stared me down then laughed at me again. After jotting a few things down he glanced my way again making me feel all too nervous. "So, are you sure you don't know anything about any babies being sold? You don't know Marcia Edmonds, Constance Lyons, or Angel Hymes?"

All those names I knew but I wouldn't dare admit to it. Those were people that my connections back in Atlanta had turned me onto. Those were people that I had Latrell meet to make the transactions work smoothly. I had been the organizer of it all and now my own son had just been taken away from me. "No, never heard of them."

Agent Miles laughed again. "You're going to prison young lady if you don't start telling me the truth. They don't call us the F.B.I for nothing." He stopped to hit me with a nasty smirk. "You think we don't know what you and your husband Latrell were into and might still be into?"

"Look, I know my husband is crooked," I confessed. "He was into a lot of illegal dealings but that's why I left him. I did nothing and you have nothing on me." I switched my stance and tried to appear more at ease. I was smart enough to know that if he really had any evidence on me he wouldn't want to talk, he'd have me in handcuffs by now.

"Mrs. Pratt, I know from your bank account history that large sums of money were put into your account. All that's being traced now."

The hairs on my arms stood up. Oh shit, I thought. Yet, I had to remain calm.

"And I also know that Latrell has been named by several people in this nationwide investigation. I'm sure with you being a big star and all now, someone will recognize you, too." He smiled broadly. "You'll be international soon."

"I think you should leave."

He stood up quickly.

"I will, but just know that someone gave you up. I just need the evidence to make all this work against you. It will work, Mrs. Pratt. And you will go to prison. But I'll tell you what," he announced as he made it to my door.

He turned to look at me showing his sincere desire to take me down. "What? What is it?" I asked impatiently.

I want the entire team of people. The people at the top. I'm looking for your husband now. But if you'll give me some other people who were involved or still dipping into things now, I'll lessen your time."

"I don't know anyone," I said quickly, opening the door for him to leave.

"Here's my card." He grinned. "I'll be nearby at all times. Interviews, shows, radio appearances. You name it, I'm there. Give me somebody," he added as he stepped into the hallway. "Enjoy your trip to Miami."

Damn, how'd he know that? I just booked that flight. I slammed the door as hard as I could and burst into tears. My emotions had exploded like a timed bomb. By the time I made it across the room to grab my phone my face was soaked. I dialed his digits all too fast. Of course his answering machine came on.

"Romello, where are you? Call me, as soon as you can. I need you."

Chapter 27

India

After weeks of arguing back and forth, I'd finally won. Gerald and I decided to have a luxurious backyard wedding at our home, our mansion in Miami. It felt good to be in a strapless, mermaid shaped Vera Wang gown, smiling from ear to ear, being treated like the Queen of Sheba. Of course, there were four assistants on call answering to my every snap along with a celebrity make-up artist and hair stylist, all on the payroll. We were crowded into my over-sized bedroom, with them gawking over me and me glaring out of the window at an unexpected guest.

The total spent so far on the wedding was in the hundreds of thousands, but that was without getting the final miscellaneous invoices. My event designer had truly outdone herself. From a champagne bar, towering table centerpieces that featured fresh flowers flown in from Ecuador, an eight-tiered wedding cake made by the one and only Sylvia Weinstock out of NYC to a Moroccan themed tent filled with opulent silk pillows just for our guests to relax during the reception. You name it, we had it. I wanted it to be the most talked about wedding of 2012. I wanted it to be featured on MTV's *Most Lavish Weddings of the Year*. It had to be. It was all in my destiny. It was what I had waited for my whole life. That shine.

"You're a beautiful bride," Royce announced, handing me a

blue butterfly broach that I planned to pin on my garter. "And stop looking out the window," she added. "Everyone is here."

"Thanks," I responded real snobby like. I snapped my fingers for one of my assistants to grab the other items Royce had in her other hand.

"Gerald looked really nice, too," she complimented. "I saw him when I first walked in."

"Wow, he's still here," my mother announced from the loveseat across the room. She'd been sitting quietly for the last hour never saying too many words at one time. "If he knew what I knew, he would escape while he still had the chance."

Royce snickered then whispered in my ear. "Don't worry. This is your day. Don't let anything bother you."

It was good advice but my emotions were split on Royce. A part of me was glad that she showed up since there weren't many people on the guest list from my family and friends. Certainly, most were jealous and never RSVP'd. I'd purposely excluded Tyesha, my former roommate after she tried to extort money out of me once she knew Gerald was a constant in my life. I wasn't having nothing like that in my camp. We were royalty now.

Fortunately for Royce, she made the cut. She'd declined being a bridesmaid even though she was the only one I asked to do the honor. She said she had to jet off right after the nuptials to make it back to New York to take care of some trouble she'd gotten into and for another show tomorrow.

How rude? I thought. She really did think she was on some V.I.P status nowadays. And I prayed her trouble was with Agent Miles.

"I'm still not clear on why you're doing this?" my mother said loudly interrupting my thoughts. "I mean, you know you don't love this man, India. So why? Please tell me why?"

I wanted her to shut her trap! Immediately. Maybe she was depressed since it had cost her lots of money to get here. I guess her health still wasn't that great either. I thought about hiring her to cure her money problems, but she'd have to show me and my new hubby some respect first.

"Respect the institution of marriage, mother," I belted.

"Uh. That's funny," she shot back. "You've never respected anything or anyone your whole life. But God has a way of fixing it all."

If she kept coming out the mouth wrong, I'd have security to escort her ass off the property; mother or not. I had planned on running a tight ship like a militia in my home, everything precise and on point. It would have to be that way since I would now be the wife of an NBA executive.

There was a knock at the door. We all turned with one of my workers asking, "Who is it?"

When the person replied, "It's me," chill bumps spread up and down my arms.

I placed a hand across my chest. Gerald should've known better. Seeing the bride before the wedding was forbidden. It was bad luck and not going to happen. "You can't see me yet, honey!"

"They're ready to begin!" he yelled from the other side of the door.

I smiled at the thought of my man wanting to see me before I walked out to take his hand in marriage. Things had been shaky over the last week after finding out that his ex-wife, Carmen who I'd met at the basketball game, was trying to persuade him not to marry me. I remembered almost slitting my wrist when I first heard someone call her Mrs. Haskin during the game. That tramp was no longer a Haskin as far as I was concerned and neither were her despicable daughters. I laughed at the remembrance of me not letting them into the house the other day. They banged and banged until their grimy hands could bang no more. I thought it was hilariously funny, but from what Gerald told me they didn't.

Suddenly, we could hear someone talking to Gerald, ushering him back downstairs. People had gotten antsy, and the music had begun. It was show time, obviously. Before I knew it, a tall, white guy had entered the room and escorted my mother out. No sooner than she walked out, my uncle, my mother's brother appeared at the doorway with a salt and peppered beard and a crisp white tux. I hadn't seen him in fifteen years, but he was the only person I hadn't pissed off who could give me away.

Quickly, he ushered me down the stairs where we were told

to wait in the foyer until it was time for the grand entrance. I couldn't see much through the oversized palatial windows that separated where I stood from the back yard, but I could see the minister take his place and the backside of all the guests in attendance.

A small part of me was nervous thinking about how my life was about to change. Gerald was a protector, a good man, one who would do his best to make me happy. He'd already gotten the FBI off my back, stopping all calls from Agent Miles and he'd wiped my slate clean of all my bills. Nothing could have been better. Nothing could make me happier than this very moment. It was a game changer for me.

"Wow, you look gorgeous," a voice said.

Where was security when I needed them? No one was supposed to be in the foyer of the house but me. I breathed a heavy sigh and thanked Rachel, hoping my cue to begin walking would come soon.

"Thanks for coming," I finally said to her. I did a double take after noticing Chris' fine ass standing slightly to her left.

"Thanks for the invite," she replied with a bright smile.

Rachel crossed her arms and stared at me for seconds then she smiled again. I wasn't certain if it was sincere or not.

"India, I just want to apologize for all that drama over Chris. You were right, his loyalty was to me, not your responsibility. As you can see, I've forgiven him and we're together now." She reached out and grabbed Chris' arm pulling him close. "I'm glad you and I were able to talk and mend things."

I tried to ignore her as I watched the pale looking flower girl start down the aisle. My nerves had gotten the best of me. And seeing Chris with her made me nauseous. "No problem, Rachel," I said nonchalantly. "I'm glad you came."

She kept staring like she had more to say. It was way too weird.

"The sex is good so I know why you did it," she finally said then kissed Chris on the cheek, grabbing his butt cheeks.

That was her way of trying to shit on me. Flaunting Chris at my damn wedding and now talking about their sex life. Oh hell, no! I was too embarrassed to admit that Gerald and I hadn't had sex yet so I didn't have a comeback ready. We'd gotten naked on one occasion and he attempted to put it in, I just don't think Gerald ever actually penetrated me. But I was fine with that. I'd find me a gardener or swimming pool attendant to put my fire out later. It was all about securing my place as a Haskin for now.

"I'm just happy you found someone," Rachel added.

She just wouldn't stop.

"Thanks." I hit her with the most plastic grin I could muster. "It's not too late for you, Rachel," I said with pity in my voice. "There's someone for everyone, so after Chris cheats on you again there'll be someone else; even for you, darkie."

I could tell her veins were about to pop from her head. I just wanted the bitch to know she didn't have nothing on me. Just who in the hell did she think she was?

She showed up to my wedding in a rented Maybach hoping someone would notice. I'd seen her from my window earlier, but prayed she didn't flaunt her success to everyone else. Hell, I was the only superstar today and for the rest of the year as far as I was concerned. With that said the 'Here Comes the Bride' music began and I started my march down the aisle with all my haters drooling.

"Oh, she looks lovely," I heard someone say.

It made me sway my hips even more and strut as if I were royalty. I felt just like Kate Middleton.

"She looks young enough to be his daughter," another commented followed by a smirk.

"Oh my, she's black," another said.

The diameter of my smile never changed even though my insides burned at the comment. My focus remained straight ahead watching Gerald standing at the altar in his white tuxedo with a wide grin upon his face. My uncle guided me to the spot we'd practiced right in front of the minister and to Gerald's left. As soon as the services began I let his words fade out in the background of my selfish thoughts. I wondered if Gerald would object to having kids with me. We could do artificial insemination or I could simply work on a donor on my own. The more children I had, the more I could have Gerald stuck mentally and financially.

Time passed quickly and the boring words of the ceremony

had me wanting to yawn until I heard Gerald say, "I do."

It was all happening so fast and I hadn't heard a word of what had been said. Before I knew it, my turn was up. It seemed as if the entire crowds' eyes were glued to my lips.

"India, do you take this man to be your lawfully wedded husband, to have and to hold..."

"I do," I said quickly.

After just three more minutes of torture, the minister had finally finished all the words and the rings had been exchanged. The best part followed in a dash. The words, "You may kiss the bride," were spoken.

I wanted to make it quick so I pressed my lips against Gerald's like a speeding bullet and pulled myself back a little with a heavy sigh. Damn, I had finally become a married woman. A woman of worth. And married someone with status. We turned to face the crowd hand in hand with me grinning from ear to ear. Even though Gerald maintained his smile his hand perspired along with several jerks.

I rushed him down the aisle as people clapped, smiled, and made their way out into the aisles. When we reached the back of the yard we stopped to take a picture for one of Gerald's co-workers. I loved the feeling of it all but my husband didn't.

"I can't stay out here honey. I'm hot...don't feel too well," he told me.

"You'll be fine, baby. This is the moment we've been waiting for. They all want to shake our hands," I added with excitement.

"You- you- don't- don't..." he stuttered.

I clutched his hand tighter refusing to let him leave me standing alone. Everyone had gotten up out of their seats. "Chello, chello, chello, everyone," I spoke.

The attention felt great. It made me think about all the parties I would host and all the charities I would head. I just didn't understand why Gerald didn't feel the same way. Before long he rushed away from me and attempted to walk toward the glass doors to enter the house. I had no idea what was wrong, but knew nothing was right about what I saw. He had his hand held tightly across his chest, moving slower and slower by the second. His moves were robotic and his face had lost most of its color.

"Baby, what's wrong?" I shouted running toward him.

"My chest!" He could barely make out the words. "It's tight. So tight," he complained.

"Oh God!" I cried out. "Sit down honey!"

"He needs water!" someone yelled.

"He doesn't need water, he needs me," I hissed. By the time I reached the doorway, Gerald fell to the ground, still clutching at his chest. The scene was like something out of a movie with the crowd rushing to form a circle around us. "Somebody help him, please!"

I remained hovered over Gerald's body contemplating doing CPR, something I didn't want to do. Besides that fact that his breath had been smelling old again over the past week, I began thinking about my relationship with Gerald wondering how long our matrimonial thing would last. Would I be better off with or without him I wondered? I would now be his sole beneficiary by law and all his money would belong to me if he died. Then again, I didn't want to wish death on him, it was my wedding day.

"Somebody do CPR," an older woman announced looking like she couldn't kneel down to the floor if her life depended on it.

I remained on my knees but leaned backwards in a state of shock. My husband was on the floor in dire need of help. His stomach had completely stopped moving and no breaths were heard. "I don't know CPR," I said slowly.

Before I knew it his youngest daughter burst through the crowd and pushed me out of the way knocking me onto my side. Mercilessly, she blew her breath into her father's mouth and did stupid looking chest compressions in between. I wasn't sure why she thought she was the savior of the day. I was the bride, the one people came to see.

Pump after pump, nothing that Eliza did worked. Gerald remained frozen, out of breath. No color at all. Suddenly, I became distraught, watching the scene unfold. My breaths quickened, followed by loud shouts and outburst. I couldn't control myself.

"Oh my God! Please, please, no! Save my husband!"

Several more minutes went by with people panicking, some crying and then the sirens sounded. The ambulance was near, but the results were clear.

"You fucking killed my father!" his daughter cried out.

I got up off the ground in a daze, snot oozing from my nose, wondering how this could happen to me. It wasn't long before the paramedics rushed inside and moved everyone away. Royce rushed over to me helping me walk over to a nearby chair. Tears streamed from my face at the mere thought of Gerald really being dead.

Soon the confirmation came. "Mrs. Haskin, your husband has died from cardiac arrest."

I'd finally had my chance at getting married and now my new husband was dead? "What kind of shit was this? *Fuck love*, I told myself. I was tired of trying. Maybe my life needed to end, too.

Chapter 28

Royce

I was already seated at the table when Tyesha arrived. She walked toward me, pimping just in time to see a fan in high spirits after I'd signed her napkin. The star-studded attention that had been given to me since I sat down made me feel superior inside. I had no idea that many people recognized me behind my five hundred dollar shades. My hands were covered with expensive looking gloves even though the temperature had hit nearly fifty degrees, but it was all a part of my needed costume for the day. When Tyesha approached the table, I stood and welcomed her warmly with a hug. She seemed shocked.

"It's about time you know how to treat *real* friends," she blasted then sat down grabbing a piece of cornbread out of the basket.

"You hungry?" I asked sarcastically.

"Yep. But I'd rather hear the details of what we discussed on the phone yesterday." She rubbed her hands together swiftly. "You know I love the taste of money, baby. Talk to me. Talk to me," she rattled on.

Little did she know, I'd made a deal with Agent Miles just two days ago to bring him someone big in Latrell's organization. I hated to give in but it was my only choice. With Latrell being dead he'd have no one to contradict my story. It was my word against the F.B.I. If they didn't have any proof on me, how could they arrest me for anything? My best bet was to give them Tyesha, fulfilling my part of the bargain that I'd agreed to. All that had to be done on my end was to give Agent Miles the time and location that the transaction was to take place. I had to make it good. He needed the person responsible for selling babies illegally caught in the action. I did, too. It would be my own personal retaliation against Tyesha for all the wrong she'd done to me.

"C'mon, give up the details," Tyesha asked leaning toward me.

"It's simple. You'll meet the woman at Bryant Park, tomorrow at five."

"Got it."

"And be on time."

The little money hungry bitch rubbed her hands together again briskly damn near rubbing the skin from her palms. I cringed at the thought of using up mostly all of my advance money to get myself off the hook. It didn't really matter though, I had lots of money coming my way soon.

"Then what? What do I do next?"

"You give her the thirty grand. Take the baby and call this guy here immediately."

I handed her the card. It was a card that didn't have my prints or my handwriting on it. It did have a number to a guy that Latrell use to deal with. He wouldn't know me at all, even though the plan was for Agent Miles to intercept before she ever got a chance to make the call. All ends were covered. I had to think like a pro. Tyesha didn't respond right away. Her mind seemed to do tricks while she stared off into space looking like a zombie.

Pulling the yellow envelope from my red Hermes Burkin bag, compliments of Romello, I slid it across the table.

"It's all there," I told her with confidence. "Thirty is for you to give to the woman and the other thirty is for you to keep."

"Damn, that's hot. Never knew you had it in you, baby."

"If you only knew," I commented.

"I see you, Butterfly."

Once again those words confirmed that what I was doing

was so right.

Tyesha seemed excited and understood how to make it all work. My only fear was that she'd cut out with all the money and never meet Niecy, so I added a little insurance to the game. "And look, when you're done with this, there's another lady in Jersey, who's giving up her child. Her name is Shelby. You'll make fifty off that sale."

Her expression changed at the thought. "Hell yeah! Way to work!" she finally belted. "So what's this lady's name?"

I thought about the words she'd told to India and decided to use them against her. "C'mon now. I can't tell you that. Let's just call her the woman with the baby."

All of her common sence must've flown out the door. Maybe it was just the thought of being involved in something illegal that soothed her soul. She loved the idea of it all. Tyesha never questioned me again about the woman's name. In all actuality it was my old roommate, Niecy. She was an easy person to pull into the mix considering she hated being a mother and was dead broke. When I mentioned the concept of giving up her child to another family for cash, Niecy grasped on all too easy. Shameful, were my only thoughts.

However it all played out, I hoped Niecy's baby would go to a family who really loved her and not back into her non-maternal arms. As for Tyesha, I knew where she'd end up. I grinned when Tyesha said she understood the whole deal. She was ready to put in work as she called it.

We both got up ready to leave with me feeling like my revenge was close enough for me to touch. "I gotta stop by the restroom. Call me tomorrow when it's all done."

A part of me felt uneasy about the whole idea of meeting her in public and wanted to play things safe. If there was an FBI car out front watching my moves or anything like that I didn't want Tyesha in the photos when I walked out.

"No doubt. I'll do that." She paused. "Aye, you talk to that tramp, India?"

"Not in a few days."

"The bitch flaking on me since she about to be a millionaire."

"Give her a break. She just lost her husband," I said softly.

"Yeah okay. The bitch owe me money though. Time is money, baby. I'll wait a couple of weeks and that's it."

Armed with cash in her hand, Tyesha jetted from the table with her usual smug strut without caring where I went or what I had going on in the restroom. "I'll wait for your call tomorrow for the meet up spot, a'ight?"

She doubled back, grabbed hold of my hand then attempted to do some thuggish handshake. I pulled back, let my eyes roll up into my head and walked toward the restroom area, waving her off. I waltzed inside, fixed my hair, then let another two minutes pass before I was out and ready to leave. Unfortunately for me, a horrible sight flashed before my eyes. Each step he took sent me further into a frenzy. His swagger, his smile and everything else about him confirmed that it was him. It was Romello, dressed in his best attire walking behind the hostess with confidence, but with a chick on his arm.

At first glance, I tried to make myself believe it was just a business associate. The woman had a beautiful face, looked to be in her mid-thirties and wore a purple headdress covering her head and neck area. Although gorgeous, she wasn't Romello's type at all. The moment she sat down, Romello pushed her chair up slightly and blessed her with an affectionate kiss letting me know my wishful thinking was dead wrong.

That did it for me. I turned with fury in my steps and walked toward them with the steam of a bull. How dare he? I was tired of men treating me any kind of way. Romello was about to get told, and his chick slapped.

"My, my, my. What a surprise," I said, standing above them both.

Luckily, Romello had pulled his usual strings allowing them to be seated in a partially private area and couldn't be heard by most.

"I've been calling you, but I see why you couldn't answer!"

Romello lowered his head. He then mouthed to the woman, "I told you it would happen this way."

Oh, so she knew about me obviously, but I had no clue about her.

"Who is she, Romello?" I asked, realizing she had on a loose pair of jeans and a basic sweater from the 80's. The two of them didn't mesh at all.

"Royce, sit down?" he begged with both his eyes and mouth.

"No, I'm fine standing." I crossed my arms and developed my kick ass stance even though my gut told me not to do a repeat of the lobby scene with Trae and his girl. I was on another level now, known by lots of people in the city and wouldn't dare stoop to that level again. "Who is she?" I repeated.

"This is Trinity. My second wife."

What in the hell did he just say? My anger subsided a little. Maybe this was all some sort of joke since the female was smiling at me like she liked me or something. "What did you just say?"

"Look, Royce, let's walk outside so we can talk." He stood then grabbed at my elbow, but I quickly yanked away from him.

"Who are you?" I asked the woman. My eye's had become larger than a baseball. "What's your name and what are you doing with him?" Romello had told me his wife's name was Kya so who was this chick. My level of confusion had just hit an all time high.

She looked to Romello for what seemed like an eternity. The fact that she waited for his approval had me stunned.

"Go ahead, tell her," Romello said as he sat back down and leaned across the table calmly.

"Like he said, I'm Trinity, his second wife."

My eyes darted to her hand where she fiddled with her not so fancy wedding ring. "Okay, okay, okay," I kept repeating while pacing slightly. "What kinda bullshit is this?" I just couldn't wrap my head around what was before me. "So, Kya's your first wife and this lady is your second wife?" I stopped to point at Trinity then banged on the table.

For the first time, we caught the attention of some people nearby. I really needed to know if this multiple wife thing was true. It seemed so unreal. After all, it was illegal to be married to more than one person.

233

Romello nodded repeatedly, silently confirming that it was indeed all true.

"Royce, you gotta understand, I was going to tell you everything. I told you before, Kya is my first wife. We just didn't discuss Trinity, but they both know about you."

First, my hands intertwined with one another. Then, I raised both hands above my head. My next move was to get up in Romello's face. I didn't care who heard me. They could call the police as far as I was concerned. A crime was being committed against me. Finally, I realized I needed to take a seat at the table. I'd gotten dizzy and began to control my rapid breaths. It was the only way I knew to calm down. My mind pressed rewind on its own and reminded me of all the weird phone calls where he argued about his whereabouts and running out on me unexpectedly. Then I thought about how he could only spend the night with me on Tuesdays and Wednesdays. Now, things were coming to light.

My voice trembled at the thought. "So, this is real. You're really married to two people?" I said in a much slower tone than before.

Trinity decided to step in. She placed her hand softly over top of mine, answering for Romello. "He is married to us both and it's okay, Royce. We're all family."

I snatched my hand back then leaned into Romello's face, ready to stab him with the fork in front of me. My body felt empty yet the pain was so severe. I was tired of being hurt, tired of always choosing the wrong men.

"Royce, baby. It was bad for you to see me out like this, but you needed to know. This is how I live and I want you to be a part of this."

My eyeballs tripled in size. I simply stared at him with the look of death. "You know in the U.S. marrying more than one person is illegal, right?"

"Yep." He answered with confidence. "But in my world it's not. I'm Muslim."

"Muslim? Really?"

"Yes," he answered calmly.

"So that's what the beard is all about?"

"Not really. But understand this, we marry in a religious ceremony, not civil, so no laws are broken. We just have love for one another. You love me, right?"

I hit myself in the forehead with a loud slap. "Any more surprises!" I shouted. This was crazy. I'd heard from a girlfriend in Philadelphia about a few guys in her circle who practiced the multiple wife tradition. It was a world where some regular looking dudes practiced the culture of having several wives yet didn't respect the other laws and traits of being a Muslim man. To me, they were disrespecting the religion and needed to be called out from the top.

Romello didn't dress like a Muslim, eat like a Muslim, nor had I ever heard him speak religious words. Romello was a fake as far as I was concerned and just wanted the benefit of having multiple women who knew about one another.

Romello stood again after seeing the detrimental expression that covered my face. "Royce, I can make it all better, I promise." He grabbed my hand. This time I allowed it. I wanted him to tell me it was all a joke. Then he spoke sincerely, "Baby, I want you to be my third wife. Will you marry me?"

After biting my lip for the third time, I stood then began to back up. I'd had enough.

"Royce, don't leave," he blurted. "You have too much to lose. I brought you a long way. We got this record deal together. We got your success, together. No need to give all that up now. And you and I both know about the Latrell thing."

I stopped then froze.

"Marry me," he repeated.

Those were the last words I could hear.

Chapter 29

Royce

The next day rolled around with my anxiety level at an all time high. I needed things to go perfectly so the pieces of my life could start to mend themselves back together again. It seemed nothing had gone right for me over the last week; of course I'd lost my son to a man who wasn't even his father. The Feds were down my throat to bring them someone they could charge, and my main problem, the man I'd fallen in love with already had two wives. Nothing could've been worse.

I sat in my car curbside in a rented Chevy Traverse next to Bryant Park totally depressed. There were no more tears to shed. I was all out, dry as an empty well. When my cell rang, I jumped wondering if Agent Miles had spotted me. He told me to stay away from the meet up spot, yet I couldn't resist. The anxiety damn near killed me.

"Hello," I answered nervously, looking from side to side.

"Have you given any thought to what I said?"

"Ughh," I breathed heavily. "Now is not the time, Romello."

"What do you mean it's not the time?"

He sounded angry but I didn't care. He'd hurt me immensely. More than he knew.

"I'm busy. That's what that means. I've got a show tonight

at eight and I don't want to be upset when I perform. So let me call…"

"What?" he interrupted with extra bass in his voice as he roared through the line. "You don't understand that without me there will be no show tonight. You understand me?"

His words caught me off guard. I was so use to him being my savior that his threats had me shell shocked.

"I make shit happen for you! So know that. I run your career. Do you understand?"

I remained silent, not sure how to respond. I'd heard Romello talk to others that way but never me.

"Royce, I need you to understand something else, sweetie." His tone became calmer but the sting remained. "I made you the mini-star that you are! So show me a little appreciation. Besides, you owe me lots of money so slow your road when you speak to me."

"What money?" I shouted.

"C'mon now, there's studio time, wardrobe receipts, admin fees, and countless other fees that have to be paid back before you really start making a dime. So it's my personal money that's taking care of you right now. Be grateful."

My heart skipped several beats as he ran down all these other expenses that he said I accrued. I wanted to ask more questions disputing what he claimed I owed until I spotted Tyesha walk down the walkway headed into the wooded park area.

"Look, Romello, we really need to get together and discuss all of this, but I'm having a family emergency at the moment."

"Yeah, well you better meet up with me before the show or there'll be no show."

"Are you serious? I have to get hair and make-up at six. It's five o'clock already." I banged my hand against the steering wheel. My plans were to just let our relationship dwindle away losing feelings for him overtime. "What we've got to discuss is too emotional, too personal," I told him, turning my head to see Agent Miles jet across the street headed toward me. Just then I spotted another undercover possibly trailing Tyesha. "Just let me do my show tonight and then we'll discuss us tomorrow," I said frantically.

"Okay. But just know you're either going to be my wife and reap the benefits of what I've built or lose it all."

I immediately became ill, deep in the pit of my stomach. Bile rose up causing me to feel uneasy. Then a knock came from the back passenger side window startling me. I hung up on Romello instantly and rolled down the window.

"I thought I told you to stay away from here," Agent Miles commented with a nasty glare.

"I- I-I-I-I know. I'll leave," I stuttered. "I just wanted to be sure the information I gave you was valid. I'll leave now," I repeated.

"You do that. We've got things under control. Roll your window up, Ms. Pratt."

I did as I was told, amazed at how the Feds operated. By any means necessary they had the means to get the answers they wanted, even spotting me amongst hundreds of cars passing and going. It troubled me that they could change a person's life just like that, the way that Tyesha's was about to change. From where I sat it was difficult to see the detailed movement in Bryant Park, but when Agent Miles walked toward the back of my vehicle and tapped on the trunk twice, I knew he wanted me to pull off. The countless tress blocked portions of the sights I needed to see but I could tell that something had transpired after seeing Niecy clearly walking away from the bench without a baby in her hand.

My eyes ballooned. I needed to know what was happening. I rolled my window back down just in time to hear Agent Miles on the walkie- talkie giving orders for his men to stop and confine Niecy as she left the park. My blood pressure rose at the thought of how things were going down, just as Miles said they would. I knew he wanted me to leave but I decided to disobey when I saw Tyesha strolling up the walkway descending beyond the trees pushing a stroller like a happy housewife. The wide grin on her face proved there were no reservations about what she'd done.

"Ms. Pratt, maybe you'd like to get processed along with these people?" Miles shouted from the tail end of the Cadillac as he pointed toward Tyesha who was met and surrounded by about four undercover agents.

Tyesha's face had knotted up into about three different hor-
rifying positions. I could see her mouthing words probably attempting to talk her way out of the situation. I knew none of it
would work.

"No, Sir. I'm leaving." Satisfaction soared from my
voice."Just one last thing," I said putting the car in drive. My head
peeped from the window.

"What's that?"

"Did you figure out how to indict my mother, Veronica
Hill?"

"Yes, we got your statement. Now go and leave the rest to
us."

Instantly, I pulled off feeling partially satisfied while
watching Tyesha in my rearview being rushed to the ground and
handcuffed like a hard core criminal. My work had been done as
far as Tyesha was concerned. Now my only hope was that my
mother would get the payback she deserved for setting all of this
into motion the day she sold me. Agent Miles couldn't assure me
what would stick without any evidence on her, but he guaranteed
that he'd bring her in for questioning and dig as far as he could,
hoping for an arrest.

That felt good knowing there was that possibility. Now all I
had to do was figure out how to pay India back. Agent Miles had
given her immunity but revealed to me that India was the person
who'd put my name into all this mess. For two days, I'd been
cringing each and every time I thought of her and how she be-
trayed me. After all I'd done for her this was how she chose to
honor the code of friendship. Our ties were cut. Forever. I hated
her.

Even though I wished death on India, it was clear she was
being paid back by Haskin's daughters twenty times harsher than I
ever could. I laughed to myself while turning the corner onto Grant
Avenue thinking about how India had cried her heart out just days
ago saying that the Haskin girls showed up at the mansion with
two guys from the Sheriff's office to put India out. It was funny as
hell to learn that after all of India's life-long planning for a rich and

fabulous life, she married a man who died never getting a chance to leave her anything in writing. His estate instructions had willed everything to his surviving two children. India was ass out on her way back to Brooklyn without any major money to survive off of. For now that would serve as my revenge.

I whipped another corner and hopped on the freeway. Within minutes I'd made my way downtown, just five minutes from the venue. The plan was for me to see Lil Trae the following day so I decided to call to make sure things were still on. The last time we'd planned our day together he cancelled saying he wanted to go to the circus with his father. The thought of playing second to Trae sent me into a funk as the phone rang.

"Lil Trae, honey," I said as he answered the phone. "It's mommy. How are you?"

"I'm good, mommy. Rosa's here. You wanna speak to her?"

I smiled after beeping the horn at some woman who deliberately cut me off. "Mommy wants to talk to you," I told him lovingly. "I want to know what you want to do when you come over tomorrow?"

"Tomorrow?" he asked me nervously.

"Yes, tomorrow."

"Mommy," he said slowly. "I don't want to come."

My voice rose. "Why not?"

"Because Alecia said she's taking me to see the Transformer show at the Arena."

"Who in the hell is Alecia!" I screamed.

"She's my other mommy."

My heart sank. Tears dropped. The car swerved. What in the hell was happening to my life? "Trae, put your father on the phone! Now!" I shouted as I turned into the lot of the venue. I flashed the badge Romello's assistant had given me to get back to where the V.I.P parking was located and jetted into a space.

"He's not here. Do you want Rosa or Alecia?"

"Hell…" I caught myself. "No, Trae," I sighed then placed my hands over my face. I prayed he couldn't tell I was distraught. "I want you to tell your father to call me when he gets in! And I want you to tell Rosa to get your stuff packed tonight. You're coming with me tomorrow, no ifs ands or buts about it! Don't you miss me?"

"Aweeee, mommy, no, pleaseeee, nooooooo," he begged. "Don't make me go, mommy. I promise I'll see you next month. Pleaseee, mommy, pleaseeeee."

"Next month?" More tears flowed but the shock of hearing my son say those words so easily stabbed me deep within. The reality hit me dead on. It didn't matter to him if he ever saw me again. He was perfectly content with spending one hundred percent of his time with his father.

"Hold on, Mommy. Alecia said, why are you calling?" he asked so sweetly.

"Tell Alecia, whoever she is to go straight to hell!"

I hung up ready to spit venom from my lips and darted from my car within seconds. I needed a drink badly. It didn't take long for me to make it to the first doorway where a humungous bouncer grinned at me.

"C'mon in, Miss Royce."

I rushed inside, barged through the stage hands and countless groups of workers. Certainly they noticed the dried up tears on my face, yet I didn't care. My pace remained steadfast, eager to get to a super strong drink.

By the time I entered my dressing room my breaths had quickened from the brisk walk. Yet another shock stood before me. "Oh my, God! Let me have some peace! Are you serious?" I asked him placing my hands on my hips. "I've got to get ready?"

"No, we've got to talk…like we said we would. Did you think I wouldn't be here?"

I glanced at the two ladies and the three children who stood close to Romello. At first I figured maybe they were reporters that Romello allowed in the room until I noticed the familiar headdress from the day before. As I zoomed in more, one woman I now recognized as Trinity. The other who dressed more up to date, I'd never seen. Somehow I just got a bad vibe. A vibe that both women had a similar connection to Romello. And then there were the children, standing in a straight, horizontal line reminding me of the children from the movie, *Children of the Corn*. They were so mannerable and resembled Romello all too much.

"Oh God," I whispered to myself, knowing that drink was really needed.

"Why are they here, Romello?" I finally got the nerve to ask.

"It's Friday. It's the one day we all get together. You met Trinity already. And this is Kya. I figured I'd bring them to your show."

I waved slightly but remained silent. I couldn't wrap my head around his words 'the day we all get together'.

"Everything's already set in motion, Royce. We're family. We support each other. That's why I brought them here.

"We all get together on Fridays?" I repeated like a zombie. I just couldn't get the words out my head.

"Yep. You get Mondays and Tuesdays. Trinity gets Wednesdays and Thursdays. And Kya gets Fridays and Saturdays. I spend the night at the appropriate houses on the planned nights. It's simple and everyone's happy."

I turned my head slowly like either drugs or a pack of aliens had overtaken my body. Trinity stood smiling at me with every single tooth showing while Kya had her hands crossed, nodding her head toward Romello, approving his schedule. It only took a few seconds for me to make out the iced out bracelet and vintage Chanel purse on Kya's arm. She was a modern woman, more like me. I stood wondering how she'd fallen into Romello's web.

I finally pulled myself together. "Okay, I can't do this right now," I told them all, walking toward the door. "I've only got a little bit of time to get hair and make-up before the show. You guys have got to go."

Romello picked up a flyer off the table with my picture plastered all over it.

"Look at you," he said turning to make eye contact with me. "You made it, baby girl. And I think you could go all the way to the top, but without me you'll be just another struggling, hungry artist waiting for that big break."

"What are you saying?" I asked bluntly. His demeanor had

begun to scare me.

"I'm saying, marry me. Become my third wife or you know the deal." He shrugged his shoulder.

"Wait a second, Romello. You already have two wives, so you don't need me. Besides, I shouldn't have to marry you to be a popular singer. I can do this on my own," I smirked.

"You think so?"

"Yes, I do. I've got the voice."

He laughed.

"This business is about connections. Don't you remember all the has-beens in this biz?" Should I name all the one hit wonders for you?"

My eyes narrowed.

"I will make it, with or without you, even if I never earn a dollar while under your label. Keep your damn money, but I'll have my dignity. I don't want to be a part of a threesome. That's crazy!"

"Royce, you either agree to marry me at this very moment or forget about even doing this show. I'll pull the plug on everything tonight. They'll be no more songs by you played on the radio as of tomorrow and all show dates and future shows and appearances will be cancelled."

My jaw hung low as I listened to him rant. He was dead serious and no one in the room seemed to think it was harsh. They were still smiling.

"This is bullshit!" I said throwing a chair across the room. "This is my success," I said to no one in particular. "And I shouldn't have to share it or have it contingent on anyone else." I glared over to Romello wondering why he'd done all this to me. Had he planned it all along or had Trinity and Kya been singers, too? Hell, none of it made sense to me. I didn't want to be his wife, but I did want my singing career. It was all I'd ever wanted. I'd lost Lil Trae, lost the opportunity to have a relationship with my mother and now was about to lose my man.

The thought of success popped into my mind again. That word had a different meaning to everyone who walked the earth. For some, it meant happiness, while others financial security. For me it was all about accomplishing a goal, being a celebrity.

"Make your decision, Royce," Romello said when the stylist knocked on my door ready for me to come out for hair, make-up and wardrobe.

"I'm coming!" I shouted, not sure if I would even perform.

"Royce, what are you willing to do to be famous? You walking away from it all? Or are we all family?"

His menacing scowl warned me that he meant business. I paced the floor becoming more worried as seconds passed. If I stayed with Romello, I'd have a flourishing singing career. I'd be financially stable and be happily married on Mondays and Tuesdays. If I decided to pick up my purse and walk to my car I'd never fulfill my dreams in its entirety, but I'd be sane and would find a man of my own to love solely me.

"C'mon Royce, time is money. My money. We're expecting a packed house tonight," he added with a devious smirk

"Why Romello?" I knew I'd asked that before, but had to ask again. "Just tell me why?"

He tapped his Cartier watch as someone knocked again.

Happy versus sad.

Rich versus struggling.

No integrity versus inner peace.

All those thoughts ran through my head.

"V.I.P. for life," I finally mumbled to myself walking toward the door. "Romello, you win. I'll marry you," I told him snobbishly. "I gotta go get ready."

I opened the door, exited, then shut it, leaving my new family inside until after the show.

ALSO BY AZAREL

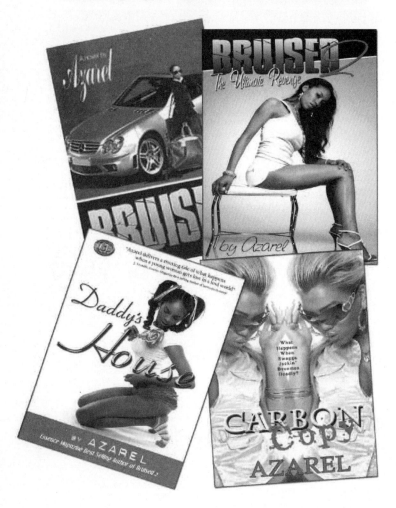

IN STORES NOW

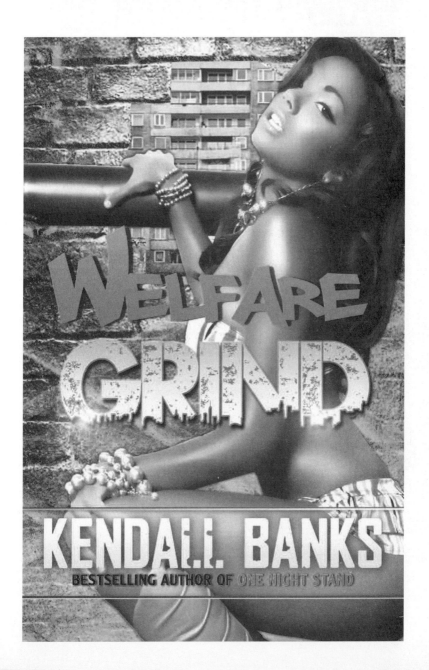

WELFARE GRIND

KENDALL BANKS

BESTSELLING AUTHOR OF ONE NIGHT STAND

CHECK OUT THESE LCB SEQUELS